The SECRET LIFE of
COPERNICUS

STRINGFELLOW

The SECRET LIFE of

COPERNICUS

STRINGFELLOW

Surreptitious SUPERHERO

Lorin Barber

SWEETWATER BOOKS

AN IMPRINT OF CEDAR FORT, INC.

SPRINGVILLE , UTAH

ISBN 13: 978-1-59955-929-2

Published by Sweetwater Books, an imprint of Cedar Fort, Inc.
2373 W. 700 S., Springville, UT, 84663
Distributed by Cedar Fort, Inc., www.cedarfort.com

Cover design by Angela D. Olsen
Cover design © 2012 by Lyle Mortimer
Edited and typeset by Melissa J. Caldwell

Printed in the United States of America

10 9 8 7 6 5 4 3 2 1

Printed on acid-free paper

FOR ROBIN, MY FIRST CRITIC, BIGGEST
FAN, AND ETERNAL COMPANION,
AND
KACEE, MY EDITOR AND TEACHER

CONTENTS

HITCHHIKER

Pull over, mister!" the young hitchhiker ordered in as gruff a voice as he could muster. He was brandishing a .22-caliber pistol aimed at Nick's chest.

"Sure, kid," Nick replied and began to pull off at the exit. They were just west of George, Washington. The road featured nothing but sagebrush and two lanes giving access to a few lonely farms or, on summer weekends, the Gorge at George, where concerts were held in a natural outdoor amphitheater.

Not again, Nick thought, as if such encounters were tedious. *Now what?* He pulled to a casual stop on the gravel shoulder.

"Give me your wallet! Get out of the car! Leave the keys!" the kid barked, trying to sound confident.

"I'm not going to do that," Nick answered bluntly. He hated it when situations came to this. This poor dumb kid was about to bring a lot of suffering on himself, and even then, Nick doubted he would learn his lesson.

Copernicus (Nick) H. Stringfellow had been in George, Washington. He'd just gassed up and had dinner at Martha's Inn. As he pulled onto the ramp to re-enter I-90 westbound, he noticed the young man trying to hitch a ride. Nick enjoyed picking up hitchhikers. He would never recommend it to anyone else because of the dangers involved, but he'd made many new friends that way, and it helped pass the lonely hours he'd spent on the road these last years. Nick was clad in a short-sleeved,

1

white-collared shirt, a light blue windbreaker, and Levi's that were slim-cut and not quite long enough for his lengthy frame. If he'd had a flattop haircut, he'd have fit well in a 1950s movie.

He wished all hitchhikers could be like the one he'd picked up just a few days before. The Mamas and the Papas were on the stereo. Nick had broad taste in music, but his mother's favorites were the Mamas and the Papas and the Lovin' Spoonful, so he was kind of partial to them. They brought back memories. "Young girls are coming to the canyon" had been the current selection. Nick had never known just why the young girls came to the canyon, but he sang along anyway.

That time he had just gotten gas on the east side of Gary, Indiana, when he spotted a young girl with a backpack standing on the corner with her thumb out. She was about five feet three inches, with straight dark brown hair that hung down well past her shoulders. She was dressed in low-rider jeans and a pink top that, per the fashion of the day, didn't cover her belly. Nick pondered how none but those with a model's sculpted abs looks decent with her belly poking out of a too-short shirt.

She had on a jean jacket that was worse for wear, several necklaces, and big hoop earrings. It gave the impression of a poor kid who had gone to the thrift store to deck herself out the way she thought rich people look. He pulled up to her and, leaning over, rolled down the passenger side window of his 1969 Chevy Impala SS 427. It was cherry, white with a deep red interior. It was Nick's most cherished and nearly his only possession.

"Cool car, mister," the girl said.

"Thanks. Where you headed?" He could see she was way too young to be out on her own.

"New York," she answered.

"Hop in," Nick offered.

She opened the door and climbed in, throwing her backpack to the backseat.

"What's your name?"

"Molly."

"How old are you?" Nick asked, entering the westbound on-ramp without her noticing.

"Sixteen," she answered, obviously lying. Nick guessed she was more like thirteen.

"Where are you from?"

"South Chicago," she said truthfully.

It was hard to lie to Nick. He wasn't really good-looking, more like unique. He was six feet six inches tall but weighed only 190 pounds. His legs were disproportionately long, as were his arms, which hung like a gorilla's when he walked. He was fair complected with a head slightly large even for a body like his. It was covered with a mop of light brown hair reminiscent of Shaggy, Scooby Doo's friend. He was thirty years old but had a hairless baby face that could have passed for sixteen. His expression was soft, like a genial grandma, and he had a perpetual smile unless angered, which was rare. The look in his eyes showed genuine concern. "What's in New York?" he asked nonchalantly.

"A new life," she answered.

"What's wrong with your old one?" he gently prodded.

"Just about everything. It's just totally bogus," she spat out through quivering lips. After a shivering pause for emotional control, she began to spill her story like water over the lip of a stopped up sink. "My mom can't handle me right now. Like, she's been unemployed for seven months and her benefits have run out. This morning she was way mad—like, she started ranting about me wasting food and how if I had to pay the bills I wouldn't squander a bite and went on about how public schools shouldn't charge to take students on outings and how keeping me in clothes was breaking her bank and how I was getting more expensive the older I got and how I couldn't expect to have the same things other kids had and—"

"Do you like your mother?" Nick interjected.

"Of course I do. I love her, and I know she loves me, but the pressure keeps building up. She's, like, two months behind on the rent, and she can't afford the next payment on her car insurance, and if she loses the car she'll never be able to get a job—"

"What does your mother do?" Nick butted in.

"She's a secretary or a receptionist or a clerk. She's totally awesome at it too; she has a letter from her last boss that says so, but she was laid off for lack of seniority. It's so lame. We didn't have much in the first place, but since she's been out of work, unemployment didn't cover everything, and, like, we didn't have any savings or anything, and we were living from paycheck to paycheck before and sometimes she'd even have to go to one of those paycheck loan places to pay the bills on time. She's been getting more and more uptight and we argue a lot and, like, she cries a lot, and she sits around staring at the TV a lot, and I know I'm just a drag on her, and I can't take watching her like that anymore and when she went to the store I just got my things and bugged off . . ."

"If you could help your mother, would you go back?"

"Sure I would."

"What are you going to do in New York?"

"I don't know, but I'll find something, and if I make some money ,I'll send it home to Mom, and if I don't, at least she won't have me to drag her down anymore and, like, I won't have to watch her suffer and things will be cool for her . . . Hey! What's that sign—Chicago twenty miles? What are you doing?"

"Relax, I'm taking you home. We're going to help your mother."

"How can you help?" She looked Nick up and down, seeing his clean but bargain basement attire and noticed the two battered suitcases in the backseat. "I don't want to dis you, but it doesn't look like you've got anything but this car."

"Well, I don't have much," he admitted. "But I do have friends. I happen to know a guy with a little business in the south side of Chicago. Let me give him a call." He pulled his cell from his pocket and paged down through his listings. Molly could see that they were numerous, as he must have gone through over a hundred to get to the one he wanted. When he reached the one he was looking for, he pushed "call," and Molly heard someone answer on the other end.

"Garin, it's Nick . . . Yeah, great. You? . . . I'm just driving through town. . . . No, I can't stop, I'm headed for Seattle. Can you do me a favor? . . . Great, I have a friend." He held the microphone against his chest and turned to Molly. "What's your mother's name?"

"Jean. Jean Nothom."

"Jean Nothom," Nick repeated into the phone. "She needs a job. She does any kind of office work, and she's really skilled. Can you help her? Great, I knew you could . . . and Garin, pay her well. Thanks."

"There you go, Molly. Your mother's got a job. Let's go see her."

Nick got Molly's phone number and called her mother. After giving

Molly a couple of minutes to apologize and cry, he took the phone back and got directions.

They arrived at the Nothoms' apartment. It was in a large tenement complex not distinguishable from a slum. The exterior was stark concrete garnished with multi-colored, artistically applied graffiti. The grass was brown where it wasn't worn through to dirt. The few trees were scarred, carved, and ravaged.

Nick followed her to the door and loomed over them, smiling as she and her mother hugged and cried and hugged some more. Molly's mom was in her late thirties, though her circumstances had added ten years to her face. She had permanent wrinkles around her lips from a lifetime nicotine addiction intensified by recent stress. Her hair was sandy brown and pulled into an electrocuted bun atop her head. She was dressed in worn-out jeans and a cast-off, bleached-out Chicago Bulls T-shirt.

Nick glanced into the sparsely furnished room. The couch was threadbare. The TV had rabbit ears. The walls hadn't been painted since "The Great Society" created them forty years earlier.

"I'm sorry. Come in, Mr. Stringfellow. I don't know how to thank you."

"No need to thank me. I can't stay anyway. Here's Garin Huard's number. Call him tonight. You can start work tomorrow."

"I don't know what to say."

"Don't say anything. Just love Molly and have a good life. You'll need something to get back on your feet and keep you till the paychecks start coming in. Here, take this," he said, reaching into his pocket, pulling out a roll of bills, and thrusting it into her hand. He took her hand in both of his and covered it so she couldn't see what she was getting.

"I can't take your money. You've done too much already. How will you get by?"

"No problem, I don't need it. I'm okay, really. I've got your number in my cell. I'll be calling to see how things go. Got to get along now. Bye."

"Thank you so much," Mrs. Nothom said through steady tears.

"Good-bye, Nick. You're, like, way totally awesome," Molly said, throwing her arms around his waist and burying her head in his stomach.

"Bye. Take care," Nick said, breaking free and leaving them at the door.

Mrs. Nothom, who'd been too polite to look at the money in Nick's presence, closed the door and, looking down at the wad, gasped. It was all one hundred dollar bills. She counted sixty-three. The next morning she showed up at Garin Huard's "little" company that had thirteen thousand employees worldwide. She started a job as an administrative assistant at $48,000 a year.

Nick had seen this young man near the freeway entrance a few minutes before. He slowed and stopped just past him. The kid picked up his pack and ran forward, opening the door. "Give me a lift?"

"Sure," answered Nick. "Hop in. Where you going?

"Seattle."

"What's your name?"

"Joe," the kid answered, sliding in and keeping his backpack on his lap.

Nick doubted it. He could sense that the boy was trouble and guessed he was sixteen or seventeen. The teen had shoulder-length hair that looked like he hadn't changed the oil for over a month, and his face reminded Nick of that timeless tale of teen angst: "You can lock me up in jail, but you can't keep my face from breaking out." Nick accelerated westbound onto I-90. "What are you going to do in Seattle?" Nick asked, trying to make conversation.

"Going to see a friend," Joe said quickly, obviously not wanting to talk, as Nick noticed a tremor in his voice and a jittery hand.

"I'm Nick. I'm moving to Seattle. I've got a friend there too. He's going to give me a job. Could you use a job?" Nick guessed he could by the looks of his ragged clothes and scruffy appearance. He watched out of the corner of his eye as the kid slowly slipped his hand into a pocket of the backpack. Perspiration shimmered on Joe's forehead like wet sand in the moonlight, though it was a cool evening. He avoided looking at Nick as he fumbled around in the pocket.

Suddenly, but shaking like the palsy, Joe pulled his hand out of the bag, and what Nick was sure was only the kid's latest mistake commenced. Nick anticipated the scene as the black nose of the pistol gradually cleared the canvas. Joe grasped the weapon as if an iron lifeline.

"Pull over, mister! Give me your wallet! Get out of the car! Leave the keys!" the kid barked, trying to sound confident.

Nick pulled off at the exit and stopped the car.

"Give me your wallet! Get out of the car! Leave the keys!"

"I'm not going to do that," Nick answered calmly.

"Give me your wallet, or I'll shoot," Joe blurted nervously. He had braced himself hard against the door, pushing his feet against the transition hump in the floor. The gun wobbled as his hand opened and shut spasmodically. His elbow was pulled back against his gut. His lips quivered.

"You don't want to do that," Nick said. He also pressed against the door, wanting to put distance between himself and Joe.

"I'll do it," Joe assured him.

"Give me the gun, kid," Nick said sternly, slowly extending his left hand across his body. He had no desire to spook the youngster.

"You're making me do this!" Joe squealed; his pitch rose with tension. The beads of sweat glistened on his forehead. His eyes squinted in taut agitation.

"Nobody's making you do anything. Give me the gun," Nick repeated in a marshmallowy tone, inching his hand forward. Nick's heightened concentration slowed the action as if it were a football instant replay.

"Don't!" the kid yelled. He squashed the trigger with a nervous twitch.

Focusing on the finger, Nick anticipated the pinch and projected an alternative outcome.

As Joe began to pull, the barrel bucked downward as if yanked by an unseen hand, sending the bullet tearing through the thigh of his own left leg. The searing projectile bolted like lightning through the sinew. Joe shrieked in pain as he dropped the gun, which, instead of falling, zipped immediately to Nick's outstretched hand. Joe was writhing like a snake with a stomachache and didn't notice.

Blood gushed like an inverted geyser from the exit wound on the bottom of Joe's leg. The bullet had continued down through the upholstery of Nick's front seat and twanged against the frame of the car. The pulsating wound throbbed like a muscular migraine, knowing no bounds.

"Now you've ruined my car," Nick said, suppressing a grin and trying to look concerned. "I told you not to shoot."

"You're insane, mister. I'm going to bleed to death."

"You'll be fine," Nick assured him, reaching over to remove Joe's hands from his punctured pants and examine the wound. "See, the bleeding has stopped."

It *had* stopped. The holes on both sides of the leg had scabbed over. "How did you do that?" Joe asked.

"I didn't do anything," Nick insisted. "You're a quick healer. Now get out," he said. Leaning across Joe, he thrust open the passenger door. Joe slid out, hopping storkedly on his good leg.

"That'll be okay in a few days," Nick said. "Here, kid," he said, reaching into his pocket and pulling out a hundred dollar bill. "Go home, and never use a gun again. Next time you might not be so lucky."

"You call this lucky?" Joe asked, snatching the bill. "Who are you, mister?"

"A better friend than you know," Nick answered and pulled back onto the freeway.

Still hopping, Joe's foot slipped, as if pulled off the edge of the shoulder, and he fell face-first onto the gravel embankment.

"Sorry, Mom," Nick said as he smiled to himself.

He reached to the backseat and grabbed the smaller of his two suitcases, pulling it to the front. Unzipping it revealed a dozen ten packs of Hostess Twinkies and a small shopping bag stuffed with one hundred dollar bills. He opened a box of Twinkies and pulled out a few of the Flavor-Filled Fillets, re-zipped the suitcase, and re-stowed it in the back. He stuffed the cakes whole into his mouth and gulped them down. He breathed a soupish sigh and within a few minutes felt relaxed and refreshed. A little further down the road, at the Vantage Bridge, he opened his window and, with perfect timing and a left-handed hook shot, flung the pistol between the girders into the Columbia River.

NEW BEGINNING

Nick had never been to Seattle. He'd only read about it. He walked into the office of Theodore S. Furney, MD, medical director at Harborview Hospital in Seattle. Harborview was *the* hospital in Seattle. In fact, it served as the regional hub for burn treatment, trauma care, and many other specialties for Washington, Alaska, Idaho, and Montana. It had 4,000 employees and served close to 500,000 patients per year, with nearly 100,000 emergency room visits. It was run by the University of Washington and located at the north end of First Hill, overlooking downtown Seattle and Elliot Bay. It was surrounded by other hospitals, clinics, and so forth, and the area was known to Seattleites as "Pill Hill."

Nick approached Dr. Furney's secretary, a middle-aged woman with a pleasant smile. "Hi, I'm Copernicus Stringfellow. Dr. Furney should be expecting me."

"Yes, he said to expect you. He didn't say you'd scrape the top of the doorway as you entered," she said, gaping up at his long, skinny frame. She thought he didn't look too intelligent with that dumb grin on his oversized baby face, but she buzzed Dr. Furney, who said to let him right in.

"Nick, come in. It's great to see you," the doctor said in an enthusiastic voice that surprised his secretary. He rose from his chair, met Nick at the door, and gave a big grizzly bear hug to the tall stranger. *Doctor Furney is a decent guy but not usually this ebullient, at least not first thing in the morning*, she thought. Nick entered the office and closed the door.

The office was plain, even somewhat stark, as was most of the hospital. For decoration it had only Dr. Furney's medical diplomas, a picture of his family on the credenza, and an oil painting of a serene farm setting on the wall. The furniture was monotone, and cases of books were the featured items.

"Great to see you, prof," Nick greeted him.

"Have a seat, Nick. You know you don't look a day older than last time I saw you. What's it been, six years? How do you do it?"

"Just good clean living, I guess."

"You left Columbia when I did. What have you been doing all of this time?"

"Mostly traveling around the country."

"Hard to imagine you just sightseeing."

"I really haven't seen any sights. I've been trying to help out where I can."

"You've always tried to help out. Have you kept up with your old gang?"

"Sure. We text each other, talk on the phone, and when I drive through I often stop in for dinner."

"Nothing like those wild parties you had when you were in school?"

"No, I've tried to cut back on the root beer. Sugar's not that good for the body, and pizza clogs the arteries. Besides, the gang are all older than me. They have families, kids, and mortgages. In fact, a lot of my schoolmates have kids in high school."

"You're not getting any younger yourself. Why haven't you married, bought a house, and settled down? I know you're not trying to make your first million."

"I've bought a few houses. As for the married part, I don't know, prof. I just haven't found the right woman."

"What's the problem?"

"No problem. I just have to find someone who's attractive, has the right values, and challenges me intellectually."

"I'm sure it's that last one that makes many drop out of the running. We were sure fortunate to have you for three years at Columbia. After all, I know you only spent two each at Princeton and Yale, and you did Harvard and MIT at the same time."

"I just wanted to take the best that each had to offer. Harvard was best for business and law. I could hit MIT for engineering 'cause it was close by. Columbia kept me for longer 'cause of my desire to master medicine."

"Well, you sure did that. What brings you to Seattle?"

"I'm not sure, but I felt like I should get a job here at Harborview. Do you have anything available?"

"Let me see," Theo said, pulling out a file labeled "vacancies." "Looks like we have quite a few things. We have a need in cardiology, we're looking for a neurosurgeon, an endocrinologist, a dermatologist . . . oh, and I know we need a supervisor for the ER. Would any of those interest you?"

"No, you know I've done all of that. I'd really just like to be a nurse."

"A nurse? What kind of nurse? Sure seems like a waste of talent to me."

"I just want to be kind of a nurse at large, so I can wander around and get involved wherever I'm interested. You wouldn't have to pay me."

"We could make you a doctor at large. Wouldn't that be better?"

"No, I'd like to stay under the radar. In fact, I'd like you to promise not to tell anyone about me or my background."

"Sure, Nick, if that's what you want. I know you never liked taking credit for anything, but wouldn't you be more effective as a doctor?"

"No, I'd rather be a nurse, but I would like the flexibility to wander around."

"Well, you know I'll do anything you want. You'd have to be paid though—at least the nurse's minimum or the union would have my hide."

"Okay, I can live with that. Can I wait till tomorrow to start? I've got some things to take care of this afternoon."

"Sure, Nick. I'll arrange it with HR. Hey, could you come over to dinner this Sunday? I know Monica would love to see you again."

"Sure, prof. Hey, thanks a lot."

"Anytime, Nick. I look forward to having you around again."

HOME SWEET HOME

Nick got to his car and began scoping out the neighborhood in ever-enlarging circles. Actually it was a half circle, because to the west was downtown Seattle. About six blocks to the east, he found a large, old, run-down house with a For Sale sign in front. It was on a block of shabby homes surrounded by low-class apartment buildings. Rusting cars were parked on the neighbor's lawn, every yard was overgrown, and every house needed painting.

The road on each side of the block was cobblestone. It was obviously not maintained. Nick mused how streets were always well cared for in rich sections of town. The cross streets showed that there were several layers of pavement over the original cobblestone base, but here the stones were bare. They had sunken and swollen in different spots, and just in front of this house was a depression about a foot and a half deep. He slowed to a crawl, not wanting to damage his Chevy, and pulled into the driveway, which led to a basement garage. Taking out his cell, he dialed the number on the sign and asked for Rita. She agreed to hurry right over and was there in about twenty minutes.

Nick used the time to stroll around the block. There wasn't a nice house on it, though a few inhabitants made an effort to mow the lawn, and a couple looked like they'd been painted sometime in the last few years. There were fences around most of them. Many must have had more cars in the yard and on the street than they had occupants. Wild blackberry bushes were common, and moss covered many of the roofs.

He stood and stared directly across the street at a home where

12

blackberries engulfed the entire yard. All of the windows were boarded up. The front door and window each had a half-sheet of plywood covering it, and there were painted warnings of "No Trespassing" and "Stay Out!" Nick pictured a loaded shotgun aimed at his chest and wondered if he might ever get to meet that neighbor.

"So pleased to meet you, Mr. Stringfellow," Rita greeted him as she stepped out of her car. "Are you new in town?" Rita was in her late fifties. She had brown hair ratted in the style that was popular when she was in high school. Dressed in a chocolate brown pantsuit, she was thin, energetic, and had a salesman's friendly manner.

"Yes, I just got in last night."

"So you don't have a real estate agent?"

"Just you."

"Great! I can show you a number of wonderful houses. I know the area very well. What price range are you looking in?"

"It doesn't matter."

"Well, is there any particular style or location you prefer?"

"This house looks good." The roof was obviously aged and covered with a couple of inches of moss. Two windows had been shattered and boarded up. The yard was jungled over with ivy and wild blackberries to an extent it could never be in a warmer, dryer climate. The grass was three feet high, and the bushes had not been trimmed for several years. The paint on the siding was peeled bare in several places. "May I see the inside? Is it as nice as the outside?"

"Of course," she went on seriously. "This house needs a lot of work. The previous owner was an old man, long incapacitated, who lived here forever till he died about six months ago. His estate is selling the house."

"It's not haunted, is it?" Nick asked with a straight face.

"Oh goodness no," Rita replied. "I haven't heard a word about anything like that."

"Good," said Nick, breaking into his usual grin, "the last couple of places I've been have had very disagreeable poltergeists. It makes it hard to sleep."

Rita unlocked the door. "You're a joker, aren't you? Watch your step here," she said as they entered. Some of the oak flooring was missing, exposing the sub-floor.

Just in from the doorway, a flight of stairs went straight up to the second floor. The newel post was about twenty degrees off plumb, and several of the balusters were missing on the way up. The carpet was worn through on every step. They took a right into the living room, which had a huge stone fireplace with only a couple of stones missing, but it was blackened in an inverse triangle above the opening. A huge water stain was on the ceiling.

The dining room to the left was in the same run-down state. The wallpaper was peeling above some beautiful wood paneling that reached three feet up the wall. At least, it *would* be beautiful if it were refinished, Nick told himself. They walked quickly through the house. Upstairs and down were in similar states of disrepair.

"I'm sorry," Rita told him as they finished the tour. "I told you it was run-down. I can show you several of the same style that are in great shape."

"This one's perfect," replied Nick. "Couldn't be better. What is the asking price?"

"Five hundred thousand," Rita answered apologetically. "It would be much cheaper in the suburbs, if you could find anything so decrepit in the suburbs."

"That's fine," Nick said.

"I'm sure the bank won't finance this without a lot of work being done," Rita warned. "They'll want an inspection."

"No problem. I'll pay cash. Here's my lawyer's card. He'll handle the details. Can I move in tomorrow?"

"Even with a cash payment, it couldn't close faster than a couple of weeks," Rita answered, somewhat agog at the speed of the transaction.

"Surely you could arrange a rental agreement until then," Nick assured her.

"Well, I'm sure I can."

"Good, I'll be here tomorrow afternoon around four. And, Rita, I'll be needing your help on a few other purchases." He left Rita, mouth agape like a hungry carp, and strode to his car. He'd looked up Sears in the phone book at the hospital and took off for First Avenue to do some shopping.

FURNISHINGS

Nick walked into Sears on the first floor and approached the information desk. "I need some furniture, appliances, and other odds and ends. Would there be a sales person available to help me?"

"I'm sure we could find someone," answered the young woman at the desk. The request struck her as odd, but coming from a person as unusual as Nick, she took it as a matter of course. She called the furniture department, and they sent up Waleed, a twenty-five-year-old Syrian immigrant.

"Hello, I'm Nick," he said, raising his long arm for a handshake as if drawing a gun from its holster.

"I'm Waleed. What can I do for you?"

Waleed was about five feet six inches tall, a little chubby, and going prematurely bald. His accent was Middle Eastern mixed with British, as that's where he'd learned English.

"I just bought a house, and I need a few things. If you could show me around and bring a pen and pad of paper, I'd really appreciate it."

"Sure," he said, reaching behind the information desk for the pen and paper. "Where to first?"

"Let's go for furniture," Nick answered, and Waleed led him to the escalator for a trip to the third floor.

They wandered the store as Nick chose a king-sized bed, a kitchen table and chairs, a couch, a big screen TV, pots, pans, dishes, linen, a refrigerator, a washer and dryer, and various other items. Waleed followed, noting the items and the prices. "Will that be all?" he asked as they finished the entire spree in about forty-five minutes.

"I think that's fine for today," Nick replied. "Could I have it delivered at four o'clock tomorrow evening?"

"I'm sure we can arrange that," Waleed answered, trying to suppress a grin. He worked on commission.

"So what's the total?" Nick inquired.

Waleed stepped to the nearest register and rang it up. "It comes to $12,147.38, including tax. Will you be putting that on your card?"

"No thanks, Waleed," Nick said, pulling a wad from his front pocket and counting out 122 hundred-dollar bills. "You can keep the change."

"Don't you worry carrying around that kind of cash?" Waleed asked.

"No, I think it's the best kind to carry. I've tried spending Canadian dollars, but people seem to frown on it." Nick searched the salesman's face for a smile but saw that the joke had gone right over his head.

"I mean, with that much cash, aren't you worried about getting robbed?" Waleed went on looking like he'd seen a pink rhinoceros.

"Not in the least," Nick answered as Waleed stood in awe. "I appreciate your help. Here's my address," he said, jotting it on Waleed's pad. "Four o'clock tomorrow evening, okay?"

"Four o'clock," Waleed echoed.

Nick often got that reaction. "Thanks," Nick waved as he strode away.

SUSTENANCE

Nick drove to the Hostess bakery on Aurora Avenue just below Queen Anne Hill and asked to see someone in sales. Natalie Mauer, a prim thirtyish woman in a navy blue tailored suit greeted him and invited him to a small conference room off of the lobby. It had the typical fake wood paneling, a table that seated six, and a magazine rack off to the side.

"So Mr. Stringfurrow, how can I help you?" she asked, trying to appear to take Copernicus seriously.

"It's Stringfellow, ma'am, but that's okay—it's not too common."

"What can I do for you, Mr. String*fellow*?" she asked, emphasizing the "fellow" with a bit of peevishness.

"I'd like to get on your route for weekly deliveries of fresh Twinkies."

"Really, do you have a retail operation?"

"No, but I use quite a few. I'd like a case a week." (A case was forty ten-packs.)

"That's a lot. Do you have a large family or an organization?"

"No, it's just me," Nick informed her.

"I'm afraid we don't deliver to individuals. You could come to our outlet store, but if we sold door to door, our retail outlets would revolt. If you're not a business, we just can't accommodate you."

"But I like them fresh, and coming to your outlet store would be a bother. I am incorporated. If you'll contact my lawyer, he'll give you the relevant tax ID number and so on," Nick said, extracting his lawyer's card. "Please have a case dropped off at this address weekly. Just leave

17

it on the porch," he added, jotting his new home address on the back of the card and handing it to her. "I'll be happy to pay top dollar; my lawyer will handle the billing."

"I'm still not sure we can do this," she stated hesitantly. "I'll have to check with my manager."

"That's fine. If there's any trouble, just call Hugh Prewitt; he's an old friend of mine." Nick said, casually dropping the name of the CEO of Hostess's parent company.

"Sure, we'll do that," Natalie said now in a more sarcastic tone. *This guy's looked at our website and is trying to impress me,* she thought.

"Just give his secretary Lillian my name, and she'll put you right through to him," Nick assured her.

That caught her attention, as she was sure the secretary's name wasn't on the website and she didn't know it herself. "Wait here, please. I'll be a few minutes," she said with tentative respect in her voice.

It was about ten minutes before she returned. Nick had read every word in thirteen magazines while he waited. "Mr. Stringfellow, the delivery will be no problem. I hope my skepticism didn't offend you," Ms. Mauer said, entering the room.

"Not at all," Nick assured her. "Can we start delivery tomorrow? I'm running low."

"Sure, anything you'd like," Natalie offered graciously.

"Well, it's been a pleasure," Nick said, extending his hand.

"The pleasure's all mine," Natalie said, looking as if she'd plugged her finger into a live socket.

Nick drove back to his cheap motel on Fourth Avenue South. He called his New York attorney, gave him the address of his new home, and asked him to take care of phone and utility hookups.

"Do we proceed with the usual drill?" the lawyer asked.

"Yes, the neighborhood is ideal. Can you see if we can arrange for street repair? It's cobblestone, and I think it could be quite charming if it didn't have so many sinkholes."

"You want me to work through the city of Seattle?"

"No, they've ignored this neighborhood for years. Let's just get a private crew and get it done without the bureaucratic hassle."

After the conversation, he flipped on the TV to the cartoon channel and began to write on a stack of 3 x 5 cards that he took from his suitcase. He got hungry, left his hotel, and drove south until he found a supermarket, where he bought a bag of mixed fresh vegetables and various pieces of fruit.

Returning to the motel, Nick got out of his car, strapped on a fanny pack from the backseat, and walked a couple of miles north to the main branch of the Seattle Public Library, munching fruits and vegetables as he went. He spent the rest of the evening in the anthropology section, finishing three large books. The walk back to the motel was uneventful, and Nick settled down to sleep as only those who are at peace with the world can sleep.

HARBORVIEW

The next morning, Nick was at the hospital at seven
o'clock. He found the employee bulletin board in the cafeteria and
tacked some 3 x 5 cards on it. Each had his cell phone number and said
"Wanted." They respectively asked for a "Part-Time Housekeeper," a
"Gardener," an "Interior Decorator" and a "Handyman." He knew the
HR (Human Resources) department wouldn't open until eight-thirty,
so he decided to wander around and see what was going on.

On the third floor in the burn center, he felt drawn to enter room
322. Lying there with her face encased in a thick, soft plastic sheet
and with moist bandages covering much of her upper body was Jamie
Preston. Jamie was a pretty, vivacious, five-year-old blonde from a middle class family in Yakima. Unfortunately, while playing in the kitchen,
her three-year-old brother Jarl had knocked over a deep fryer, scalding
his sister with 350-degree oil that had hit her square in the face. Sedated
to allow relief from the relentless pain, Jamie was unaware of Nick's
presence.

Her face had been swaddled in a flexible plastic much like shrink-
wrap. Beneath the wrap was a layer of collagen, then silicone. Nick rec-
ognized it right away as the newly developed French technique known
as the Integra Dermal Regenerator. He'd read papers on it and immediately approved of its application, making a mental note to compliment
the doctors on their approach.

Nick sat next to the bed and leaned over Jamie. He put the middle
finger of his left hand under her neck at the base of her skull. Focusing

his entire immense mental prowess on Jamie's pituitary gland, he massaged it, mentally encouraging growth and follicle-stimulating hormone production. The hormones streamed immediately to Jamie's ravaged face. After about ninety seconds, he drew back from the bed, leaned back in his chair, and took several deep breaths. He reached in his fanny pack and nabbed a couple of Twinkies.

Recentering his concentration, he put his right index finger on Jamie's sternum and again closed his eyes. Deep in her chest cavity Jamie's thymus kicked into high gear. It began generating many times its normal level of thymus oil. The oil was quickly pushed by Nick's fixation to converge at the sublayers of her facial skin, greatly reducing the levels of nitrous oxide, which the body had produced in reaction to the burn. With the nitrous oxide (which causes clotting and stems blood flow to the wound) wiped out, her capillaries cleared of their tiny clots and again provided ample blood to the affected skin. Once more Nick leaned back, took a couple of deep breaths, and relaxed his brain.

After a couple more Twinkies, he placed a finger on Jamie's stomach and centered his mind on the Peyer's glands located near the end of her small intestine. After a few seconds of deep concentration, he rested. Absorption of vitamin B12 would from this point on greatly increase, speeding the healing process.

Just as Nick was finishing, the door flew open and in walked Dr. Prescilla Spurbeck (Press to her friends).

He sensed the overload on his occipital lobe. She was the most beautiful woman Copernicus H. Stringfellow had ever seen.

"What are you doing there, praying?" she demanded.

"Yeah, sort of," Nick answered sheepishly. He was wearing his hospital blues, so she assumed he was staff of some kind.

"Do you work here?"

"Yes."

"Where's your badge? Who are you? Are you supposed to be in here?" she fired at him.

"I'm, uh, Nick Stringfellow. I'm, uh, a nurse. I, uh, just started and can't get my badge till HR opens at eight thirty.

"It's eight fifteen now. You shouldn't be anywhere till you've been assigned. You may leave now." It wasn't a suggestion.

At twenty-three, Prescilla Spurbeck was the youngest resident in the history of Harborview Hospital. She was the only child of Drs. Bill and Anna Spurbeck. She was five feet seven inches tall, thin with curves in the right places, and had ebony hair and golden brown eyes. Her skin was a light olive color, and her facial features were not chiseled but softly Greek.

Dr. Spurbeck was in the nineteenth month of a three-year residency. She was assigned as an assisting physician on numerous cases in various departments throughout the hospital. She had entered the University of Pennsylvania Medical School at nineteen with degrees in biology and chemistry. She had completed the four years of med school in three, had done a year as an intern, and was anxious to complete residency so she could specialize. Her supervising doctors saw her as a "no-nonsense," "hurry and get on with it," "type A" personality driven to succeed. She didn't lack for confidence.

Nick walked slowly toward the door. He kept his eye on Dr. Spurbeck both because of her breath-taking beauty and because her demeanor frightened him. He stumbled over a chair next to the door.

"Are you clumsy as well as impertinent?"

"I, uh . . . yeah, I guess I am clumsy, but I don't mean to come across as impertinent."

"Then you shouldn't be visiting patients to whom you haven't been assigned."

"Yes, doctor." He sidled out the door.

HR

Dwelling as long as he dared in the hall to absorb her beauty, Nick meekly walked on, took the elevator to the basement, and staggered to his locker. He turned the dial on the combination lock he'd brought in, opened the door, and reached for the Twinkie stash in his backpack. Unzipping it, he grabbed six Golden Gobs of Goodness from one of the three ten-packs inside and sat down on the bench to quickly polish them off. He rested a few minutes. By then it was eight thirty, so he wandered up to HR.

"Copernicus H. Stringfellow," began the HR assistant, looking at his paperwork.

She was tall, stout, middle aged, and had the compassionate expression of a Marine drill sergeant.

"Call me Nick," Nick offered.

"Okay then, Nick, there's nothing on this application; it just says 'Qualified' in large print and is signed by Dr. Theodore Furney."

"He knows me from earlier times," Nick said.

"Well, can we at least have your current address and other relevant information?"

"Sure," Nick agreed and filled out the statistics, listing his lawyer as who to contact in case of emergency.

"We've not been told what department you'll be working in," she said accusatorily.

"I'm a 'nurse at large,'" answered Nick.

"Nurse at large—I'm sure we don't have any such classification." She glared at him over the top of her reading glasses.

"Dr. Furney created the position just for me."

"And what did Dr. Furney say was your pay level?"

"Just the minimum."

"This is highly irregular. I'll have my manager check with Dr. Furney." She growled. "Step over to the yellow line and smile at the camera."

MONTY

Nick did so and in a few minutes walked out with his ID badge to further acquaint himself with the hospital and deduce where he could be of service. He wandered from department to department, emptying bedpans, refilling water pitchers, helping patients to the restroom, and studying charts. He often stopped to chat and answer patient questions regarding their ailment or hospital procedures. He enjoyed himself so much that he completely forgot lunch till about three in the afternoon, when he returned to his locker and retrieved his brown bag. He had celery, broccoli, cauliflower, an apple, and a plum. He went to the cafeteria and sat down next to an orderly named Monty.

"Hi, I'm Nick," he opened the conversation as he pulled out his chair.

"I'm Monty," the guy answered, not sounding eager to talk. Nick could tell it wasn't out of discourtesy but from shyness. Monty was six foot two inches tall and weighed 190 pounds. He had dark curly hair and brown eyes. Nick thought he was a handsome sort of fellow and projected intelligence. He felt he should get to know him better.

"I just started working here today," Nick told him. "How about you?"

"I've been here a little over a year."

"You're an orderly?"

"Yeah, but I'm studying to be a nurse at Seattle Central JC."

"Is that a good program?" Nick asked.

"It's good enough to get me another rung up the medical ladder."

"You a native of Seattle?" Nick continued his questioning, though Monty seemed reluctant to get involved in a lengthy conversation.

"Yeah. You?"

"No, I grew up in the Midwest and went to school back East," Nick answered. "What inspired you to choose a career in medicine?"

"I don't know. My dad died of cancer. I guess since then I've wished I could help people to not suffer so much."

"What family do you have?"

"Just my mom and my little brother, Matt. He's in junior high."

"What does your Mom do?"

"She's a waitress."

"So you've had to work your way through school?"

"Yeah, no choice. It drags out the process."

"You'd rather go more quickly?"

"Yeah, I'd rather go to premed than nursing school. I was accepted but couldn't afford it."

"You'd like to be a doctor?"

"Sure, if I could. I think I'm smart enough, but at the rate I'm getting an education, I've given up on it."

"You shouldn't give up on a dream so easily."

"It's more like the dream's given up on me."

"You never know. Life can change dramatically with no warning."

"I don't have any rich uncles to die and leave me a fortune."

"You could adopt one."

"Yeah, I'll be on the lookout.

"Really, you never know about life. Do you have any friends in the hospital?"

"Acquaintances. I'm too busy between work and school to get to know anyone very well."

"You eat lunch, don't you?"

"Yeah . . ."

"If you let me be your friend, I'll bet we can pick up a few more."

JEMIMA

Nick had been taking calls from his "want ads" all afternoon. He wanted to meet with the potential hirees in person before offering them a position, and most of the calls had been from hospital employees looking for jobs for friends or family.

Nick met Jemima Jones at the bulletin board as arranged.

"Hi, I'm Nick Stringfellow."

"I'm Jemima."

Nick thought she was plumper than any Tetraodontidae.

"Like Aunt Jemima?"

"Yeah, it's not my born name. When I was a kid, I was fat and black and the white girls called me Jemima. I didn't mind, and the name stuck. I'm still fat and I'm still black, so I still use the name. My mom named me Jerusha."

"Have you got a family?"

"Yeah, I've got three kids—a boy and two girls."

"What does your husband do?"

"Never had one."

"That's got to be tough. How do you take care of your kids?"

"I get here early for the breakfast shift. The kids are old enough to get themselves off to school. I'm always home before they get back. I'm hoping this housekeeping gig will have flexible hours so I can work around my kids' sports and school events."

"Sure. You can bring them along if you'd like."

"Really? That'd be nice. Where's your house?"

"Just a few blocks from here."

"I don't live far myself. That's wonderful."

"If you'd like, you could have your kids come straight to my house from school."

"What would your family say?"

"It's just me. I live alone."

"I'd really like the job. I'm a whiz at cleaning."

"Why don't you meet me there this afternoon?"

"I sure will. Thank you."

Nick arrived at his new home at 3:58 p.m. The Sears truck was in the driveway waiting. A case of fresh Twinkies was on the porch. Nick was supervising the unloading of his purchases when Jemima Jones showed up at four-thirty.

She opened the front door and hailed him. "Mr. Stringfellow, you home?"

"Coming," Nick answered and strode out from the master bedroom to meet her.

Jemima wanted the job but wasn't known for her tact. Looking around, she said, "You don't need a housekeeper. You need a bulldozer."

"I know it's a mess, but I have plans," Nick told her, smiling. "Let me show you the place."

The Sears guys were just finishing up, and Nick thanked them and slipped them each a hundred-dollar bill as they left.

Jemima Jones was only about five feet five inches tall; Nick guessed that she was nearly that wide. She had a broad smile and bright white teeth, and Nick knew right away that he liked her.

"This place looks like a sty that was so dirty the pigs hightailed it," she told him as they walked through the living room to the hallway. "If my mama saw this, she'd puke up scouring pads," she commented as they walked into the master bedroom with its torn curtains, worn through carpet, and graffitied walls.

As they entered the kitchen, she just shook her head. Spying the narrow doorway to the pantry, she asked, "How am I supposed to get my fat hind end through there?"

"Steatopygia," Nick interjected.

"Who do whatchea?" Jemima asked.

"Steatopygia," Nick explained. "The genetic disposition to accumulate fat in the buttocks. It's a hereditary trait of the Khoi people of south central Africa. They're not actually a people anymore because they were vanquished and engulfed by the Bantu. I assume your family carries it as a dominant gene."

"You speaking English?" she asked, shaking her head.

"I'm just trying to strike up a conversation about your probable ancestry. I thought you'd be interested."

"Look, I can comment about the size of my hiney, but anyone else that says anything will wake up spitting teeth," she warned, shaking a hamlike fist at him.

"Sorry, sometimes I get off on tangents. Tell me about your family."

"My boy James is in high school. He's a big kid and plays football. He's on the line; they never get much credit on the line, but he most always blocks his man. He says he only gets noticed when he lets someone get by."

They took a glance at the living room and walked down the hall.

"Does he do well in school?"

"Absolutely. He's got a B average. I should have been so smart."

"Is he planning on college?"

"He sure is."

"Will he get a scholarship?"

"No, he says he's too slow to play football in college. I'm getting this job so he can go where he wants."

They entered the master bedroom and peered into the bathroom and the closet.

"Well, if he does well in school, I'm sure he'll succeed."

"Yeah, he's worried though. He doesn't do too well on tests. He's smart, but he's a slow thinker."

They made their way up the stairs.

"How about your other kids?"

"Next is Cassy. She's in junior high. She's big like me."

"How's she in school?"

There was another bathroom and two bedrooms on the main floor.

"She doesn't care for it too much. I have to kick her along."

"Is she into sports?"

"No, the only thing that gets her excited is singing."

"She's got the voice?"

Nick pointed out the basement, but Jemima had no desire to go down.

"Yeah, she always gets the solos in the choir, church or school. These windows got more dust than the Sahara desert."

"I don't think anyone's been in here for years."

"You don't expect me to clean this whole place at once?"

"Of course not. You have two children then?"

"Three. Last comes Tilly. She's nine. She's not like a Jones at all. She's skinny and real active. She's our scholar. She gets real mad if she gets anything less than an A. Her teachers say she won't let them alone till they give her extra credit assignments."

"I can't wait to meet them."

"I'll bring them tomorrow. You'll know all about Tilly right away. She won't quit talking till you do, and once you know all about her, she'll keep telling you more. James and Cassy are a bit more shy."

"Like their Mama?"

"No one ever called me that."

They were back to the entryway.

"It sounds like you're proud of your children."

"Nothing else matters."

"Will you take the job?" he asked. "I won't expect you to clean it all up at once. You can start with the kitchen and the bathroom."

"You expect me to spend the rest of my life here?" she asked.

"Just a couple of hours a day. I'll be patient," Nick answered.

"Are the hours flexible?"

"Whatever is convenient for you."

"How much are you going to pay?" she asked accusatorily.

"Would $3,000 a month be okay?"

"Honey for $3,000 a month I'd clean between your toes with a Q-tip," she answered.

After a quick fruit, vegetable, and broiled chicken dinner, Nick returned to the hospital to make the rounds again.

CATHY

Cathy Starr was a twenty-four-year-old LVN (licensed vocational nurse). She was pretty in a plain sort of way, though she didn't see it herself. She wore no makeup and didn't spend any time on her hair. She thought her figure straight and uninteresting. She'd worked at Harborview for two years.

Cathy always dreaded the walk home when she worked swing shift. At one in the morning, anyone else walking the street was suspect. She lived several blocks south of the hospital in a low-rent apartment with her alcoholic father. It was a drizzly gray night, typical for Seattle at any time, except for the two weeks of high summer. There wasn't enough moisture to puddle or even to make the sidewalk seem wet.

Seattleites live with drizzle like dogs live with fleas—a minor annoyance to occasionally scratch or bite at but not enough to keep their tails from wagging. The wet was blanket-like: comforting, buffering, and sound dampening. The Northwest personality, though friendly, is close, private, and somewhat reclusive. The hills, trees, and weather form barriers that make each neighborhood a village, each house an island. About a block from the hospital, Cathy felt more than heard someone tramping behind her. The same comforting drizzle quickly became chilling.

Her nerves tightened and her senses sharpened. She jogged daily, motivated by the potential need to outrun a pursuer in a situation like this. She'd taken some self-defense courses, but at five feet five, 110 pounds she knew she was no match for a man of any size. Judging by the clop-clop on the concrete, she figured he was about thirty feet behind

31

her. His shoes had to be large to create such a deep echo. He didn't seem to be closing in; his step even had a certain easy gait to it as if he were meandering about seeing the sights.

She reached stealthily into the pocket of her jacket and used her thumb to pop the lid off her can of pepper spray.

She passed a lamppost, and as her stalker cleared it, she could see the shadow of his head at her feet. *If he's thirty feet behind me, he must be a giant to cast a silhouette that long*, she posited.

Her hand was still in her pocket, pepper spray at the ready, as she approached an alleyway a block and a half from her apartment.

She mulled over the possibility of darting down the alley and approaching her place from the next street over.

Would thirty feet be enough of a head start for her to out-distance a long-legged man?

Would she be better off just continuing casually on her way? Was he really following her or just walking the same direction?

The steps hadn't gotten any closer. Probably it was just someone going the same way.

She'd never experienced someone going this way at this time of night.

She tried to imagine why anyone would head this direction.

The only answer would be to get to her neighborhood.

He either lived there or was going for a visit.

Either that or he was following her.

The alley was upon her, and she couldn't take the suspense any longer. She took a quick step to the right and began her sprint.

Before her second stride hit the ground, the darkness seized her arm, stopping her in midair. Two large, dark humanoid vapors confronted her.

"Look what we got," one of the hazes grunted in the voice of a hungry grizzly. "We can have some fun with this one."

She started to scream, but the second ghoul slapped a paw over her mouth and held it there.

"Let her go!" a quiet but powerful voice murmured from the sidewalk.

"It's the Jolly Green Giant," one of the shadows said, pulling a gun from behind his waist. "Get out of here. This is none of your business." Cathy was writhing and struggling in the grasp of the other phantom.

"I said let her go," the giant repeated sternly but with a startling calm.

The specter raised the gun, but before he could fire, it flew from his hand into the street.

He was flung against the cinder block wall on the right side of the alley. A loud crack split the air as his head whiplashed into the bulwark.

The other apparition dropped Cathy and started toward the human telephone pole, drawing a knife. One step, and he was dashed against the brick on the left side of the alley, dropping unconscious to the pavement.

Across the street, two men in a plain, dark, late model four-door sedan sat quietly and chronicled the event on film.

"May I walk you home, miss?" the tall man politely asked the stunned Cathy.

"Uh, sure, I'd be delighted," she answered dazedly without thinking. "Who are you?"

"Nick Stringfellow, ma'am," he said, extending his over-sized hand.

"What are you doing here?"

"I saw you leaving the hospital, and I didn't think a lady should be unescorted at this time of night."

"Maybe I shouldn't, but I have no choice."

"Perhaps you have one now."

"I'm Cathy Starr. I don't know how to thank you. I was walking down the street, worrying about you following me, and didn't see them at all."

"Sorry to worry you, Cathy. Which way is home?"

"Just down the block and around the corner. How did you do that?"

"Do what?"

"Throw those guys against the wall without touching them."

"Oh, you noticed that?"

"I certainly did. Do you think I'm blind?"

"No . . . uh, would you mind if we didn't discuss it right now?"

"If you insist. What can I say, but it was pretty impressive."

"It's just a form of martial arts, really. It's nothing special."

"I've never seen Jackie Chan do that."

"Could I ask that you don't talk to anyone about it?"

"How could I refuse my rescuer? I'll keep it quiet if that's what you want."

"Thank you. Let me walk you home."

"You've already saved my life. You don't need to accompany me home."

"Wouldn't let you out of my sight till you're safe."

"Okay. You work at the hospital then?" she asked.

"Yeah, I just started this morning."

"Lucky for me, you did."

"I'm glad too." They walked in silence for a moment. "Listen, I don't want you walking home alone at this time of night," Nick said as they approached her door. "You should let me escort you from now on."

"You don't have to . . ." she started. But then, "I'd like that," she said shyly, and being two steps up, she leaned over and gave him a peck on the cheek. "Good night and thank you," she said as she went through the door.

"Who's that?" Chuck Starr demanded, half rising from his drunken stupor on the couch. The coffee table was littered with beer cans, cigarette packs, ash trays, and cheesy magazines. It smelled like a cheap tavern at closing time. Chuck hadn't shaved in three days and seemed not to have changed clothing in at least that long. He was a thin almost skeletal figure with a perpetual scowl and a gruff gravelly voice.

"A nice guy from work; he saved me from a couple of muggers on the way home," Cathy answered with lamb-like humility.

"Got a new boyfriend, huh? You little flirt."

"He's not a boyfriend, Daddy. He's just a gentleman."

"He ain't no gentleman. I know what he's after, and so should you."

"He's not that kind of guy—really."

"Sure, and I'm not a stinking drunk. Get me a beer, brat."

"Yes, Daddy," Cathy answered timidly.

Nick hurried home with long-legged strides while slurping a few of his Palatable Pellets of Power. After following from a distance, the late model sedan pulled off into the night.

BABY NICK

The next morning Nick hung around the nursery. He liked babies. It had always bothered him that he couldn't remember much from when he was that age. Nick had been born thirty years earlier in Galena, Kansas. The town was two intersecting streets with a few barely paved lanes branching off. Main Street had once been part of the historic Route 66, but now Galena was history. Its heyday had come and gone, and the inhabitants who had gone hadn't much reason to come back.

Galena was in Cherokee county, the poorest county in Kansas, which had to make it one of the poorest in the country. It was at the southeasternmost corner of the state, bordering on Missouri and Oklahoma with Arkansas about an hour's drive away. Joplin, Missouri, a town of about forty thousand, was the nearest big city. Nick was born to Chad Robert and Carol Andrews Stringfellow. That is, he was born to Carol; Chad was out drinking with his buddies.

Carol was eighteen. She was a beautiful girl with sandy blonde hair, skin as smooth and translucent as mother of pearl, and a figure to be whistled at—at least, before she got pregnant. She'd been a cheerleader, student body vice president, and valedictorian of her class. She had an academic scholarship and planned on going to KSU in Manhattan, Kansas. She was going to major in sociology and return to Cherokee County as a social worker to help poor people turn their lives around.

Her parents had died of cancer, which was prevalent around Galena due to the high lead content in the ground, which had seeped into the

35

drinking water. Galena (the word means a type of lead ore) had once been a booming mining town of forty thousand, but as lead went out of vogue, so did Galena. It barely topped two thousand now, and there were lead contaminated cleanup sites just outside of town. Carol lived with her sister and brother-in-law in a well-kept double-wide on the north side of town. Then she met Chad Stringfellow.

Chad was from nearby Joplin, Missouri. He was a friend of Carol's best friend's boyfriend. He fit his name, with a six-feet-two-inch wiry frame and tight, muscular body. He was three years older and super cool. He had a job at a battery factory in Joplin, a hot car, and money to spend on Carol, which few people in Galena could match. He swept her off her feet. By the time she graduated, she was pregnant, college was forgotten, and they were married, as was the custom in that part of the country in cases like theirs. She expected to live happily ever after.

Carol hopped cars at the local Sonic drive-in to help pay the bills and worked tirelessly at home to cook and clean and be everything she supposed a perfect wife would be, but as her belly expanded, Chad's interest waned. By the time she delivered, she hardly saw him except when he stumbled into bed drunk.

Copernicus H. Stringfellow was born in a shabby trailer attended by Carol's older sister and a local midwife. Carol had always admired the original Copernicus whom she'd done a report on in her junior year European history class. The "H" had no meaning, but she thought it sounded good between Copernicus and Stringfellow.

All Nick could remember of the experience was pressure all around him followed by the shock of being expelled from the warmth and security of his mother's womb. He cried but calmed immediately upon being wrapped in a blanket and laid in his mother's arms. He smiled as she sang to him, and the familiar voice soothed him like aloe on sunburn after the trauma of being expelled down a drainpipe.

Within a few days, Nick was looking brightly at the world around him in a way that told Carol he was no ordinary baby. He never cried, only making faces and moaning softly when messy or letting out an occasional squeal when hungry. He seemed to listen to every word his mother spoke to him. She began reading to him when he was just a couple of weeks old and held conversations as if he would respond to her.

Chad came to loathe the little intruder as Carol doted on him. She increasingly worked to ignore her drunk and disorderly spouse. He spent even less time at home, and when he was there, barely a word was spoken that wasn't accusatory or argumentative. He refused to have the least bit to do with Nick and demanded that Carol wait on him as if the baby had no need of her.

Nick's memories were vague, but he knew that even as a baby resented his father's treatment of his angel mother. To say Nick was a child prodigy would be like saying Hitler was an inconsiderate guy. He was speaking full sentences by the time he reached six months old. He talked nearly nonstop except when Chad was home. Then he would clamp his jaws like a clam on a finger.

Nick's memory was very clear from that point on. In fact, he never forgot anything. His photographic memory was more like streaming video. He could play it back and pick out the minutest detail in the background.

The relationship, or lack thereof, between his mother and father was foremost of these early memories. Nick still woke up screaming when he saw in his dream his drunken dad slapping his mom around. Chad would arrive in the middle of the night after an evening with the boys at the bar and wake Carol, demanding that she love him and serve him, or just to harass her about supposed faults she had as a wife, mother, and homemaker. Things came to a head just before Nick's second birthday. Carol was sitting on the couch with Nick beside her. He was reading her a Dr. Seuss book.

It was early June, and a towering black thunderhead had just over-shadowed Galena. The bucket-bursting clouds were cascading over the trailer like Niagara in spring. The 1812 Overture was exploding in the blackened sky when Chad seemed to rupture the door, drunk as usual.

"Witch, you've blown all our cash. How am I supposed to pay the rent?"

"I haven't bought anything but food and a few clothes at the thrift store for the baby," she meekly replied.

"You blow it all on that baby. When's the last time you bought me any new clothes?" he demanded.

"But Nick is growing. He can't wear what he wore three months ago."

"And food! You never have anything but slop around here."

"I'm sorry, Chad. I do the best I can." Then cowering and in a palsied voice, she whispered, "Maybe if you'd go to the bar less often."

Chad's face tomatoed, and he inhaled a tropical depression. "You smart-mouthed little twit!" he bellowed as his right hand drew back and began a concussive swing at Carol's cringing face.

Time crawled like a slug on the freeway for Nick as he watched that long arm careening toward his beloved mother. His entire little genius mind focused on the projected point of impact. Half an inch prior to contact, Chad's digits struck armor and bent back 90 degrees as his arm continued forward, breaking all four fingers at the first joint.

Chad screamed in pain and blasted every word of profanity in his limited vocabulary. "What have you done to me, you sorry little . . . I'm going to beat the . . . out of you, you two-bit . . . !" He fashioned a fist with his big left hand, pulled it back like the string of a crossbow, and then let it fly.

Once again little Copernicus focused on his mother's befrighted face. Chad's fist again came to about a half inch from it and slammed into a brick wall tearing his flesh and busting his bones. His wails were like a bevy of banshees fleeing hell. The sound was still crystal clear in Nick's memory. Chad burst through the door of the trailer with his shoulder and ran off like a wounded tiger fleeing a charging elephant into the howling rage of the night.

Carol called her sister Lily, who came over immediately with her husband, Stan. She retold the story, in awe of what had happened. She couldn't fathom it. It never occurred to her or Lily that Nick may have been involved, and he didn't say a word. Lily made Carol talk to the police, which she'd always refused to do before. The sheriff got a restraining order and served it on Chad, not allowing him within one hundred yards of the house.

Carol was inconsolable as she blamed herself for ruining a marriage covenant she'd made for better or worse. She tried to reach Chad at his friends' places and at the taverns she knew him to frequent. She wanted to suggest counseling to plaster up the crumbling walls of their once beautiful love affair. Chad was not to be found.

Two weeks later, Chad showed up. Keeping the specified one hundred yards from the trailer, he waited till Carol stepped out to the porch holding little Nick's hand. This time there was nothing Nick could do as a .30-caliber hollow point bullet entered his mother's head. She slumped against the side of the trailer.

Chad Stringfellow was never seen in Cherokee County again despite an intense manhunt. The rifle was found with his fingerprints on it, and in the minds of the people of Galena, he was convicted in absentia of first-degree murder. Copernicus moved in with Stan and Lily Bennett and his two older cousins.

NIHONGO

Nick was walking the halls on the fourth floor the next morning when his cell phone rang. It was a nurse asking about the gardener's job on behalf of her grandfather. Nick agreed to meet her at lunch in the cafeteria. He described himself and assumed she could pick him out. He was right.

"Hi, you must be Nick." She was a compact, dark-eyed, beautiful, black-haired Japanese-American, which Nick had already deduced from her slight accent on the phone. Her hair fell several inches below her shoulders in gentle waves. Her face was not the classic oval of the Japanese floating world art, but longer and thinner, almost European. Though slim, she had more than the typical Japanese stick figure from over two decades of a high-protein American diet.

"That's me, and you are?"

"Yukiko Ishikawa."

"Ah, Snow-child Rocky-river," Nick answered, translating her name.

"You speak Japanese." It was half question, half statement.

"Yeah, I've picked up a bit."

"Where did you learn?"

"Oh, when I started college, I thought I'd like to go there someday, so I took a class."

"That's wonderful. Have you ever been?"

"No, I've been kind of busy, but I'm sure I'll get there someday. Why would you want a landscaping job?"

"It's not for me; it's for my grandfather."

40

"That's great that you're looking out for your grandparents."

"They're more like my parents. I live with them."

"Where are your parents?"

"They died when I was three, and I'm an only child."

"How old is your grandpa?"

"He's sixty-nine, but he's in great shape. He's always done farm or landscaping work."

"How about your grandma?"

"She's sixty-eight, but not so healthy. Nothing specific, but she just seems worn out. She can't work, but she keeps the house clean. They won't let me help out with the bills. They say I should save my money for when I have a family."

"So is a family on the horizon for you?"

"Maybe somewhere *over* the horizon. Right now I'm too concerned with my grandparents."

"Do they discourage you from dating?"

"No, but when I had a gaijin (foreign) boyfriend, I could tell it bothered them, so I broke up with him. Unless I can find a Japanese guy, or until my grandparents die, I'll probably be single. Grandpa doesn't speak much English. He's issei."

Nick knew that *issei* meant first generation, or an immigrant direct from Japan. "So that makes you sansei (third generation)," he answered. "Anata no Nihongo was doo desu ka?"

"My Japanese is fine. It's all we speak at home."

"Great. Could your grandfather drop by my place this afternoon? He's got the job if he wants it. I'll be able to brush up on my Nihongo." (It didn't need brushing.)

SUNDAY DINNER

Monica Furney opened the door, looked up at Nick's tall figure, and grabbed him in a big bear hug. "Nick, it's been so long. How are you? You really need to put on some weight. I've got a big dinner waiting for you. How are you?"

"I'm great, Mrs. Furney. It's great to see you."

"I think you know me well enough not to call me Mrs. Furney, Nick. Monica will do."

"Okay, Mrs. Furney."

"Nick!"

"Okay, Monica."

"That's better. Come in, sit down. Theo, Nick's here!"

"I'll be right down."

"Make yourself at home, Nick. Theo will be right down. I've got to check the roast."

The Furneys lived on a hill overlooking Lake Washington a few blocks north of Leschi Park. It was a large two-story home about one hundred feet up from the water. The living room was sunken three steps from the entryway at the right corner of the home and the dining room to the left of that. Both rooms opened onto a stained cedar deck with an unencumbered view of the lake.

Dr. Furney came down the stairs, and Nick stood to greet him.

"Sit down, Nick. Old friends needn't be so formal. I'm so glad you've come to Seattle. I seldom see anyone from the East Coast anymore."

"I'm just grateful you could give me a job."

"You've always got a job with me, Nick, not that you need one. Why haven't you retired yet?"

"Why would I want to retire? What would I do then?"

"Anything you want, I suppose. It's not like you need the money."

"You don't need the money either, prof, but you can't quit, can you?"

"No, I guess not. It won't be too long though. The old mare ain't what she used to be."

"You still look great."

"Boys, come and sit down for dinner." Monica Furney was five feet ten inches tall and was stately and trim. She was clad in a navy blue dress and was hanging her apron on a hook in the kitchen. She asked her husband to say grace, which she let him get by without except when company was there.

"Nick, tell me what you've been doing with your life. It's been too many years."

"I've been kind of a rolling stone, Mrs. Furney."

"Monica."

"Monica. Before coming here I was working in Ohio. Do you remember Brad Clawson?"

"Brad . . . ?"

"You remember him, dear. A psychiatrist. Right, Nick?"

"Yeah, he was at Columbia with us—played the drums in our band."

"Oh, him. I never really knew him, but I sure enjoyed your music. Do you still play?"

"I try to at least a couple of times a year. I don't want to get out of practice."

"Well, what were you doing with Brad?"

"He has a mobile psychiatry clinic servicing small towns north of Columbus. He specializes in mood disorders."

"What made you leave?"

"It just drove me crazy."

"Still a wisecracker, eh, Nick? How is Brad?"

"He's got a pretty wife and a couple of teenagers. He's very happy, despite the teenagers."

"Speaking of children, Nick. Shouldn't you have some of your own by now?"

"I thought I'd wait till I got married."

"Well, Theo and I will take care of that while you're in town. How long were you in Columbus?"

"About a year."

"And where have you been all of the other years?"

"I spent a couple of years in North Carolina and a couple in Memphis. I was in Alabama and Mississippi about a year each. I could name just about every state east of the Mississippi and account for a month or two."

"Goodness, what have you done in all of those places, and why don't you settle down?"

"I've mostly just spent time with friends or made new ones. I like to dabble in different things."

"Has it all been related to medicine?"

"No, I've parked cars and pumped gas and cleaned toilets."

"Cleaned toilets. I thought only us housewives did that."

"No, ma'am. I worked as a custodian in an office building in Mobile."

"Why would you want to do that when you could be a doctor?"

"I love being a doctor, but sometimes it just feels right to do other things. There are good people everywhere."

"Sure there are, but a janitor? Anyway, I'm glad you're in Seattle. Theo tells me you're playing a nurse. You remember I was a nurse. But why wouldn't you want to be a doctor?"

"I will be a doctor. I'm always a doctor, whatever else I do. I just think while I'm here, I'll do better if people see me as a nurse."

"He just wants to remain anonymous, honey," Theo joined in.

Dinner was delicious. Then they had pie and ice cream on the deck. Nick declined a second piece, saying too many sweets can be detrimental to one's health.

QUESTIONS

That afternoon Nick was once again in the burn center in the room of little Jamie Preston.

"Who are you?" she asked, awake but groggy, with her eyes bandaged.

"I'm Nick. I'm a nurse, and I'm here to do some things that will help you heal. Is it okay if I go ahead?" Nick didn't want her to talk much because it would tax her and the facial movement might disturb her wrappings.

"Sure, go ahead." Something in Nick's manner spoke of love and safety, and she willingly submitted to the same routine he had performed the day before.

The stimulation of the pituitary gland, aside from its healing effects, produced endorphins, which gave Jamie an overwhelming feeling of happiness and peace. Jamie had sensations she'd describe as tingly as Nick focused his psycho-energies on her internal organs.

"I don't want you to talk much," he said. "It wouldn't be good for your bandages. I think, though, that your healing process has quickened. I'm hopeful that you won't have to be here much longer. I'm sure you'd rather be home."

"I would," she whispered.

"Well, these kinds of burns are very severe, and I don't want you to get overly optimistic, but I think you're coming right along."

After the therapy, Nick didn't stay long, wanting Jamie to get the rest necessary to her healing process. He left her happy and hopeful.

Dr. Press Spurbeck was approaching Jamie's room when from about twenty feet away she saw Nick exiting and heading the other way with a Twinkie held to his lips. "Excuse me!" she said, hurrying to catch him. "Excuse me!" she repeated, grabbing him by the elbow. "Who are you? And what are you doing coming to this little girl's room every day?"

"As . . . as I, uh, told you yesterday, I'm Nick Stringfellow," he stammered. "I'm a, uh, nurse here, and I'm a friend of Jamie's."

"As I told you yesterday, you should work where you're assigned." She shot back commandingly.

"I, uh, I'm very sorry, doctor," he said, hanging his head slightly, "but I'm a 'nurse at large,' and I've, uh, been told I'm free to go wherever I'm needed."

"You're not needed here, and I've never heard of a 'nurse at large.' Who made you that? And why are you eating a Twinkie? You shouldn't eat in the hallway, and especially in patients' rooms."

"Uh, Dr. Furney, uh, he gave me the title and I, uh . . . I'm sorry. I like Twinkies." Nick slinked away, mad at himself for having upset such a beautiful woman and for feeling so tongue-tied in her presence. She was as intimidating as she was gorgeous.

Prescilla stood there fuming. The mention of Dr. Furney had shut her up. He was at the top of the hospital ladder, and she was down several rungs. If he truly had hired this guy, there was nothing she could do, but she didn't trust this "nurse at large" thing. The HR manager was the mother of one of Dr. Spurbeck's college roommates. She'd check through back channels to find out about this Stringfellow fellow.

Nick shuffled off to his locker to refill his fanny pack.

NUMBER 1

That afternoon at 4:20 p.m. nine-year-old Gina Dealva was walking home from school at Hawthorne Elementary in the Rainier district. She'd just turned left, as she did every day from Genesee Street onto Forty-First Avenue South when a man stepped out from a windowless van and greeted her.

"Hello, Gina. How are you?"

"Fine. Who are you?" she answered cautiously.

"I'm a friend of your mother's. She asked me to pick you up," he said, drawing closer.

"I've never seen you before." She was worried.

"Don't give me any trouble," he said angrily and grabbed her right arm, pulling her into his body while slapping his left hand over her mouth before she could call out. Looking around and seeing no one, he carried her to the van, where he duct-taped her mouth closed and hand-cuffed her to a ring hanging from the ceiling behind the passenger seat.

QUALIFIED

Just before her shift ended at five, Dr. Spurbeck made her way into the office of Laura Lebow, Director of Human Resources.

"Hello, Prescilla. What brings you here?"

"Hi, Mrs. Lebow." Press couldn't be informal with the older generation.

"How's your residency going?"

"I'm learning a lot and really enjoying it. The doctors on staff are great at taking extra time to teach."

"Good. I'd hate to have to censure any of them for disappointing my favorite employee."

"How's Jan?"

"Great! I think she'll be engaged soon."

"Really? Anyone I know?"

"He's a nice young man from her office. He's been over several times, and we really like him. You should do a double date with them sometime."

"I'd love to if I had anyone to double date with."

"Are you letting work interfere with your love life?"

"If I had a love life, I wouldn't let it interfere."

"Well, you've plenty of years left before you hit old maid status. Jan's a couple of years older than you, and she's still young."

"That's true, but it seems like all of the fish in the sea work somewhere besides Harborview."

"We're not exactly the Dating Game here, I suppose. Now, I'm guessing this isn't just a social call."

"No, actually there's a strange character I've run into a couple of times. I wondered if you could check into him."

"Personnel records are confidential, Prescilla. You know that."

"I know. I'm not asking you to show them to me, just read them yourself. That's allowed."

"Sure, I guess if that's all you want. Who is it?"

"He says his name is Nick Stringfellow."

"Stringfellow, huh? Probably Nicholas." Depressing her intercom switch, she made the request. "Sheri, could you get me the file on a Stringfellow, probably Nicholas?"

"Right away," Sheri answered.

In a moment the file was delivered. "There's no Nicholas, but here's the file for Copernicus Stringfellow."

"That must be it," Laura answered, opening it. "Well, the address and phone number are here. I shouldn't be reading this to you, but it's so unusual. There's no resume, and in the experience and education section it just says, 'Qualified' and is signed by Dr. Furney. The assignment is given as 'nurse at large.'"

"That's what he said," Press told her, "'nurse at large.' What does that mean?"

"I don't know. I'm sure I've never seen it in my twenty-five years in health care."

"Can a person be hired without providing their qualifications?"

"Well, I've never seen it done, but I sure wouldn't question Dr. Furney's judgment in the matter."

"Could you ask him about it, and about the 'nurse at large' title?" Press pleaded. "I can't get him out of my mind. There's something odd about him."

"Well, sure, Prescilla. If it's bothering you, I'll ask Dr. Furney about it. I've got to see him on another matter before I leave today anyway. Come and see me in the morning."

"Thank you, Mrs. Lebow. I'm very grateful."

GARDENER

Yaburo Ishikawa showed up at Nick's home at about five thirty, accompanied by his granddaughter, Yukiko. He was short and skinny, as befitted his race. He was permanently bent from decades of bending over on the farm. His skin was brown, wrinkled, and leathery from long exposure to the sun.

"Hajimemashita Ishikawa-san. Nikku to moshimasu." (*A pleasure to meet you, Mr. Ishikawa. My name is Nick.*) Nick didn't try to transliterate Copernicus or Stringfellow because the length and combination of Ls and Rs would have frustrated a Japanese tongue.

"Hajimemashita," he said, bowing low. "Oshigoto o domo arigato gozaimasu." (*Thank you very much for the work.*)

Nick bowed equally low, "Doo itashimashite." (*You're welcome.*) He went on to explain that Mr. Ishikawa could do whatever he thought best for the yard, that he only expected a few hours of work a day, and that he'd pay $3,000 per month.

Ishikawa-san went right to work.

MISSING PERSON

At eight o'clock at night a call was forwarded to Detective Terry Kimura. A Mrs. Dealva was on the line, hysterical that her daughter Gina had never come home from school. He started with the standard questions.

"How old is your daughter?"

"Nine."

"Have you checked with the school?"

"Of course."

"Is she out with friends?"

"No, I've called all of them."

"Has she ever run away before?"

"No."

"Does Mr. Dealva know she's lost?"

"I'm divorced."

"Where does your ex-husband live?"

"Newark."

"Might he have come and gotten her?"

"I haven't heard from him in five years. He doesn't care about Gina."

"Relax, Mrs. Dealva. I'm sure she'll turn up. I'll come right over and check things out."

"Thank you so much. Please hurry." She gave him the address.

Detective Kimura was a ten-year veteran of the Seattle Police force. He'd grown up in the Rainier District and liked working there. There was a lot of crime, most of it drug and gang related. They didn't have any active kidnappers in the area that he was aware of, so he was confident this would turn out to be a short-term missing person case. Kids ran away and wandered off and went places on their own all the time, but he felt he should provide a balm for Mrs. Dealva. He was there by eight thirty.

Arriving at the Dealva home, Terry was greeted by an agitated mother.

"Come in, detective. Sit down. Have you heard anything yet?"

"No, ma'am," he said, taking a seat in a wing-backed chair by the front window. "I'll need to get a description and pictures before we can have our officers start looking."

"Sure, I'm sorry. Can I get you a cup of coffee or something?"

"No thanks. Let's start with a photo. Do you have anything recent?"

"Sure," she said, grabbing a frame from atop the TV. "This is her school picture from just a couple of months ago."

"That'll work great. Can I take this with me?"

"Sure, anything. Do you think she'll be okay?"

"In most of these cases, the child is found within hours of when we start looking. Usually they just go someplace new and forget about the time."

"Oh, I don't think she'd do that. She's very responsible."

"Still, we're very good at this. It happens all of the time. Now how tall is she?"

"About four feet ten inches, I believe."

"And she has brown shoulder-length hair?" he asked, looking at the photo.

"That's right."

"And what does she weigh?"

"I don't know . . . about average, I suppose."

"What was she wearing today?"

"She had a sky blue jacket with a hood, Levi's, and a red T-shirt that said 'Top Gun' on the front."

"Does she do well in school?"

"Oh yes. She never gets less than a B."

"Do you know her close friends?"

"Yes, and their mothers. I'm careful about where I let her go."

"Could you provide me with a list?"

"Sure," she said as she retrieved a pen and paper and began writing.

"Are there others whose families you don't know?"

"She's very outgoing. I'm sure she has many friendly acquaintances."

"There's a good chance she's with one of them then."

"No, she wouldn't do that without calling."

"What are her hobbies? Is she involved in any extracurricular activities at school?"

"She plays basketball and T-ball, but those are done outside of school and neither of them are going right now."

"Are there any men in your life?"

"No, not right now."

"How long has it been?"

"I haven't been seeing anyone for over a year now."

"Would any friends or ex-boyfriends have any interest in Gina?"

"No, I don't think so."

"If you could remember contact information for any men in your life over the past few years, it would help."

"Okay, I'll add it to the list. Can you issue an Amber Alert?"

"I'm sorry, ma'am. Gina doesn't meet the criteria."

"Why not? She's missing!"

"First, we have to confirm she's been abducted, and then that she's at risk of serious injury or death."

"Death! You don't think she'll be killed, do you?"

"No, ma'am. Like I said, it's very likely we'll find her with a friend or something. If you've finished that list, I'll begin working on it and get Gina's picture out to our force."

"Yes, detective. Please hurry."

"We'll get right on it. Don't worry."

"I'll worry."

"I understand. I'll get back to you as soon as we have anything to report."

"Thank you."

ABOUT FACE

Dr. **Spurbeck was in Jamie** Preston's room first thing in
the morning. Mrs. Preston was there, because she was about half of
the time. It was time to change Jamie's facial mask.

She slowly began the process of cutting the connecting tape at the
back of Jamie's head and gently lifting the plastic from both sides. This
was often painful, because the scabs could be ripped away or healing skin
torn open. Jamie's face had been a mangle of both atrophic (depressed)
and hypertrophic (elevated) scar tissue.

Though she did her best to stay emotionally detached from her
patients, Press really cared for this little girl whom she had helped treat
from the day she came in a couple of weeks ago. She'd also spent a
good deal of time with Mrs. Preston, consoling her and explaining that
even with the best of care and reconstructive surgery, Jamie would likely
never again be a pretty girl. No one had told Jamie, and so far she had
faced her trials with courage.

The compress began lifting free of the side of Jamie's face, and Jamie
drew a deep breath through gritted teeth but didn't cry out. Press continued to lift as carefully as she could, and after what seemed like ten
minutes but was really about twenty seconds, the pad floated free.

Standing to the side, Mrs. Preston gasped, as she was the first to see
her daughter's face. She'd been prepared for carnage but not for this.
Drawing the pad to the side, Press saw it too. Bright pink raw skin, new
and tender but smooth as a baby's behind. Press stood there, astonished.
Mrs. Preston burst into tears.

"What's the matter, Mommy?" Jamie asked worriedly.

"Nothing, baby. You're beautiful," she said, squeezing Jamie's hand, too fearful to hold her in her arms like she wanted to. "You're beautiful."

Press gained her composure. She bolted through the door and shouted at the nearby nurse's station. "Nurse, call Dr. Wetstone, STAT!" she yelled, referring to Jamie's primary physician.

Dr. Wetstone was there in two minutes, having been just down the hall. "What is it?" he asked, looking at Press, who, with Mrs. Preston, could do nothing but stare at the patient.

"Look," Press answered, and he did.

After a long pause to drink in the miraculous sight, he spoke. "I've never seen anything like it," he said. "I've used this new French method several times now. It's good, but not this good. Have you done something I don't know about?"

"Nothing, doctor," Press answered. "Look at this," she said, pointing just above Jamie's eyes. "Eyebrows."

"Impossible," he said, bending closer for a better view. After a disbelieving hesitation, he admitted "You're right, the beginnings of eyebrows. That's impossible."

"Maybe so, but there they are," Press replied.

Mrs. Preston stood silently, tears streaming down her cheeks, caressing the hand of her once again beautiful little girl.

THE NEEDLE

Nick was taking the Joneses to the Space Needle's Sky City Restaurant for dinner. The kids had all been to the observation deck, as had Jemima as a teenager, but never could they afford to eat there. The kids already knew Nick was a walking encyclopedia. On the ride up the windowed elevator, Tilly asked, "Nick, how tall is the Needle?"

James butted in. "It's fifty stories."

"Actually," said Nick, "it's fifty-one, but then that's another story."

Jemima jabbed an elbow in his side for that one.

As they exited the elevator, the hostess greeted them. "May I help you?"

"Reservations for Stringfellow," Nick told her.

"A party of five?"

"Yes."

The Space Needle was originally built for the 1962 World's Fair. It consisted of three immense steel beams reaching 500 feet into the sky topped with a round, almost saucer-like edifice.

They were seated by the window. The dining area was a ring around the outside of the Needle's core about fifteen feet wide. The dinner guests orbited the center core, which included the elevators, kitchen, restrooms, and so on, at a speed that gave them a 360-degree view of the city once every hour.

"Wow," Tilly said as she jumped in the seat closest the window and did her best to look straight down. "This is way cooler than the observation deck."

"Tilly, you should let Nick sit there. He's new in town."

"It's okay, Jemima. I'm the tallest, and I'll sit the furthest from the window. I'm not too interested in seeing straight down anyway."

The window they were seated next to opened to a large bucket used by the guy who cleaned the glass outside. "Whoa," said Nick. "This is a poor location for defenestration."

"Say what?" asked Jemima.

"What's de-fen-es-tration?" Tilly sounded it out.

"Oh, that means being thrown out the window. I can only imagine it might hurt more through that window than through most others."

"You use too many big words," Jemima scolded.

"If you don't use them, they'll go to waste."

"Look, Nick, there's the University of Washington." Tilly quickly moved on from the vocabulary lesson and pointed northeast over Lake Union to the school's campus. "James is going there year after next."

"Provided he keeps his grades up and passes the SATs," added Jemima sternly.

"You don't have to keep telling me, Mama. I won't quit working. Look at these prices!" James exclaimed as the menus were placed on the table.

"Shhh." Jemima shushed him. "That's not polite."

"It's okay, James," Nick said. "I'm taking employees to dinner. I'll write it off as a tax deduction."

"It's a really good school. It's got—" Tilly continued.

"Tilly, let James describe the college. He'll be going there before you do," interrupted Jemima.

"What are you going to major in, James?" Nick asked.

"I haven't decided yet. It's the best university around here, and I think I'll be more employable with any degree than if I went anywhere else. Besides, it's close to home and I can save on rent."

"I hear they've got a good medical school there," Nick commented.

"Excuse me, excuse me!" Tilly said, raising her hand as if in school.

"Go ahead, Tilly," Jemima allowed.

"It's one of the best," Tilly assured him.

"You don't know it from any medical school," Cassy thrust in.

"Well, I'm sure it's a good one." Tilly was defiant.

"You're bragging like you invented it."

"You girls, stash it." Jemima warned them.

They were looking out on Lake Union, a small freshwater lake connected by canal to both the Puget Sound on the west and the larger Lake Washington on the east. There are locks, allowing boats and small ships to travel from freshwater to saltwater and back.

"That's the Montlake Cut," Tilly said. "And that's the University of Washington stadium. When there's football games, rich people drive right up in their yachts and take a shuttle to the stadium."

As they began with an appetizer of Dungeness crab cakes, the view made its way to the southeast. "Look, Nick, Mt. Rainier!" Tilly nearly shouted.

"Keep your voice down. This isn't McDonald's," Jemima warned her.

"Sorry, Mama."

"It's beautiful, Tilly. I've heard that the Indians used Mt. Rainier to predict the weather."

"Really?" asked Cassy. "How did they do that?"

"Well, they said if you could see the mountain it was about to rain. If you couldn't see it, it was already raining." That earned Nick another elbow in the side from Jemima.

"Nick, do you make up this funny stuff or do you steal it?" James asked.

"There's no new thing under the sun, James."

As they got to soup and salads, they were facing south toward downtown. "There's the Columbia Center Tower," Tilly said, pointing to the tallest building in town. "It's seventy-six stories tall."

"Actually, its seventy-seven," interjected Nick, "but then that's—" An elbow from Jemima stopped him short and exacted an "Ouch."

The daylight was ebbing out to sea, and downtown began to twinkle. They ordered entrees, king salmon for Nick, New York strip for James, Jemima had the seafood pasta, and the girls both got Short Ribs.

"You can't get what I get," Tilly accused.

"I can get what I want. I liked ribs before you were born."

"Looks like you've eaten too much of them to me."

"Better than anorexia . . ."

"You girls stash it or I'll defenestrate you," Jemima scolded.

To the southwest, the view turned to Elliot Bay, Seattle's port section.

"That's where the Duwamish River enters the Sound," Tilly said, pointing. "Did you know that Chief Sealth was chief of the Duwamish Tribe and he's who Seattle is named after?"

"Really," Nick replied. "Is that the truth or is it just another story—" An elbow stopped him short.

By the time they faced west, the sun was in the throes of a red and purple struggle, waging war with the summits of the Olympic mountain range. In the end the sun lost, leaving nothing but the jagged edges of the mountains to stand as shadowy sentinels in the sky.

Tilly's guided tour of the Seattle skyline was into reruns as they rounded out their 360-degree vista. They topped off the gourmet meal with the Needle's signature dessert, Lunar Orbiters, all around the table. A Lunar orbiter is a chocolate or berry sundae served atop a goblet of dry ice over which the server pours hot blue water as it's set before the recipient. The gush of steam covers the table and spills over the side to the floor. Five at once nearly caused a death-fog throughout the restaurant.

"This is way cool!" Tilly exclaimed.

"Such a juvenile," said Cassy.

"Well, it is cool; you're just not cool enough to admit it."

"Girls, stash it."

CONFESSION

Nick had walked Cathy home the night before and now sat with her at the swing shift lunch hour. "You asked me if we could discuss the happenings of that first night later," she reminded Nick. "Is it later yet?"

He paused, thinking. He'd never talked to anyone about the special things he did. Some had asked, but he'd put them off. Many previous victims and rescuees had wanted to ask, but he'd left the scene before they could. Others were unconscious, drunk, or just too dumbfounded to believe that anything out of the ordinary had really happened. Even his aunt and uncle were quiet about things they knew to be true but didn't want to discuss.

He looked Cathy in the eyes. She was pretty in an unadorned way. She was obviously kind, humble, and in a way quite innocent. He felt a special affinity toward her that he'd never felt before. "I've never talked with anyone about this," he began. "Can you keep a secret?" He looked around as he spoke, noting that no one was seated in any of the adjacent tables.

"I've kept them all my life," she answered and put her hand over his.

Her touch was warm—not romantic, but comforting. Through its warmth Nick knew he could trust her like he'd trusted no one before. "I'm smart," he said simply.

"I know you're smart, Nick. What's that got to do with the things I've seen? We're talking about more than smart," she prompted him.

"No, I wasn't bragging. I can do things because I'm smart."

"There's lots of smart people in the world. Are you smart and a magician?"

"No, magic is illusion. I do real things. I'm not tricking anyone. I can do things that seem like miracles to other people because they don't understand them. They're not really miracles. When I concentrate, things just happen."

"What do you mean 'things happen'?"

"Well, when that guy pulled a gun on me, I focused on the gun and ripped it from his hand."

"You just *thought* the gun out of his hand?"

"Sort of."

"I don't get it."

"It's not difficult. I just focus on his hand and make it let go of the gun. Then I focused on him and threw him against the wall. I turned my concentration to the other guy and did the same. That's what I mean."

"How can you do that? It sure sounds like magic."

"Magic means it's something that can't be explained or that someone is fooling someone else. You've heard of telekinesis?"

"Moving things with your mind? Yeah, I've heard of it, but I never believed it. Is that what you do? How does it work?"

"I've been studying all of my life to understand it," Nick explained. "I've studied physics, medicine, religion, everything I can think of. I think I understand it, but I haven't been able to prove anything, physically or mathematically."

"What is it then?" Cathy pushed harder, trying to understand.

"As near as I can figure, it's thought waves," he answered.

"Thought waves?"

"Yes, waves. You know about sound waves and light waves. There are also thought waves. I'm reasonably sure of it."

"And you can move things with thought waves?" she asked, incredulous.

"You know a sonic boom vibrates objects, and you know a laser can cut materials. Thought waves can move things too. The trouble is, despite all of my efforts, I've not been able to devise a method or an instrument that can actually measure them. They're too fine, undetectable."

"Then how can you use them?" she asked.

"I guess my powers of concentration are just greater than anyone else's. I'm really not bragging. That's just the truth."

"So waves of thought shoot out of your head and make things move?"

"Yeah, that's what I figure. I can't think of anything else that would explain it."

"How many times have you done things like this?"

"Actually quite a few. Trouble seems to follow me around."

"In my case, you seemed to come looking for trouble."

"I guess I'm kind of foolhardy because I feel like I can handle myself."

"Have you been doing this kind of thing all your life?"

"Most of it. It was quite a while before I developed my theory of thought waves though."

"I'd like to hear about some of the other times you've done this."

"I'd really rather not talk about it. Can you just take it on faith?"

"I believe you," she said, squeezing his hand.

"Please promise you'll never talk to anyone about this," Nick asked.

"Promise," she assured him.

JEALOUSY

Frank Brunk worked in hospital maintenance. He was thirty-three years old and six feet tall, with a belly that crossed the county line well before the rest of him. He weighed close to 280 pounds. He had thick, stringy black hair and a five o'clock shadow that showed up around nine in the morning. His dark shirt always had darker stains under the armpits, and people never seemed to stand too close. He didn't have any friends in the hospital, or at home for that matter. He lived with his widowed mother, who still treated him like a kid.

Because of his mother's possessiveness, he developed his own. He cherished his time away from home, his van—which he never shared with her—and many other prized possessions that he kept locked in his van so his mother couldn't get to them.

Frank sat at a table in the corner of the cafeteria watching as Nick and Cathy talked. He nearly left his seat when Cathy put her hand on Nick's. Who was this guy anyway? Frank hadn't seen him around. He was dressed in blue, so he must be some kind of medical puke. Frank sat and seethed till the guy finally got up and left, his head nearly scraping the doorway as he exited the cafeteria. Frank walked across the room and sat down facing Cathy.

"Who's the geek?" he asked.

"A friend," she answered frostily.

"I ain't seen him before."

"He's new."

"You were holdin' his hand."

"Yes, I was."

"You shouldn't do that to me."

"I didn't do anything to you. You don't own me."

"You're my girl, and you'd better act like it."

"I'm not your girl! I only went out with you once."

"You'd better not disrespect me. I'll hurt you."

"Leave me alone, you freak," she said, pushing herself away from the table.

"I'd better not see you hanging around with him again," he called after her as she left.

NO ANSWER

Dr. Spurbeck ran into Laura Lebow in the hall outside her office. "Hi, Mrs. Lebow. Did you find anything out about the qualifications of this Stringfellow character?"

"Yeah, I brought it up to Dr. Furney. I asked him about the 'nurse at large' title. I told him there was no provision for it in the collective bargaining agreement."

"I don't know much about unions. Does that mean it can't be done?"

"I told him it concerned me, and he just said if there were any problems he'd handle it. Then he asked me not to make any problems."

"That doesn't sound like him. He's usually so nice."

"I'm sure he was at least half joking."

"And what about the qualifications thing?"

"He just said, 'Trust me, he's qualified.'"

"Great. Is there anything else you can do?"

"I don't think so, not unless someone makes an issue of it. Are you going to make an issue of it?"

"Of course not."

"Well, I suppose that's the end of it then."

"I'll not bother you about it anymore, but I'm going to do some digging of my own."

"Sounds like your good old determined self. Good luck."

"Thanks."

THE SEARCH

Terry Kimura had spent the day looking for Gina Dealva. Terry was about five feet ten inches tall. He was thin with dark hair. He had a three-year-old daughter, who was cared for primarily by his mother. His wife had died of a virulent type of lymphoma a few months after the baby was born. The shock and suddenness of it caught him totally off guard. He was still in love with her and engulfed himself in his work and his little girl. Finding another mate wasn't even on his radar.

Terry's time on the force had taught him that there wasn't much chance of recovering a missing child after the first day, at least not alive. He'd read of the girl in Utah that was found after nine months but knew that was either a miracle or the rarest of good luck. If a child wasn't found in forty-eight hours, odds were astronomical against a happy conclusion.

The Newark PD had checked on the father, a primary suspect in most child disappearances, and found him to have an airtight alibi. Gina hadn't shown up at any friends' homes. Her teacher had seen her leave school at the regular time, and she was really too young to have run away and stayed so long. There was nothing he could conclude but that she had been abducted.

Terry's heart ached for Mrs. Dealva. He seldom went to church, and then only on Easter or Christmas, but he'd been raised by religious parents and often said a prayer in his heart hoping for the intervention of a higher power. The fact that these prayers were nearly always answered in the negative didn't deter him.

He ran a listing of the known offenders in the area. It was a lot longer than any of the voting public would imagine it. Terry knew that if the media made a bigger deal of it, laws would get tougher and more perps would be kept off the street. He and others in the department would spend several days tracking these guys down and checking out their alibis. It was a tedious process that seldom produced results. He visited Mrs. Dealva to let her know their lack of progress.

"Detective, have you found her yet?"

"No, ma'am, I'm afraid we haven't."

"Well, do you have any leads?"

"We've been to the school and are following up with the parents of all of the children in her class as well as any others that are possible friends of Gina's."

"She wouldn't be missing at a classmate's home for this long, would she?"

"No, not likely."

"Well, what other leads are there?"

"I hate to say it, Mrs. Dealva, but the only other leads we have would be criminal."

"You mean, she's been kidnapped?"

"I'm afraid that's the most likely scenario at this point."

"Do you have any suspects?"

"We keep a list of convicted child molesters. We're checking on all of them."

"You don't think she's been . . . ?" Mrs. Dealva sat on the couch, put her face in her hands, and began to sob.

"We don't know anything yet, ma'am. There's always hope," he said, trying to sound like he believed it.

BLOCK AND TACKLE

Nick joined the Jones family at James's next football game. It was Friday night and James's Franklin Quakers were playing their rival the Garfield Bulldogs in Memorial Stadium at the Seattle Center.

"What number is James?" Nick asked.

"He's number seventy-five. He's a tackle. He plays offense and defense. When he's on offense, like, nobody ever gets by him. He's mass strong." Tilly was excited.

"Do you come to every game?

"Yeah, when Mom lets me."

"It sounds like you're a real fan."

"I like football okay; mostly I just like to watch James. He's way good."

Franklin took the opening kickoff, and soon James was in action. On the first play they took it over James's side of the line for a twelve yard gain.

"He must be strong," Nick commented. "He opened a big hole for the runner."

"He always does. The runners get all of the credit, but they wouldn't get anywhere without James blocking for them."

"Is James's dad a big guy?"

"Mom says so. I've never met him. I haven't seen my own dad since I was four."

"Does James work out?"

"Of course—all football players do. James goes early to school every-day to lift weights. During the summer, he goes to his friend's house."

The next play was a pass, and James kept his defender in front of him.

"It's good that he has such dedication. Whatever you do, it's important to give it your all. Does he do his schoolwork?"

"Oh yeah. Mama wouldn't let him near a football if he got anything less than a C. Mostly he gets Bs and sometimes As."

Over the next few plays Nick could see that James was like a rock—big, strong, and immovable, even when he should have moved. Once when pass-protecting, James's man put a quick sideways move on him and had an open path to the quarterback. Suddenly the guy's feet went out from under him and he missed the sack.

"Sorry, Mom," Nick said to himself.

"See, I told you his man never gets to the quarterback."

"You're right. I've watched every play, and nobody gets by."

Nick opened his backpack to extract some Twinkies. Jemima would only let Cassy and Tilly each have a couple of those Choice Chunks of Channeling.

Franklin scored, and James went on the defense; he was equally immovable in that position.

He seldom got in on a tackle but often occupied two of the other team's linemen.

"How about those cheerleaders?" Nick asked. "Would you like to do that when you're older?"

"I'd rather play football. Did you play football?"

"No."

"I'll bet you played basketball, didn't you?"

There was a roar as the enemy team scored a touchdown.

"If they would have run on James's side, they wouldn't have scored," Tilly assured him. "So did you play basketball?"

"I've played it a few times, but never on a team."

"But you're so tall."

"I'm not what you'd call extremely coordinated."

The Quakers lost that game, but James had a perfect night. Nick apologized to his mother several times.

Seated a few rows back were a couple of men in dark suits. They didn't cheer for either team.

REVIEW ANEW

A couple of days later, Nick was wandering through the Hepatitis and Liver Clinic when he felt the need to step into room 12-C. The patient, a man looking to be in his fifties, was sleeping. Not wanting to wake him to inquire after his condition, Nick went to the nurse's station, where recent ultrasound pictures had been forwarded to the primary physician from the radiology lab.

Nick opened the folder and read the diagnosis of the pictures as negative for any abnormalities. It was signed by Dr. Drosdick, a radiologist. He began to scan the attached photos showing various views of the patient's liver. As he was doing so, the primary physician, Dr. Kelleran, walked up.

"Ah, I see my ultrasound results have arrived."

"Yes, sir," Nick answered. "But there seems to be a discrepancy."

"What's that?"

"Well, the radiologist concluded that there are no abnormalities, but when I looked at this anterior left side view, I noticed a faint change in gray scale for about one thirty-second of an inch past the external surface. I'm afraid it might be the beginnings of a malignancy."

"Let me see that," Dr. Kelleran demanded, examining it more closely. "I believe you're right, son. Good catch."

Nick reached in his fanny pack for a couple of Pleasant Portions of Perspicacity and walked on to the next room.

FISHING

Dr. **Spurbeck ran into Dr.** Furney in the doctor's lounge. He was reading the paper and looked relaxed. "Excuse me, Dr. Furney," she interrupted.

"Yes? Oh, Dr. Spurbeck. How are you?" He didn't always remember all of the young doctors' names, but when they were this pretty, it was hard to forget.

"I'm fine."

"How's your residency progressing?"

"I really enjoy it here. The breadth of exposure is fascinating. I still haven't made up my mind on which area I'd like to specialize in."

"Are you getting enough variety in your assignments?"

"Oh yes. Harborview has some of everything, and I'm seeing quite a medley of afflictions.

"We're not overworking you, I hope."

"No, sir, not any more than any other resident."

"We count on all of you to carry a lot of the load."

"It is a benefit for us as well as the hospital. It's all so interesting, it's hard to choose a specialty."

"Well, I'm sure you'll succeed whatever you do. Was there something you wanted?"

"Actually, yes." She hesitated. "I've been running into a nurse named Stringfellow, kind of an unusual guy." (She would have said weird but knew Dr. Furney was his friend.) "I'm told you know him."

"Yes, I've known Nick for many years. An amazing person."

71

"I've run into him in several different locations. It's almost as if he too were a resident assigned to multiple disciplines."

"I believe he's been categorized as a 'nurse at large.'"

"I've never heard of a 'nurse at large' before. Is that some new sort of thing?"

"Well, I made it up for Nick. He likes to poke around in a lot of different disciplines."

"That's what I've been wondering about. Can a nurse be effective moving around so much? Wouldn't he be better staying in one department, at least till he learned all about it?"

"Oh, he knows all about it, whatever it is," Dr. Furney assured her.

"Really? I was kind of wondering about his education and experience," she said, trying to prod him along.

"I really don't think I should go into that." He paused. "But Dr. Spurbeck . . ."

"Yes?" she answered, hoping he'd reveal something.

"If he ever offers a suggestion . . ."

"Yes?"

"Do it!"

"Yes, sir. Thank you, sir," she said, walking away more curious than before.

HANDYMAN

Nick had several contacts from within the hospital for his handyman posting, but none of them felt right. He was walking down Second Avenue between Yesler and Jackson at lunch hour when he came across the Union Gospel Mission. It was a pleasant day, and men were standing around smoking and joking. As he was passing the door, he noticed a guy seated back against the wall, head down.

"Hey there," Nick greeted him as he tapped him on the shoulder.

The man looked up. He looked to be about thirty-five, with close-cropped hair and several days' growth of beard. His normally thin frame was emaciated, evoking scenes from a concentration camp. His clothes were ragged. "What do you want?" he asked in a voice that said "leave me alone."

"You look like you could use a job," Nick told him.

"Very observant of you. Anything else?"

"What's your name?"

"Russ. What's yours?" the man asked, getting annoyed.

"Nick. I'm in need of a handyman for some repairs to my house. Would you be able to do that kind of work?"

"I've done everything from finish carpentry to plumbing," he answered with a hint of pride in his voice.

"To look at you, one might doubt your reliability."

"Lately all you can rely on is that I'll be unemployed, but when I work, I'm good and dependable."

"Sold," Nick said excitedly. "Here's my address. Can you be there around five?"

"Can I be there? Was Caesar a Greek?"

"I believe he was Roman."

"Well, I'll be there anyway."

HIT ME AGAIN

At the hospital, Nick was in the room of a patient in the Endocrinology Clinic. It was Ekatarina Ivanov, a sixty-six-year-old woman suffering from type 1 diabetes. She had atherosclerosis (narrowing of the blood vessels) causing peripheral limb ischemia (lack of oxygen in her leg tissues).

From her knee down, the skin had a purplish gray hue, and she had several large ulcers exposing raw flesh on her feet. The measurement of her systolic blood pressure was 24 mm Hg at her ankles. Anything below 50 was considered critical. Nick knew from reading her charts that her condition was advanced to the point that amputation had become inevitable.

"Hi, Ekatarina, I'm Nick Stringfellow. Do you mind if I check out your leg problems?"

"I guess that's why I'm here, isn't it?"

"Yeah. Are you enjoying your stay?"

"I had more fun in the principal's office during grade school."

"But isn't the food great?"

"Is that what they call the gooey stuff they bring around three times a day?"

"From your name, I'd guess you're Bulgarian."

"That's right."

"Mnogo mi e priatno da se zapoznaem! Ot kade ste?" (*It's good to meet you. Where are you from?*)

"Az sam ot Shipka." (*I'm from Shipka.*)

"Oh, tova blizo do Shipchenskiat Prohod li e, kadeto niakoi ot nai-vajnite bitki v Rusko-Turskata Voina sa se vodili pres 1800ta godina?" (*Oh, is that near Shipka Pass where some of the most important battles in the Russo-Turkish War of the 1800s took place?*)

"Da, bili li ste tam?" (*Yes, have you been there?*)

"Ne, prosto sam chel za prohoda." (*No, I've just read about it.*)

The conversation continued in Bulgarian.

"You're Bulgarian is very good," the woman said. "Have you been to our country?"

"No."

"I'm amazed."

"Thank you. I'm here to check your legs. Is it okay if I touch them?"

"Of course. Please do."

"Are you in pain?" Nick asked.

"I was, but they've given me some wonderful drugs," the patient replied.

"That's good. I'll need to concentrate. If you could remain silent I'd appreciate it."

"Certainly."

Nick focused on his first target, which was the tissue just below the skin. These ischemic cells produce a protein known as VEGF (vascular endothelial growth factor) that if propagated in sufficient quantity could promote regeneration of the vasculature. He mentally focused, running his mind up and down each leg psychogenically, stimulating the tissues to greater production.

Next he focused on the bone marrow in her pelvis. His mental microscope picked out the stem cells there and ignited their multiplication to produce endothelial progenitor cells that would replace the damaged capillaries in Mrs. Ivanov's legs.

"Tova triabva da e dostatachno za sega. Blagodaria vi. Utre shte se varna. Dovijdane." (*That should do. Thank you. I'll be back tomorrow. Good-bye.*)

"Dovijdane, Nick. S netarpenie shte ochakvam da se vidim." (*Good-bye, Nick. I'll look forward to seeing you.*)

Holding a conversation in Bulgarian then concentrating on a healing exercise was doubly hard on Nick's psyche. Knowing he'd have to return for at least one more treatment, Nick walked out the door and reached into his fanny pack for a Twinkie infusion. Partway into the hall, with the Helpful Hunk of Healing halfway into his mouth, he ran into Dr. Spurbeck again.

Nick stopped in mid-bite, struck with her beauty, but before he could savor that Rich Round of Remedy, he was struck with her sardonic utterance. "So, the great nurse Stringfellow is actively involved in the fight against diabetes, I see."

Nick fought to gulp down the Twinkie and respond, but he was too slow.

"I see your table manners are as magnificent as your bedside manners. Excuse me," she said, pushing her way past and into the room.

Press felt guilty about her abruptness, but the guy just seemed to bring out the villain in her.

RUSS

Russ Pauley was a hard luck story waiting to be told. He'd been raised in Renton, just south of Seattle. He never was much for book learning, and he'd dropped out of school after his high school sophomore year, taking the first of his many construction jobs as a roofer. He wasn't unintelligent, just easily distracted. He was a good worker, and roofing paid by the square (one square yard of roofing laid) rather than the hour, so he did okay. He changed employers a couple of times when offers of a higher rate came along.

At twenty, Russ ran into Amber at a friend's party. She was a petite redhead with a freckled face and a figure that was a carpenter's delight: flat as a board. She was kind of pretty though and was sitting alone on the sideline, having been invited by a friend who had subsequently deserted her for male companionship. Russ wasn't the forward type and had never had a girlfriend before. She looked like he felt, and somehow he ended up sitting next to her.

Their romance had blossomed like wisteria entwined in a common vine as they both found their first and only love. They were soon married and after a couple of years had a beautiful baby girl, who became the apple of her daddy's eye. Russ worked hard, but because roofing can't be done when it rains and he lived in Seattle, he tried to pick up other jobs. He worked as an assistant to plumbers, electricians, and framers as he bugged the contractors he knew for any kind of work to keep him occupied.

One rainy day in October, there had been a major pileup on I-5 and Russ's world was shattered. His wife and daughter were both killed instantly when a semi plowed into the back of their car going full speed. He never recovered from the shock. His wages went to alcohol, and he became less and less dependable, missing work because of hangovers or just forgetting to show up.

After a few months of such behavior, he got into a major argument with his boss and said a lot of things he shouldn't have. His boss fired him and told him he'd fix it so he never got another job in this town, and he made good on his promise. Russ eventually lost his apartment and his car. He spent the next eight years on the street. He wasn't an alcoholic, and he eventually dried out, but his reputation was shot, and he could only pick up temporary or part-time work. He hadn't found anything for over a month, and the Union Gospel Mission was keeping him alive when Nick found him.

Russ was waiting for Nick when he got home just before five. He had obviously used the Gospel Mission's facilities to shave and clean himself up. "I never did introduce myself," he said. "I'm Russ Pauley. I can't tell you how thankful I am for this job. I'll make you glad you hired me. You watch, I'll work harder and better than anyone else you could find. I've got a lot of experience, and I've just been down on my luck lately."

"That's fine," Nick said. "Relax, I know you'll work out fine; you're just what I need. Let me walk you through the house."

"I'd like you to start with the obvious repairs: the windows, floor boards, and the roof. Then you can check out the integrity of the plumbing and electrical. That should keep you busy for a while. I'll be hiring an interior designer to come and spruce the place up, and I'll expect you to handle the painting, wallpapering, and so on that she specifies. Have you got your own tools?"

"Uh, no. I pawned them all."

"Here's some money to get what you need and a bit more to get you a place to stay and some food and clothes," Nick said, pressing a wad of hundred dollar bills into his hand. "I'll expect at least forty hours a week, and I'll pay you $5,000 a month. Is that okay?"

"Okay? I can't believe it. Why would you do this for me and how can you trust me with all of this?" he said, holding out the wad of money. "I'm just a bum off the street. How do you know I won't run off and spend it all on booze?"

"It's in your eyes, Russ. I can see the person you are in your eyes."

Just as they stepped out onto the porch, the gardener rounded the corner. "Ishikawa-san O genki desu ka?" Nick greeted him.

"Go kage same de, genki desu," Mr. Ishikawa replied.

"Kore wa Pari san desu. Daiku desu."

"Hajimemashita," Ishikawa said as he bowed to Russ.

"I just introduced you to Mr. Ishikawa, Russ, and explained what you do. You should bow too."

Russ did so but was too stymied to speak.

Across the street and down about a block, two men in a dark sedan looked on.

RECOVERY

Dr. Spurbeck came in for her regular morning check of Mrs. Ivanov's condition. Press knew that within a couple of days the decision would be made to amputate both her legs at the knees. Her overall physical condition would mean that even if she got prostheses, she would likely never walk again. She'd be confined to a wheelchair or motorized scooter. Press was outwardly all business, and many considered her somewhat callous, but the tough exterior was built to hide the natural feminine compassion so deeply rooted within her. The wall was built subconsciously to protect her from her own emotions. She felt she needed it to maintain strength in the eyes of her patients and her peers.

She mechanically wrapped the blood pressure monitor around the patient's ankle and pumped the bulb. She stared in disbelief, then started again from the beginning as if that would make things right. Systolic pressure read 76 mm Hg. She'd never heard of a diabetic actually improving in this manner. She called in the primary physician. Dr. Holder had spent fifteen years working with diabetics. He was as shocked as she.

Press hadn't told Mrs. Ivanov the reason for her astonishment, but now that Dr. Holder had confirmed it, she explained.

"Mrs. Ivanov, your circulation has improved dramatically."

"I wondered why the pain had died down so nicely," she commented. "Is this unusual?"

Dr. Holder assured her it was extremely unusual.

"Well, that good-hearted nurse fellow assured me that things would get better real soon."

"What nurse is that?" Press asked her.

"He said just to call him Nick," she answered.

A picture of Nick Stringfellow leaving the room with a Twinkie sticking out of his mouth popped into Press's mind.

"And his Bulgarian was flawless."

"He speaks Bulgarian?"

"Better than I do, and he says he's never been there, only read about it."

DOUBLE SHOT

Nick continued to walk Cathy home night or day, depending on the shift she worked. He tended to work a bit on each of the three daily shifts. He never slept more than a few hours at a time and preferred being at the hospital to anywhere else. Their conversations were light and happy. Cathy usually gave him a good night kiss on the cheek, but somehow Nick never felt inclined to let it go beyond that. He felt more brotherly than romantic.

He often heard her father greet her with insults and profanity as she went inside, and he wished he could do something about it without seeming a buttinsky. Now, Nick and Cathy were having lunch. "How's your father?" he asked.

"He's okay. Why do you ask?"

"Is it just you and him, or do you have any other family?"

"My mom left Dad when I was three. There's been several others since then. He's insisted I call each of them Mom. They never stay too long on account of the way he treats them."

"How's that?" Nick pressed her.

"He's kind of a gutter mouth. He's really unhappy, and he has trouble being nice to people."

"I've heard him talk to you a few times."

"Oh, you have? I'm sorry. He's just kind of grumpy at that time of night. Really, he doesn't treat me bad. He never gets after me unless I deserve it."

"Are you sure you wouldn't like me to talk to him? Tell him to ease up a bit?"

"Oh no, I wouldn't want you to get involved. Everything's fine— really."

"All right, but if he ever hurts you, I'll do more than throw him against a wall."

"He's never hurt me, Nick. Really. He yells and stuff, and sometimes he raises his hand and looks like he wants to hit me, but he never has. He always catches himself. He doesn't mean anything. He's just hard to live with."

"Then why do you?"

"He needs me."

Cathy had all the psychological symptoms of a battered woman, though Nick believed her when she said she'd never been hit. You didn't need to hit a person to bruise his soul. She was trapped in a home with a worthless father, who wasted his life watching TV and drinking up her hard-earned wages as he constantly demeaned her for supposed imperfections. Nick hadn't figured how yet but was determined to break into this abusive cycle and free her to be the lovely person she was.

RADIO

Nick was in the radiology lab reviewing all of the recent
X-rays, ultrasounds, MRIs, and so on, when a doctor walked in.
He was about five foot seven inches tall and about five foot eight inches
wide. He had a full head of dark wavy hair, a round face, and rosy
cheeks reminiscent of Santa Claus except that he lacked the pleasant
countenance. His mouth was drawn down at the corners in a kind of
permanent frown. He looked at Nick over the top of his glasses.

"You a new technologist?" the doctor asked.

"Kind of," Nick answered. "Nick Stringfellow. How do you do?" he
said, extending his hand.

"Stringfellow," he answered accusatorily, not offering a handshake.
"You're the one that overrode my diagnosis on that liver scan. Who do
you think you are, waltzing in and reviewing my work? You're nothing
but a nurse," he said, staring accusingly at Nick's badge. "What are you
doing in here? You get away from those prints. I'll have your license for
this, butting your nose in where you're not qualified."

"I'm just helping out. I didn't think it would hurt to have another
set of eyes on things," Nick replied humbly.

Several other doctors and technologists stood around awed at the
fury of Dr. Drosdick's rebuke.

"Another set of 'unqualified eyes.' Do you realize the trouble you
could cause coming in and rediagnosing things you have no clue about?
I'd better never catch you interfering in radiology again. You're a danger
to the integrity of this hospital."

Nick put down the negatives and walked out, sorry that he'd caused a scene.

As he left, Dr. Drosdick's toupee flew off his head. It floated to the floor, to his dismay and the delight of all in the lab.

"Sorry, Mom," Nick said as he smiled to himself.

SNOOPY

At about three in the afternoon, Press pulled up in front of Nick's home. She'd weaseled the address out of Laura Lebow, whose curiosity won out over her professional ethics. She wanted almost as badly as Press to know about Copernicus H. Stringfellow. Press saw Ishikawa trimming hedges and Russ Pauley tearing off old shingles when Jemima Jones stepped onto the porch and yelled at both of them to come and get some lemonade. Curious, she got out of the car and walked up to the three on the porch.

"Hi, is this Nick Stringfellow's place?"

"It sure is," Jemima answered.

"Is he here?" she asked, knowing full well he was at the hospital.

"No, ma'am," Jemima told her. "He's at work."

"I'm Dr. Spurbeck. Do you work for him?"

"Yes, ma'am. All three of us do. I'm Jemima Jones. This is Russ and Mr. Ishikawa." The two men nodded their heads in acknowledgment.

"I know I shouldn't ask, but how can he afford his mortgage and three employees on a nurse's salary?" Press questioned.

"We don't actually work for him. We work for CASH Corp Nick's an employee just like the rest of us."

"Really? So he has a job besides the hospital?"

"I guess so."

"What does he do?"

"I'm not sure everything he does, but he bought the house and hired us to fix it up."

"He's a real estate developer?"

"I haven't seen him developing anything but this house."

"CASH Corp must have a lot of money to pay him to buy one house."

"I don't know, but he—I mean, the corporation—pays us well," Jemima answered.

"Yeah, and there's no mortgage," Russ chimed in. "He bought the house with cash."

"No, he didn't, Russ. The real estate lady told me his lawyer did a wire transfer."

"That's better than cash."

"He has a lawyer?" Press asked.

"Not his. The corporation's."

She paused, looking perplexed as she soaked up the information she'd just gathered. "Well, if Nick's not home, I'll go check at the hospital."

"Shall I tell him you visited?" Jemima asked.

"No need to. I'll catch him at the hospital," Press told them as she walked away more curious than ever.

DISTRACTIONS

Soon thoughts of Nick Stringfellow were banished completely from Press's mind. She was going to dinner tonight with Dr. Cyril Veshkov. It would be their second date. Dr. Veshkov was a pediatrician who had a thriving practice treating what he called "the rich brats" on Mercer Island, the home of old money in Seattle. He was affiliated with the hospital and usually spent at least an hour a day there.

Dr. Veshkov was thirty-four. He was a handsome man of about six feet and 180 pounds. The cut of his tailored shirts showed that he kept himself in excellent shape, and he was always lightly tanned, which in Seattle meant time at the fake and bake. He drove a new full-size Lexus in a deep burgundy color. Press had noticed that he liked gold, as he wore a heavy chain of it around his neck, a large gold ring on his left hand, and another heavy chain around his wrist to back it up.

Press knew that he was a bit ostentatious, but several years of dating doctors had shown her that ego was standard equipment. She did know quite a few that were not full of themselves, but they were all older and married. Anyway, the first date had been an early dinner at the Space Needle followed by "A Midsummer Night's Dream" at the Center Playhouse, and it had been fun. He didn't talk about himself the whole night, just most of it. He asked several sincere-sounding questions about her.

He wasn't the perfect man, but Press wanted a home and family someday to go with her career. And with her long hours at the hospital, she figured doctors were the only targets within reach.

LITTLE NICKY

Nick was having lunch with Cathy, Monty, and Yukiko. The conversation was centered around the growing level of obesity among the young in America.

"Speaking of fat," said Cathy, "you should gain some weight, Nick."

"That's for sure," added Monty. "I've never known anyone who could hide behind a fence post—a seven foot tall fence post, anyway."

"You must be a real health nut," Yukiko said. "All I've ever seen you eat is fruit and vegetables with an occasional broiled chicken breast."

"I do try to ingest only what's good for me," Nick answered. "If I go to someone's place for dinner though, I eat whatever they feed me. I don't like offending people."

Cathy, Monty, and Yukiko went on for a while, and Nick tried to be involved, but the subject of eating switched his brain gears to memories of his childhood.

Two-year-old Nick, the orphan whiz kid, lived with his aunt and uncle but was adopted by the whole town of Galena. Everyone figured he'd grow up to be famous, and the odds of a town that size producing fame was slim. They all wanted to be remembered when he grew up.

Uncle Stan was a supervisor at a plant that assembled cables for the military. The plant, a telemarketing business, and the school district were the only major employers. Stan was six feet two inches tall and balding, and he wore thicker-than-average glasses. At about thirty, he began his journey from husky to portly, a trip full of pies, cakes, and cookies that his loving wife would proffer him regularly. She believed in getting to his heart through his stomach and had built a four-lane highway.

Lily was five foot four. She had sandy blonde hair like her sister, though she wasn't quite as pretty. Her figure was slim, with just a small matronly bulge here and there. She was a stay-at-home mom, and because Sally was eight and Carrie Sue six, during the school day she often took Nick to the town library, which was also the school library. The school was far and away the nicest building in Galena. There was just one unit, incorporating kindergarten through twelfth grade.

Nick was reading at a junior high level by age three. Sally and Carrie Sue loved to play school with him, but he always ended up being the teacher.

Having them was like having two extra mothers. They dressed him in costumes and played house. Nick drew the line at Barbies, even if they did let him play Ken. He would read them stories even though books for first and third graders were well below his interest level. He was still a little boy and, though intelligent, appreciated having older cousins to play with. Other two- and three-year-olds held no appeal.

By the time he turned three, the school board decided that a mind like his deserved special attention. They had the first grade teacher spend fifteen minutes with him daily, taking the course work as fast as they dared give it to him, which was much slower than he was capable of. He finished two grades per year and went to junior high at age six.

FRUSTRATION

Detective Kimura was frustrated. He stopped to give Mrs. Dealva an update.

"Have you found anything yet?"

"No, ma'am. Not yet."

"Well, what have you tried?"

"I told you about the list of registered sex offenders. We've either found them or found that they've moved. So far most of their alibis check out. We're still following up on the rest."

"You can't trust that kind of person."

"No, ma'am. We just have to find ways to disprove what they say. That can be very difficult."

"How about the neighborhood? Have you searched all of the houses?"

"We can't do that without probable cause. We have talked to all of the neighbors on both sides of the street for two blocks around. We've gone back night and day until we've found them home. No one has seen anything. I've given them all my number and asked that they call with any information. A few of them call regularly just to see if we've found her yet."

"I know. This is a great neighborhood. Many have been over to comfort me. I just can't be comforted."

"Yeah. I'm sorry. We've put out her picture to every agency in the state, even the border patrol."

"You don't think they've taken her to Canada?"

"No, ma'am, but we're trying to cover all possibilities."

"Oh, detective, isn't there anything else you can do?"

"I can't think of anything. I'm sorry. We'll keep trying."

Terry felt like a lost sailor becalmed at sea. He didn't know which way to go, and he didn't have any means to get there.

REVEREND DUCK

Aunt Lily insisted that the family attend church regularly. They were in the congregation of the Free Christian Church of Galena, a non-denominational worship group. They had a small chapel with classrooms that they built themselves and were presided over by Reverend Robert "Duck" Dorsey. The nickname Duck was acquired when he got a scholarship out of high school to play football for the University of Oregon Ducks. He was six foot four and weighed close to 300 pounds. In his first year at U of O, he blew out his knee and ended his football career. Having no future in sports, he turned to religion.

Reverend Duck, as they called him, had been to divinity school but hadn't chosen to affiliate with any established sect. He was tolerant and loving of people regardless of their religion and was even kind to heathens. If you were in his congregation, his expectations were high, and he figured you had committed and were subject to the same rigorous standards of Christianity he practiced.

Duck was no paid minister. He believed the gospel should be purchased, as Isaiah said, "without money and without price." Donations from the congregation were used for building maintenance and helping the poor of the congregation. Duck had a barbershop to provide for himself and his wife. They had no children.

Rev. Duck had a rule that everyone should come to church carrying a Bible. If they forgot or didn't have their own, there was a supply of extras in a closet. Sunday school was an exercise in group learning because Duck believed no one, not even he, had a monopoly on gospel knowledge.

At age five, Nick came to church one Sunday sans Bible. Knowing his intelligence, but not wanting to embarrass the little guy, Rev. Duck took him aside.

"Nick, I see you forgot your Bible. Would you like me to get one for you?"

"No, sir, I didn't forget. I just didn't bring it."

Thinking Nick was a bit young for rebellion, Duck was surprised at his answer. "Nick, don't you think everyone should study the scriptures?"

"Sure, I do, Rev. Duck. I plan on studying with everybody else, but I couldn't see the use in carrying my Bible. I've already read it."

Duck chuckled at Nick's naiveté. "Nick, you're a brilliant young man, but scriptures are the kind of thing that no one can understand with just one reading. I've read the entire Good Book many times, but each time I do, I learn something new."

"Oh, I know that, Rev. Duck. I certainly didn't understand it all, and I intend to keep studying. I just don't see the use in reading it again. I may not understand, but I do remember. I just spend a little time each night before my prayers reviewing certain sections in my mind."

"Nick, are you trying to tell me you have memorized the entire Bible?"

"I don't really memorize, sir. It's just there, and I kind of replay it."

Duck was, of course, skeptical. "All right, Nick, tell me what it says in John chapter 3 verse 16."

"For God so loved the world that he gave his only begotten Son, that whosoever believeth in him should not perish, but have everlasting life."

"That's great, Nick. How about Matthew chapter 5 verse 48?"

"Be ye therefore perfect, even as your Father which is in heaven is perfect."

"Well, I can see you know a lot, but many people know those two. Let me try something more obscure." He flipped open his own book to the nineteenth chapter of the book of Numbers and chose verse 11.

"He that toucheth the dead body of any man shall be unclean seven days," Nick quoted. "But Rev. Duck, that's one I don't understand yet. Can't you just take a bath after you've touched a dead body and be clean again? I touched my Mom when she was dead. I didn't like it, but I didn't feel dirty."

The Reverend Duck Dorsey couldn't answer. He shook his head slowly and finally said, "Nick, I see you know your Bible. You ponder on that one for a while, and we'll discuss it later."

THE POWER

The incident with Nick's dad had stayed with him,
though he had no further manifestations until the summer of his
fourth year. He was playing in the city park with a friend, who had
climbed a tree to fetch a Frisbee that was stuck in the outer branches.
Nick watched as the boy shimmied farther and farther out on the limb
till his weight began to bend it to an acute angle. He watched as the first
fibers on the top of the limb began to split. The boy flailed his arms and
leaned backward, attempting to evade gravity.

When it snapped—as Nick had tried to warn him it would—the
boy somersaulted headfirst into a twelve-foot fall to the rocky ground.
He approached the earth chin tucked to his chest, arms waving franti-
cally but uselessly to his sides, and legs straight up. He would hit with all
of his momentum on the bare back of his neck, immediately snapping it
as his head and torso followed it downward.

Once again, Nick's mental acuity was entirely absorbed in the pending accident. Focusing on his friend, he kind of grabbed him in midair
and the last six inches of the fall were as gentle as a mother laying her
baby in a crib.

The friend thought nothing of it. He jumped up, dusted himself off,
and immediately ran to retrieve the now available Frisbee. But in Nick's
prematurely mature mind, a chord was struck. He had a power no one
else had. He wondered about it. He knew he couldn't talk about it with
anyone, but he had to figure it out or go crazy trying.

After that, when he was alone he'd practice moving pencils around

97

on the table or stopping a rubber ball from rolling. He also tried heavier objects but was unable to do any more than nudge them. He eventually realized that it was all a matter of concentration. With his dad swinging at his mom and his friend falling from a tree, the drama of the event had sharpened his senses to a honed blade.

He tried ways to improve his concentration. He quickly noticed that when tired, he was much less powerful. After Sunday dinner, he was almost worthless. He correctly guessed that an overfull tummy sapped his brain. He remembered the first time someone gave him a Coke after he had realized his abilities. The caffeine buzz completely wiped out his thought-centering facility. It would be many years till he felt he had perfected his diet, but he'd learned for certain that input affected output.

He decided to surreptitiously try to tap into Rev. Duck's knowledge. "Rev. Duck, how did Jesus cause that fig tree to wither?"

"God is all powerful, Nick. He can do anything."

"I know he can, Rev. Duck, but how? How did he heal the blind and the lame?"

"Those were miracles, Nick. We can't understand the mysteries of God."

"But what are miracles? Aren't they just things we don't understand or can't explain?"

"Yes, Nick. We can't understand them and we can't explain them."

"But if we did understand them and could explain them, they'd still be wonderful things, wouldn't they?"

"Of course they would, Nick, but we can't understand them, so they're wonderful things that are miracles."

"Well, I'll bet God wouldn't mind if we understood them. I'll bet that he being omnipotent partly means that he just knows how to do things we don't. I'm sure he'd be happy for people to figure out some of those things.

"Nick, I know you're smarter than almost anybody, but mysteries are mysteries, and God meant it to be that way so we'd have to work by faith."

"I have faith. I believe God can do anything. I just want to know how."

"Nick, I've tried to teach you all I know, and you've learned many things that I'll never know, but the doings of God are mysteries, and you'll only ram your faith into a brick wall if you don't accept it and move on."

Nick wasn't convinced. He felt that everything could be explained if you worked hard enough figuring it out. He wasn't deterred, but he knew there would be no help from Reverend Duck. "Yes, sir," he said. "I'll move on." *But not in the way you think I should*, he thought.

As he practiced his concentration, he gained strength. He would go outside when no one was looking and throw rocks without touching them. The size of the rocks he could toss got larger and larger, and his control improved greatly. He got so he nearly always hit what he aimed at. He flung one at a sparrow once and cleanly severed its head. The grief and remorse he felt afterward were part of a learning process he needed to experience.

SCHOOL DAYS

At school, though, as he sat in classes with older students, he'd complete his assignments and in boredom begin to play pranks. Peggy Spencer, teacher's pet extraordinaire, was seated to the left of Nick. She was twelve years old, as were most of the other sixth graders in class with nearly five-year-old Nick. Nick was particularly eager to bug Peggy because she insisted on treating him like a little kid. She thought he was cute and had a mother complex.

It started when her no. 2 pencil rolled out of the depression at the front of her desk and off the left side. She assumed she'd bumped it and leaned down to pick it up. Straightening up, she replaced the pencil and then the stack of about a dozen papers on her desk flew off to the right. She assumed she'd knocked them off as she sat back up. She was obviously flustered and was gaining the attention of the students around her as she leaned over to gather them. Nick was trying hard to suppress a grin as he nudged the three texts and a notebook from the cubbyhole beneath her seat. They fell onto the floor to the left with a loud clap.

"What seems to be the problem, Peggy?" the teacher asked as she strode down the aisle beside her. The entire class was watching now. Peggy righted herself, and the pencil somehow rolled out of the depression and up off the front of the desk. She burst into tears.

The boys in class were snickering uncontrollably until the teacher hushed them with an icy stare. "Would you like to step outside and compose yourself for a few minutes?" she asked compassionately. Peggy nodded, arose, and left for the hallway. The teacher cleaned up the mess and retreated behind her desk. "I don't see what humor some of you find in another person's frustrations," she chided. As she sat down, somehow her chair scooted backward, and she crashed to the floor.

That night Nick woke to someone softly calling his name. Rubbing the sleep from his eyes, he saw his mother, or the spirit form of his mother, floating a few inches off the floor next to his bed. "Is that you, Mom?" he asked the ghost.

"In the flesh," she answered. (She'd always had a sense of humor.) She was dressed in a paler translucent copy of the bib overall outfit she'd had on when she was killed. Her face was kind but stern.

"Are you real or just my imagination?" Nick asked, still not sure.

"I'm real, Nick. You still need me, so I'm here. In fact, I've always been around; you've just been too preoccupied to see me. I had to come at night when your mind was at rest."

"What do you want?"

"I just want you to fill your mission in life," she answered.

"I have a mission?"

"Yes, you do. Everyone does, and those with special gifts have special missions, though many never fulfill them."

"What is my mission, Mom?"

"It will unfold as you grow, but it doesn't include playing pranks or annoying people or in any way using your gifts for selfish reasons."

"What do you mean 'selfish reasons'?"

"Things like getting even or showing off or embarrassing someone."

"I didn't do any of those things."

"Nick, don't try to fool yourself or me. What you did to Peggy today was wrong."

"I was just having fun."

"Fun is okay, but having fun at someone else's expense isn't fun; it's mean."

"I think I knew that. Sorry, Mom, I just got carried away," he admitted. "I'm sorry, Mom. It won't happen again."

"I'm sure it won't, Nick. I love you. I'll always be near. Good night," she whispered as she slowly ascended up to and through the ceiling.

Nick fell immediately back to sleep and in the morning wasn't positive it had been more than a dream.

WHAT DAY IS IT?

Right, Nick?" Cathy jarred him from his reverie.
"Sure, I agree completely," he answered.

"What was I talking about?" she demanded in a pseudo-angry voice.

"I don't know, but I've never known you to be wrong, so I agreed."

The group chuckled. "Nick, I wonder about your mind wandering off like it does. Do you even know what day it is?"

"Sure I do. It's Independence Day in Guyana. It's John Wayne's, Jay Silverheels's, and James Arness's birthday. It's the anniversary of the edict of Worms that outlawed Martin Luther and also of the opening of the Golden Gate Bridge and the premier of *Star Wars*."

"What in the world is all that about?" Yukiko asked.

"It's just a little bit of what makes May 26 the day it is," Nick answered.

"Who is Jay Silverheels?" Monty wanted to know.

"You remember him. He played Tonto on the Lone Ranger show."

"Oh, yeah."

"Nick, you're something else," Cathy said. "Where do you learn all of these things?"

"I just pick 'em up here and there. You never know when they might come in handy. By the way, Yukiko, how does your dad like his job?"

"He loves it. He says Russ and Jemima treat him really well. They're patient with his English. He says he's already getting better at speaking and that they enunciate well enough that he understands most of what they say."

"The yard is really shaping up."

"I'm sure he'll have it in great shape. He takes a lot of pride in his gardening."

"The whole house is coming along. I still have to hire an interior decorator, but before long I'll be inviting you all over for a barbecue."

"I've never had barbecued Twinkies," Cathy quipped.

"You can get them deep fried in Arkansas," Nick assured her.

A HUNK OF BRUNK

Frank Brunk had stalked Nick for several days. He watched him walk Cathy home, and he saw him wander the entire hospital like he owned the place. He wondered why a nurse meandered around when he should have worked in an assigned department, but he had no way of finding out, and nurses were up the food chain from Frank.

There was a definite hierarchy at the hospital, and Frank knew he was at the bottom. He was sure that was a big part of why Cathy had quit dating him. She did only go to a movie with him once, but Frank was sure he'd charmed her and that she turned him down after that because she felt uncomfortable hanging with someone from the "lower classes."

Frank followed Nick to the basement locker room and confronted him. "Hey, string bean. You've been sticking your long nose into where it don't belong."

"It's Stringfellow," Nick answered pleasantly. "And who are you?"

"Name's Brunk, and Cathy Starr is my girl!"

"Funny, she's never mentioned you."

"She wouldn't, 'cause she's after bigger fish."

"And what type of aquatic vertebrate would you consider me?"

"Don't mess with me, noodle. She's a gold digger. She's only after you cause you make more money than me."

"But she makes more than me."

"That don't matter. She's working her way up. Anyway, you'd better can it. I don't want you hanging around her no more."

"I think that's up to her to decide, Mr. Brunk," Nick answered, still pleasant and polite.

"She don't know what to decide. I haven't told her yet."

"It sounds like you might have control issues."

"Don't give me any of that psychiatry junk."

"Really, your delusions may be an indicatory of psychotic depression. I'd be glad to sit with you and diagnose your particular mood disorder."

"Don't mess with me. I got no kind of disorder."

"It could be referred to as a mania."

Brunk moved in and put his extended fingers on Nick's chest. Looking up at him from eight inches away, he said, "I told you to stay away, and you'd better stay away."

He shoved Nick, trying to slam him against the lockers, but it appeared that he'd shoved a brick wall while wearing roller skates. He shot back several feet, lost his balance, and fell over a locker room bench.

Enraged, Brunk untangled the heap of himself, leaped the bench like a rhino over a sand dune, and charged Nick. As he neared, he drew back his right hand and swung for Nick's nose. Nick held up a hand, and the fist smashed into a rock-solid mass half an inch in front of it. Brunk howled like he'd slugged stainless steel.

"I'm sorry. Did you hurt yourself?"

In an effort to regain his dignity, Brunk backed off. "You'd better leave my girl alone, or you'll both be sorry." He spat at Nick.

"You'd better back off or it's you who'll be sorry, Mr. Brunk," Nick said, still in a calm but less-than-friendly voice. "And if you do anything to Cathy, it will be the last thing you do."

"We'll see," Brunk said and left still rubbing his throbbing fist.

CYRIL

Dr. Cyril Veshkov was at his office on Mercer Island. He had a medical journal open in front of him but had other thoughts on his mind. Cyril came to the United States at age two with his immigrant parents from Russia. It was still the USSR at the time, and few were allowed to leave. Some party connections and most of the family fortune had been used to get out. His parents still lived in the Russian community in Chicago. They were comfortable there, and he was comfortable with them there.

He was an only child, and with both parents working, even at rather menial jobs, he'd been spoiled. He hit the teenage years in the nineties and had made the most of it. His grades never suffered. He was brilliant and knew education was the key to his future. His parents also pushed him toward it.

Still both parents worked, so he had the house to himself a lot and was allowed to party whenever he wanted. He made use of the parent-free time as most teenage boys would, indulging in the typical excesses of adolescents.

College was the same. He breezed through it easily and partied often. Medical school had challenged him and, with specialization, he was thirty when he was finally free to open his own practice. Mercer Island had been a real find. His fees were high, but his clientele could afford them. Besides the weekends and closing early on Fridays, he took Wednesdays off golfing, fishing, or sailing. He had a lot of wealthy contacts through his practice and made the most of them, sponging free trips.

He'd been lonely during his years in med school, but with the rise of the Internet, he had found outlets online. He'd played around since then but could see that for status in his profession and Mercer Island society, he really needed to marry. Press Spurbeck seemed the ideal solution and was the first woman he'd ever dated with any kind of commitment in mind. A marriage of two doctors would leave him plenty of time and freedom just as when his parents were always gone as a teenager.

Press was gorgeous and intelligent, and Cyril figured they could have some fun and have a couple of kids, and he could still be unfettered. He made up his mind to get serious with her. He'd even taken the relationship real slow to show what a gentleman he was.

NUMBER 2

Twyla Tedford was walking briskly home from piano lessons a few blocks from her house. She was ten and a fourth grader at nearby Kimball Elementary. She'd stopped at a friend's house and spent about an hour listening to music. It was getting dark, and she knew her mother would begin to worry.

Hurrying along 24th Avenue South, she approached the corner of Spokane Street. The Jefferson Park Golf Course paralleled 24th on her left, and the thick trees and undergrowth got kind of spooky as the twilight deepened.

A lone car whizzed by, startling her. She wished there was more traffic. A feeling of dread shuddered down her spine.

She picked up her pace.

About thirty feet from the corner, a white van was parked facing the wrong way to traffic.

She slowed down. The darkness seemed to deepen. She heard each of her own footsteps echoing in the gloom. Then something sinister engulfed the echo. Even the silence seemed muted. She wanted to run but was transfixed, spellbound.

The sliding side door was open. Though spooked by it, she couldn't help but stare inside as she passed. It was pitch-black. There was no opposite side window. The front and back panes were tinted dark. She hesitated just briefly as curiosity held her.

Suddenly, from behind, a broad hand clasped tightly over her mouth. A muscular arm wrapped firmly around her.

She was in the van, duct taped, and handcuffed almost before she realized it. She hadn't had a chance to put up a fight.

Terry Kimura had another case of a missing girl.

CASH CORP

Nick arrived at home one evening just after five and found Jemima waiting for him at the door. "What is CASH Corp, anyway?" she demanded before he could say a word.

"It's your employer," Nick answered.

"I thought I worked for you."

"Well, CASH Corp is who I work for too." (He didn't mention that he owned the company 100 percent.)

"They sent me this whole packet of stuff with my paycheck," Jemima said.

"Is there something you're displeased with?" asked Nick.

"I'm happy as a pickle in vinegar. You said you'd pay me $3,000 a month; my paycheck is for $3,000 after all the government money is subtracted. They paid all of my taxes! They sent a pamphlet about insurance. It covers all expenses, no deductibles, and the company pays the entire premium. I get $300,000 of company-paid life insurance. They are putting $3,000 per month into a retirement account, and they provide a load of scholarship money if any of my kids go to college. What kind of company is this?"

"Oh, they try to provide for their employees," Nick answered.

"Do Russ and Mr. Ishikawa get the same deal?'

"Yeah, they work for CASH Corp, too."

"How come I never heard of such a bodacious company?"

"It's small and privately held."

"Well, I'm not so small, but I'm going to privately hold on to this job."

SESQUIPEDALIAN

Tilly was lying in Nick's living room doing homework on the floor while her mom worked in the kitchen. Nick flopped onto the couch, working his way through a stack of books on geology. Tilly looked up from her history book and pondered the way Nick was turning pages almost as fast as humanly possible.

"Why do you thumb through those books like that? Don't you want to read anything?" Tilly asked.

"I'm perusing them thoroughly," Nick answered. "I just do it expeditiously."

"You use big words. You probably think a little girl like me won't understand them."

"I guess I hadn't considered that. I'm just sesquipedalian."

"Sesquiped-what-lian?"

"Sesquipedalian. Do you know the word?"

"Well, from its Latin roots I'd say it was someone with one and a half feet."

"That's impressive. The Latin does mean one and a half feet. It denotes the use of longer than usual words, words that are a foot and a half long. I don't do it on purpose; I just read a lot and pick them up."

"What's the biggest word you know?"

"Chargoggagoggmanchauggagoggchaubunagungamaugg."

"What in the world is that?"

"It's the Indian name for a lake in Massachusetts."

"What does it mean?"

111

"It means 'You fish on that side, we'll fish on this side, and nobody will fish in the middle.'"

"How do you pick up words like that?"

"I just read a lot."

"So you're actually reading as you fan through those pages?"

"Yes, I try to sit down a couple of times a week and read a few books. I usually stick with one subject per sitting."

"What are you studying tonight?"

"Geology in general. This one's on sediment stratification of the Pre-Cambrian era."

"Mom said you were a nurse."

"That's my job title. I try not to get pinned down to any one discipline. Have you decided on a career yet?"

"I'd like to be a doctor and an astronomer and an electrical engineer and play on Broadway. I guess it just depends on what day it is. Regrettably, they won't let me be all of them simultaneously. Sometime I'm going to have to choose."

"Not necessarily so." Nick answered. "With proper tutoring I'll bet you could handle several fields at once. I do."

"Is that why you're so rich? Mama says no way you could spend money like you do on a nurse's salary."

"Well, I do have other sources of income, but I don't like to think of myself as rich. I just have enough to share. Do you want to be rich someday?"

"Of course. Doesn't everybody?"

"I suppose if enough people do that, you could generalize it as 'everybody.'"

"Well, why wouldn't everybody?"

"There are a number of good reasons. Not everyone wants the burden of money. It is a weighty matter to manage it correctly."

"That's lame. Isn't managing it like spending it? Isn't that what money's all about?"

"That's part of what it's about. Getting it and spending it could sum it all up, but how to spend it the right way can be as tough a decision as earning it the right way."

"What do you mean 'earning it the right way'? If you earn it instead of stealing it, isn't any way okay?"

"There can be ways that are considered earning that approach stealing."

"Like what?"

"Well, if you were a very talented poker player, you could say you earned your money."

"Sure, some people who are really good earn a living that way. I've seen them on TV."

"If someone earns money gambling, where does it come from?"

"Other people or casinos or state lotteries."

"How do casinos and state lotteries and people who gamble get their money?"

"From people who gamble."

"That's right. And who are those people?"

"Mostly just everyday folks, I guess."

"That's right. And have the casinos done any work that deserves payment?"

"Not really, but hey, if people are stupid enough to gamble don't they, like, deserve to lose their money?"

"If you sold real estate and found someone stupid enough to buy something for way above its actual value and you took their money, would that be right?"

"I guess not, but if they were stupid enough to spend it, someone else would just take it from them."

"If you advertised on cable TV and got old people to buy cheap stuff that they didn't really need, would that be right?"

"I guess I see what you mean. Taking money from stupid people is easy to do, but it hurts them."

"That's part of it, but how about on your side? If you can talk someone into spending their money like that, how does it affect you?"

"What do you mean? If I play poker or sell overpriced real estate or advertise cheap stuff for old people, how does that hurt me?"

"If you provide a worthwhile service, such as selling real estate or advertising good products, there's nothing wrong. If you rip someone off, there's no service there. It's hard to imagine gambling as ever providing a meaningful service."

"People get off on it, so aren't you providing enjoyment?"

"As you describe it, for 'stupid' people you are."

"And how does that hurt me?"

"If you make a living without providing a meaningful service or product, it detracts from your soul."

"Are you talking religion here?"

"I guess in a broad sense, if religion means the way you live and the person you are. But it has nothing to do with going to church. It just means you should earn your money in a way that adds to your character, not just your wallet."

"I guess I get it, but I'll have to cogitate on it."

Nick liked Tilly. Sometimes it was like talking to an adult in a nine-year-old body.

RE-GUNNED

Nick was walking Cathy home as usual. "Who's this Frank Brunk I met?"

"You met him? I'm sorry. What did he say?"

"He said you were his girl and I'd better back off."

"I can't believe that guy. I went to a movie with him once. That was a big mistake. I've tried to avoid him ever since, but he still comes up and bugs me occasionally."

"He seems prone to violence."

"What did he do?"

"We chatted for a while, then he tried to push me around."

"What did you do?"

"Nothing."

"I don't believe you got pushed around."

"Actually he pushed himself around."

"Huh?"

"He applied the force; I just redirected it."

"I'd have like to seen that."

"Well, he'd fallen for you, so now I guess he's fallen for me. Anyway, do I need to be worried for you? He strikes me as out of control."

"No, I'm sure he's all bark and no bite."

"How about your dad? I heard him barking at you the first night we met. Would you like me to talk to him?"

"No, I'm sure it would do no good."

"Can I meet him and see?"

"I'd rather you didn't. He's not purposefully hateful. He's had a tough life, and he's in pain and just gets grouchy sometimes."

They walked on and began discussing the beauties of the Puget Sound, which Nick had only read about before his trip to the Needle with the Joneses.

"This really is a beautiful city. I'd never spent much time sightseeing anywhere."

"An hour at the space needle doesn't qualify as 'much time.'"

"Well, it was fun being with Jemima and the kids, but I'm saying that pictures in books aren't the same as the real view."

"That's a great thing to learn."

As they came to the same alleyway where they'd first met, a couple of goons with guns drawn stepped out. It was the same two phantoms that had attacked Cathy originally.

"Hello, beanpole," the taller one said. "Whatever karate or judo you used on us last time won't work now. We're ready for you, and we won't get close enough for you to touch us." They were holding back about twenty feet.

"Don't you guys ever learn?" Nick asked. "Crime doesn't pay. Put your guns down and walk away before you hurt yourselves. I should have taken your weapons from you last time."

"You lost your chance, string bean."

"It's String*fellow*," Nick said. "Now give me your guns."

As he reached out his hand, the trigger-happy shorter guy fired, followed a split second later by the taller one. Both bullets were nudged slightly by Nick's thought waves and buried themselves in cars parked across the street, one on the left and one on the right. Intent on plastering Nick with as many slugs as possible, the men immediately pulled their triggers again. This time the guy on the right felt his arm jerk to the left while the guy on the left fired to the right. One was hit in the knee, the other in the ankle. Both dropped their pistols, grabbed their legs, and howled.

Nick calmly walked over and kicked the guns well away from the assailants. "Cathy, call 911, would you?" he asked, handing her his cell.

"Sure," she said and punched in the numbers.

As the police arrived, a man with a digital video camera—specially adjusted for night filming—turned away from the front edge of the roof across the street and descended the garage on the backside to a dark sedan.

"Same place, same two guys—but this time it was more spectacular and we've got it all on tape," he said to his waiting partner.

After the police and ambulances had come and taken care of the criminals, Nick walked Cathy back to her porch.

"How did you make them miss?" Cathy asked him. "They fired before you pushed their arms."

"It's easy enough to tweak a bullet in flight," he answered. "Just a few degrees, and it'll miss by a mile."

"Are you immortal?" she asked.

"Oh, I'm mortal all right, but you'd have to catch me by surprise. My reactions are faster than anyone else's I've met, but if a sniper fired from a hidden perch, I'd bleed like anyone else. I'm not superman."

"I think you are," she said, then kissed him on the cheek. "Good night."

"Now explain to me why all the lights and sirens came buzzing around," her father demanded.

"There were a couple of guys that tried to shoot us," she replied.

"I didn't hear nothing till the sirens shot by."

"You must have been sleeping, Daddy."

"I was, and I ought to whip you for causing such a ruckus."

"I'm sorry, Daddy. It won't happen again."

"See that it doesn't. Get me a beer."

DESIGNING WOMAN

Lisa Schaff was thirty-three. She was five feet three inches tall with medium brown hair highlighted with blonde. It didn't reach her shoulders but was long enough to swish a bit when she turned her head. She was attractive, but showed some signs of the struggles and stresses she'd experienced over the past few years.

Lisa had gone to college, majoring in interior design. While there ,she met Rick, a law student who'd given her his last name. Eight years and two kids later, Rick dumped her for a paralegal that worked at his firm, and she was on her own. Rick was a good lawyer, and Lisa was left with next to nothing. She got five hundred a month for each of her children in child support, which Rick was responsible enough to have deducted from his paycheck and sent regularly.

For the past three years, she'd been trying to make a go of it as a decorator. She couldn't land a job at a furniture or department store for lack of experience. She eventually quit trying, convincing herself that it would be better to have her own business so she could work from home. She borrowed money from her parents (the term "borrow" was used loosely as there was no telling if it would ever be repaid) to buy the necessary tools and advertise in the yellow pages.

A couple of Rick's partners' wives had taken pity and paid her to work on their homes. She guessed that they could imagine themselves in the same situation. She attended home shows and conferences and joined the International Interior Design Association (IIDA), but little came of it. You don't get much work associating with others competing for the same work, although a couple of local designers did occasionally throw her some business too trivial for their own companies.

Lisa's girls, Jennifer and Jessica, were dolls. Ages four and six, they loved their mother and were patient when she left them at daycare. She doubted whether she would marry again but took comfort in the prospect of seeing her girls grow and marry and have children. The natural cycle of life was a joy to Lisa.

Having failed to secure a decorator, Nick opened the yellow pages. There in small print, with no ad or anything except a name and phone number, was Lisa Schaff. He called, they made an appointment, and Lisa showed up at the house at five, bringing Jen and Jesse with her.

"I hope you don't mind me bringing my girls," she opened. "I couldn't get a sitter on such short notice."

"Not at all," said Nick. "In fact, if you take the job, you can feel free to bring them with you all of the time. I don't mind."

"Really? That's great. How did you get my name?"

"My fingers did the walking," Nick said, trying to be glib, as usual.

"That's great," Lisa said, acting as if it happened all the time, but the truth was she'd never had a call come through the yellow pages. "Would you like my references?"

"Would you give them to me if they were bad?"

"Uh, no, I suppose not."

"What kind of reference would you give yourself?"

"I guess I'd say I'm really good, but I haven't had much chance to prove myself."

"You really believe that?"

"Yes."

"That's good enough for me."

"You're hiring me?"

"Yes. Would you consider taking a long-term retainer?"

"How long?"

"Well, the corporation I work for will be purchasing a number of homes in this area. It could go on for years."

"I think I could fit you in to my busy schedule. What do you want done?" She looked around; the house was structurally more sound and definitely cleaner, but still plain and shabby.

"If you can come back at four tomorrow, I'll introduce you to my handyman, and the three of us can discuss what should be done."

"That'd be great. I . . ." She paused, looking at the girls. "We'll be here."

"Wonderful, and here's an advance on your retainer," he said, handing her his customary wad of hundred-dollar bills.

FOUND

The next morning, a couple was hiking Denny Creek in the foothills south of I-90 when they noticed something unusual in the bushes. It was a large, black plastic item. As they neared, they could see that something was swathed in a couple of garbage bags wrapped in duct tape. It was Gina Dealva.

MAMA CASS

Nick accompanied Jemima, James, and Tilly to Cassy's Choir Concert.

"Cassy is an awesome singer; she's going to sing a solo. She always gets to." Tilly said, excited.

"Are you a singer too?"

"I try, but no way am I like Cassy."

"Have you thought any more about our career conversation?"

"Yeah. You said there were lots of ways to make money that aren't good."

"Uh-huh, and there are lots of things you can do with your money that aren't good," Nick said.

"Sure, you could buy drugs."

"How about some not quite so obvious ways?"

"Are you about to tell me that having fun with what you earn can be bad?" Tilly asked.

"What do you call having fun? You already admitted that doing drugs would be bad. Is everything in life that black and white?"

"There are lots of gray areas. Everybody says so."

"Think about that. What makes gray *gray*?"

"I guess it's white with some black in it."

"That's right, and none of us is perfect. We all have some gray."

"You're not talking race, are you?"

"Of course not, but have you noticed some people have a dark countenance?"

"You mean an evil aura about them?"

"Yeah, like that. Look at your mother. She's black, but her face is a ray of sunshine. It has nothing to do with skin color, but with what's inside. She doesn't make much money—"

"Until she started working for you!"

"Well, even now she's not rich in monetary terms, just in character and love. So back to black, white, and gray. Black is black, white is white, and gray is somewhere in between. We can't just leave it at that; we all need to keep scrubbing our souls till they are as white as we can get them."

"What does that have to do with spending money?" Tilly asked.

"We can do things with our money, like having fun or buying things for ourselves, and that can be all shades from black to gray to white depending on the fun or the things we buy. Or we can help others—that approach is pure white."

"So we should go around giving our money away?"

"Just giving money away doesn't always help people."

"Like if they go and spend it buying drugs."

"Yes, but even if they use it for food, it isn't good for them to get something for nothing. People have to earn what they get or it detracts from their souls."

"Back to that again?"

"Yes, it's true for you or me or anybody. We have to provide a worthwhile service for what we get or we shrink spiritually."

"You sound like a preacher."

"I don't mean to preach. It's okay to give someone a hand, but in the long term, it's best to give them a chance to provide for themselves."

"You mean like hiring my mom and Russ and Mr. Ishikawa?"

"Yes, they are all talented people who deserve a chance to better themselves and are willing to work hard to do so."

"You're saturating my cerebrum with some seriously sobering sentiments."

"Excellent alliteration, adolescent. I'll give you twenty years for it to soak in, then I'll quiz you on it."

"Shush, you two. Cassy's coming on," Jemima said, elbowing Nick in the ribs.

Cass thrilled the audience with her rendition of "Dedicated to the One I Love."

SPEAKING IN TONGUES

The gang got together for lunch as usual and was engaged in lively conversation when Monty, speaking with his hands, accidentally knocked over Cathy's tray. Meat, potatoes, vegetables, and juice mixed together in one miry mess on the floor. Fortunately, very little splattered onto the inhabitants of the table.

Nick spied a Latino janitor mopping the floor in the corner of the room. "Señor, ayúdeme, por favor," he called.

"I'd be glad to," he answered in heavily accented English. "There's no need to speak Spanish. I'm an American now, and I must use English."

"Sure," said Nick. "And you speak it far better than I do Spanish," he lied.

When the mess was cleared and Jaime Beltran was converted as a member of Nick's extended family, Monty asked, "You speak Spanish, Nick?"

"Yeah, a little," Nick admitted.

"You ought to hear him speak Japanese," Yukiko said. "He's better than I am."

"That's not true," Nick said, though it was.

"How many languages do you speak?" Cathy asked.

"Well, doctors learn a lot of Greek and Latin getting through medical school, so I figured I'd learn them. Then there's lots of medical writing that's better understood in the original German . . ."

"But you're just a nurse," Monty interrupted.

"He's smarter than the average nurse," Cathy threw in. "Come on,

Nick. How many languages do you speak?"

"That depends on what you define as speaking. I've never really spoken Latin or Greek, only read them. And I don't know all the words in any language; I just pick up a bit here and there."

"Sure, like your 'better than a Japanese' Japanese," Yukiko said.

"Are you going to tell us or not?" Monty demanded.

"Let's just say it's more than most xenophobic Americans," Nick admitted modestly.

"Have you traveled the globe?" Monty asked.

"No, but I'd like to someday. Mostly I just read. I'm sure I'd have trouble if I had to actually converse in a foreign language."

"Most Americans have trouble with English," Cathy assured him.

PRESSING ONWARD

Press saw Nick's gaggle at lunch, and in her snooping she had noticed Nick hanging around Cathy a lot, so she decided Cathy would be a great source of information. She knew that walking up to her and asking about Nick would put her on guard. Instead, Press decided to become friends with Cathy.

She wondered if making friends for the purpose of gathering information was a sneaky, underhanded, despicable thing to do. Though she concluded that it indeed was all of those things, she'd do it anyway.

She began by finding out where and when Cathy worked and made sure to drop by that part of the hospital when she was on duty. She introduced herself the first night.

"Hi, I'm Doctor Prescilla Spurbeck. But friends call me Press. I've noticed you around and thought it was about time I got to know you."

"Uh, thank you, doctor," Cathy said.

"Call me Press."

"Sure, Press. I'm Cathy Starr."

"How long have you worked here?"

"Almost three years now. And you?"

"About a year and a half," Press answered. She'd prepared herself by studying the charts of a patient in Cathy's care. "Are you tending the lady in 502?"

"Yes, I've been assigned to Mrs. Custer for the last few days."

"Have you spent any time talking with her?"

"Yes, when I can. She loves telling me about her grandkids."

"Is she always lucid?" Press asked.

"I've got to admit she sometimes changes direction in her conversation for no apparent reason, and she repeats herself word for word as if she hadn't mentioned something already," Cathy answered.

"Does she know your name?"

"As a matter of fact, she asks it every time I go in."

"She's in for her broken hip, of course, but I'm worried she's in the early stages of Alzheimer's disease," Press said.

"Oh, how awful for her. Have you told her family?"

"No, I've just recently been assigned to check on her and haven't met the family yet. She likes to be called Mrs. Custer, so she must have a husband."

"No, her daughter is the primary next of kin. I think she just lived long enough as a missus that she isn't comfortable with anything else," Cathy explained.

"Well, I'm not confident of the Alzheimers diagnosis; I've ordered a brain scan for tomorrow pending family approval. I'd rather not alarm them till I'm more certain. I'll be spending more time with her, but I'd appreciate it if you could pay attention to the warning signs."

"Sure, doctor, I'd be happy to help out."

"Call me Press. It's good to meet you, Cathy. See you around."

"See you."

INTERIOR DESIGNS

Russ Pauley had been busy at the house. First, he'd torn the roof off and replaced it. He'd begun on the windows and decided they should all be replaced by the modern double pane variety to calm the draftiness of the old domicile. He was most of the way through rewiring the entire place when Lisa Schaff showed up to meet Nick and inspect the house. Ishikawa-san had the yard trimmed to the point of only needing detail work, and it gave the impression of an old house, but not the ramshackle dump it had been.

Nick greeted Lisa and introduced her to Russ. Russ had been out of circulation for years and hadn't talked to, let alone shaken the hand of, a pretty lady in all of that time.

"Uh . . . uh . . ." he began.

"Very intelligent sounding," Nick butted in. "Russ is really a pretty sharp guy. Just kind of shy," he said.

Russ turned pie-cherry red, cleared his throat, and, extending his suddenly clammy hand, blurted out, "Uh, pleased to meet you, ma'am."

"Please, just Lisa," she answered. Russ, with a steady income, had put on some much needed weight and was tan from his days on the roof. Though dressed as a workman, he had recently purchased all of his clothes, and the total package seemed ruggedly handsome to Lisa.

"Russ is employed full-time here and can do any work you deem necessary."

They entered the house, and Lisa could see that though clean, it was in a state of disrepair. "Well, it looks like I won't have to throw out any good stuff," she quipped.

"No, you can pretty much have at it," Nick answered.

"You're living here alone?"

"Yes, but don't decorate it for me. I'd like it done for a family. I would prefer traditional American décor."

"That would go with the woodsy interior," she said, "but it could use some lightening up. You're going to need some furniture."

"Yes, it's bare; I wanted to leave it for you."

"And what kind of budget are you considering?"

"I have no limits in mind, but I don't care for extravagance, just good quality."

"And what are your thoughts on my commission?"

"As I mentioned, I'd like to have you on full-time retainer. Would five thousand a month plus expenses be okay?"

"Ma'am . . . uh, Lisa, that's a deal you should jump at," Russ interjected. "Let me tell you about CASH Corp Five grand a month means after taxes. It's matched by another five into a retirement account, full no-deductible medical and dental insurance, and scholarships if you have kids. I could go on."

"That doesn't sound real," she said, turning to Nick. "Is it real?"

"Yes."

"And who or what is CASH Corp?"

"It's a good organization. I'm an employee too. They allow me to hire people according to my needs. Are you interested?"

"Just give me a couple of nanoseconds to consider. Okay, I'll do it."

"Great. Now, I really don't care to be too involved. You and Russ decide what you're going to do and do it."

"You don't want us to consult with you?"

"No," he said, handing her his lawyer's card. "Just contact this guy at CASH Corp, and he'll arrange accounts or cash advances or whatever you need."

"Just like that? You don't even know me."

"I know I can trust you."

"How?"

"I just know. Russ, will you show her the house, upstairs and down, inside and out?"

"Sure. Follow me." Lisa's two girls actually led out, curious to scope out the place.

HOMING IN

Hi, Cathy," **Press began as** she again made a point of visiting a certain ward during a certain shift.

"Uh, hi, Dr. Spurbeck."

"Call me Press."

"Sure, Press. Good to see you again."

"How is Mrs. Custer doing?"

"The same. I saw her daughter again today, as well as a granddaughter."

"I'm glad she has a concerned family. That always helps a patient's comfort level and I'm sure must influence recovery rates."

"I'm sure it does."

"So, Cathy, did you grow up in Seattle?"

"Yes, I've spent all of my life within ten miles of Harborview."

"You must have a lot of friends then. Anybody that works here?"

"I wasn't all that social as I grew up, but I've made some friends at the hospital."

"That's nice to hear. I guess I haven't taken the time to get to know anyone here very well."

"I really hadn't either until recently. A group of us have kind of gotten together over lunch."

"That's great. I guess we all take time to eat. Did you just sit next to someone and start chatting?"

"No, I wouldn't have the nerve to do that. There's a nurse named Nick that kind of got the ball rolling. He's gregarious and makes friends easily."

"I suppose people like that would help all of us be more outgoing," Press commented.

"Nick's a real sweetheart, all right."

"Sounds like you might consider him a special friend."

"He's special, but we're just friends."

"I've got to be off. See you later, Cathy."

"See you, Dr. Spurbeck."

"Press," she insisted again.

"See you, Press."

Somewhat curious at the doctor's friendliness, Cathy asked her friend at the desk, "Have you seen Dr. Spurbeck around here before?"

"Yes, occasionally."

"Has she been friendly?"

"Not unfriendly, but businesslike."

"I would have thought that by the way she carries herself. She doesn't seem like one who would take time to shoot the breeze."

"You're right. Maybe she's just lonely and you have a friendly face."

"Maybe."

By the third night, Press had gotten Cathy to call her by her first name and figured by the morrow, she'd be ready to have a chance meeting with the group at their lunch hour.

The next day Press just happened to walk by the table where Cathy, Nick, and the others were having lunch.

"Press," Cathy called, seeing her with a purposeful lost look on her face as if searching for a place to eat. "Why don't you come and join us?"

"Oh hi, Cathy. I'd be glad to sit with you."

Nick immediately recalled his previous meetings with Press, and with trepidation born of her rebuffs and his overwhelming attraction to her, he turned his face away and slunk back in his seat on the opposite side of Cathy.

"Hello, nurse Stringfellow," Press addressed him.

"You two know each other?" Cathy asked, surprised.

"We've bumped into each other a couple of times," Press answered. "Seems we share an interest in the same patients."

"That's great. Nick, aren't you going to say hello?" Cathy asked with an elbow to his ribs.

"Hello, Dr. Spurbeck," he replied dutifully.

A cloud of silence hung over the group fueled by Nick's obvious bashfulness.

"I didn't mean to interrupt," Press said, breaking the silence. "What were you talking about before I barged in?"

"Ohanapecosh," Monty blurted out.

"I've been called a lot of things, but never that," Press said, feigning offense.

"Let me introduce everyone," Cathy offered. "The Ohanapecosher over there is Monty. This is Yukiko across from you, and Jemima joins us when she's on break," she said, extending her hand toward the large cook. "Of course, you already know Nick."

"So what was that humongous mouthful Monty spit at me?" Press asked.

"Ohanapecosh," Cathy explained. "It's the name of a campground and a river and a glacier and a waterfall on the south side of Mt. Rainier. Monty was just telling us about his weekend there."

"I see. So it's a name only a native Washingtonian would know. Had you heard of it before, Nick?"

"Yeah, uh, it comes from the Indian word 'Awxanapayk-ash.'"

"Easy for you to say. What does that mean?"

"Roughly, 'standing on the edge of a deep blue pool,'" he said, still uncomfortable at being forced into a conversation with the intimidating Dr. Spurbeck.

"And I suppose you translated that from the native tongue yourself?" Press asked jokingly.

"No, I don't speak the Northwest native dialect," he answered seriously. "I just read about it."

"You've never been there?"

"No."

"So did you read up on it in preparation for this conversation?"

"No, I was just doing some geographical reading a while back."

"And what other bits of wisdom do you have on the subject?" Press asked.

"Andesite."

"Who do sight?" Jemima asked, shaking her head.

"Andesite. It's formed at accretionary plate margins by the dehydration melting of peridotite and fractional crystallization, or magma mixing between felsic rhyolitic and mafic basaltic magmas."

"What's that in English?" Jemima asked.

"Most volcanic rock is basalt, but Mt. Rainier is made up primarily of andesite, so named for the Andes Mountains where it was first observed."

"You're talking about a rock?"

"Yes."

"You could have said so without puking out all that rubbish," Jemima chided him.

The rest of the table was laughing so hard they couldn't talk. Nick, realizing that he had lapsed into his nerdic persona, had to join in, though self-conscious in front of the austere MD.

STOKING THE FURNACE

Nick was in the room of an overweight man with severe vascular deficiencies in his legs. He experienced clotting and the accompanying pain. Aside from the pain, the medical risk was that at some point plaque from the vessel wall would break off and send a clot closer to his heart, with fatal consequences.

Nick was reviewing the ultrasound images in the patient's file and engaging him in pleasant conversation when Dr. Drosdick stepped through the door.

The short man's naturally rosy cheeks turned to fire engine red, which spread all over his face and neck. Nick was seriously concerned for Drosdick's health as veins in his neck and temples protruded. He looked like a volcano expanding just before it burst.

"You . . . You . . . !" was all he could get out as he put a viselike grip on Nick's arm and dragged him out the door. Once in the hall, the lava flowed.

"I'll have your job, your career, your credentials revoked, and you'll never work in the medical profession again when I'm through with you! I told you never to review my work," he said, dragging Nick down the hall to the elevator. He punched the down button so hard it hurt his finger, but he didn't stop to feel the pain. "We're going to Dr. Furney's office. I'll put an end to this right now." He continued the clamp on Nick's arm as they descended. He then stormed down the corridor into Dr. Furney's office. They brushed right past the secretary.

"Dr. Furney," Drosdick began. "This . . . this *cretin* has been poking his long skinny nose into business he's not qualified to engage in. I demand that you fire him immediately."

"Hi, Nick," Theo Furney said, ignoring Drosdick. "How's the job going?"

"Great. I'm really enjoying it here."

"You know this fool?" Drosdick demanded.

"I hired him. We go back a long ways," Furney answered with a smile.

"I don't care if he's your firstborn son. You can't allow an unqualified imbecile to wander the hospital making diagnoses."

"I assure you, Dr. Drosdick, that Nick is qualified."

"I haven't even told you what he's been doing," Dr. Drosdick complained.

"Well, I assume he's been interpreting radiological images or you wouldn't be involved. Anyway, it doesn't matter. He's qualified. You can take my word for it."

"You, you, you . . . !"

"Dr. Drosdick, calm down. Nick is qualified. I'll personally vouch for him. You don't need to worry about spurious diagnoses. I suggest you work with him. You might learn something.

"I-I-I can't believe this. I've got twenty-two years of radiological experience. I'm a senior member of the hospital staff. You can't expect me to learn from this juvenile."

"I can and do expect that you could learn a lot. Now, if you've nothing further, I was in the middle of a serious project when you barged in. Please relax, and get back to work. I'm sure some patient requires your attention."

Drosdick stomped out the door.

"I'm sorry, prof. I was just trying to help."

"I know, Nick. This would be a lot simpler if you'd just let me announce your credentials to the staff."

"Please don't do that, prof. It changes attitudes when people learn about me, and I don't like it at all."

"All right, Nick. It's your neck, but Drosdick and others like him don't take kindly to anyone showing them up, especially a nurse."

"Thanks, prof. I'll be more careful," Nick promised.

PRESSING THE ISSUES

Press's curiosity about Nick hadn't been sated. She decided to get as much as she could from each member of the lunch group. Later that day, she spied Yukiko at her nurses' station and engaged her.

"Hi, Yukiko."

"Hello," she replied, reaching to grasp the extended hand.

"That's quite a group you had for lunch. Is that an everyday occurrence?"

"Yes, for quite a while now."

"How did you all get to know each other?"

"Each of us got to know Nick."

"He seems like a nice guy."

"He sure is."

"How did you get to know him?"

"He hired my grandfather as a gardener. Did you know Nick speaks Japanese?"

"No, only Bulgarian."

"He speaks Bulgarian too? Wow, Japanese, Spanish, Bulgarian, Latin, Greek, German . . ."

"You're kidding. Tell me about it."

"Well, whenever they're together Nick talks with my grandfather, who still struggles with English, and he's delighted."

"How did Nick learn Japanese? Did he spend time there?" Press asked.

"He says he's never been, that he just studied it. It's hard to believe, but I can't imagine him lying about it."

"You've heard him speak all of those languages?"

"Only Japanese and Spanish, but I don't doubt he speaks the others. Why would he lie about it? Bulgarian though—that's new to me."

"One of the patients told me his Bulgarian was better than hers."

"His Japanese is perfect."

"What's that about Ohanna . . .?"

"Ohanapecosh?" Yukiko filled in.

"Yes, was that for real? How can a guy spout off about a place like that? He said he's never even been there."

"It's real. He does it all the time. Someone brings up a subject, and Nick tells us everything you'd ever want to know about it and usually a lot more."

"And he gets it all from books."

"Apparently so. He never claims to have been any place."

"So does he dominate the conversation?"

"No. In fact half of the time, he seems lost in space. You have to grab him and bring him back to earth. But I've never seen you with Nick. Have you known him long?"

"Well, we're not really friends. We just bump into each other now and then, and he seems to be an interesting person," Press said.

"Oh, he's interesting, all right, and smart and about as nice a guy as I've ever met."

"It's hard to believe he's just a nurse."

"He's not *just* a nurse," Yukiko defended.

"Well, I didn't mean it as an insult. He just seems to be different."

"He's different all right."

VAN GO

Frank Brunk sat in his van and stewed. He'd seen Cathy hanging around with Stringfellow at lunch. He'd seen them walking down the halls talking and laughing. He'd even watched several nights now as they walked home, sometimes holding hands, always enjoying each other's company. He'd confronted Cathy about it. She was defiant. He'd confronted Nick, even tried to shove the beanpole around, but for some reason seemed unable to. It frustrated him, but he'd never had a girlfriend, and he wasn't about to give this one up, even if she didn't want him.

The van was idling, and he revved the engine a couple of times in anticipation. Frank was a man of action. He wasn't going to stand for being stood up.

Nick and Cathy were leaving the hospital via the employee entrance on the east side.

"Nick, what was it like growing up in Galena, Kansas?" Cathy asked.

"Same as any small town, I guess."

"Did you have the same friends from grade school through high school?"

"My cousins were my best friends, Sally and Carrie Sue."

"Were they your age?"

"No, they were older."

"Didn't you have any friends your own age?"

"Not really. I guess I just liked hanging around with older kids. Sally and Carrie Sue let me play with their friends."

"That sounds unusual. I don't have any cousins or siblings, but on TV the older ones seldom want the younger ones hanging around," Cathy commented.

They moved beyond the portico and around a trash bin. "My family was different. They always included me in everything. Uncle Stan, Aunt Lily, and my cousins let me get involved in games and stuff for as long as I can remember."

"Why is it you talk about your family, but never about yourself?"

"I don't. They're just the core of my life, that's all."

Across the street, Frank exhaled, took a deep breath, and jerked his van into drive. He jammed the pedal to the floor. Turning quickly to square himself with his target, he swerved, screeching and squealing toward his prey about thirty feet ahead.

The two had just stepped past the dumpster that stood to the right of the oncoming battering ram. The screaming of the tires alerted Nick. Time slowed as he saw instantly that there were no escape options.

Frank obviously intended to pancake them against the concrete hospital wall. Nick had knocked bullets from their intended paths but never stopped anything as large as a van.

Cathy looked up, frozen with fear as the headlights blinded her. It took a moment to register that it was charging forward with no intention of stopping.

In another split second, she knew it was too late for her to take action. Knowing that death was certain, she sorrowed that for the first time in her life she had begun to know true happiness and now it was about to end.

She wished she had told Nick she loved him. She wished she had told her father that she loved him too.

Her dad had never seemed to like her, but she knew he loved her. She knew Nick loved her, at least like a brother.

Monty, Yukiko, Jemima, and even Press had become the happy family she never imagined she would have.

All of her years as a wallflower at school flashed before her. The taunts and teases, but especially the total disregard of the other girls, had hurt more than she had ever admitted to herself until now. Now that she had friends and finally felt whole and loved, it was about to end.

She closed her eyes and tried to scream. A vision of smashed bones and mangled flesh flashed through her frantic mind.

As she opened her mouth, it immediately felt as though it were filled with a cup of peanut butter. Her entire body vibrated, beginning with her right hand and extending outward in teeny, furious waves. She knew she must have been dreaming.

It felt like falling backward into quicksand, but instead of her body oozing through the sand, the sand was squirting through her body.

It felt like bathing in honey.

It felt like landing on a stack of pillows and melting into it as it melted into you. It was one of those dreams that seemed to have no end though they only last a few seconds.

The van met the wall at about thirty miles per hour with a crunch of metal as the front end collapsed. Glass crackled as the headlights shattered. Frank, who had forgotten to put on his seat belt, was thrust forward with unanticipated force.

The full momentum of his 280 pounds met the inside windshield. His forehead rammed into the rearview mirror. His skull and neck absorbed the shock and was knocked senseless.

Cathy's dream continued. She tried to close her mouth as she vomited a continuous stream of rock.

She tried to escape but Nick's grasp was too strong on one hand and the other was being drawn through a brick wall. Her feet were cast in stone. Her innards ossified and her neck was rigid. Even her brain seemed frozen in sludge.

Steam and hot antifreeze spewed in all directions as the van's radiator ruptured, temporarily obliterating the view of two young men in dark suits parked down the block. Sure that the victims were dead or badly maimed, they bolted from their car and sprinted to the scene.

Cathy was near comatose as even her cognitive powers seemed infused with muck.

All of a sudden, her one hand broke free of the ooze.

Her arm and then the aft of her torso escaped the grasp of the gunk. Her head followed as once again she perceived reality.

The balance of her person seemed to pop out of thickness like a cork from a bottle, and she was free at last.

In the hospital's boiler room, Cathy, still grasped tightly by Nick's big left hand, felt like Captain Kirk must have when being rematerialized after Scotty beamed him up. She'd finally awakened from the eerie reverie.

She had the sensation of being Jell-O sucked through a screen door with a vacuum cleaner in slow motion. "What happened?" she asked Nick incredulously.

"Well, I think your boyfriend just broke up his van," Nick answered weakly. Then he released her hand and collapsed to the floor.

"Nick, what's wrong?"

"Please, in my backpack . . ." he croaked just above a whisper.

"What is it? What do you need?"

"Twinkies," he gasped. "Hurry."

Cathy unzipped the backpack and pulled out one of four ten-packs of Twinkies. She ripped it open and handed it to Nick.

"Open them," he begged.

Cathy opened the first and passed it to Nick's gaping mouth. He hungrily gulped it down and breathed out, "More!"

She fed him another and another till all ten were gone. Nick swallowed the last of those Rocks of Rapid Renewal and leaned back against the wall, taking a long, slow breath. "I'm sorry," he said. "That took a lot out of me."

"What happened? Why aren't we busted up?" she asked.

"He missed us," Nick replied.

"Don't mess with me, Nick. How did we get here? Why aren't we smashed against the outside wall? I feel like I've been dragged through a strainer, like my every molecule has been sanded with 60 grit."

"We slipped through a crack."

"I'm going to slug you if you don't tell me the truth."

"That is the truth. Don't you know that in every atom over ninety-nine percent of its volume is empty space?" Nick said.

"Sure, but—"

"We just moved the space in our atoms through the space in the wall's atoms, and here we are."

"I don't believe you," she said.

"Then you explain it," he retorted.

"Well, I can't, but I still don't believe it. And what's with the Twinkies? I always thought you were a health food nut."

"I am a health food nut. I only eat what's good for me."

"You're telling me Twinkies are good for you?"

"You'd never guess how good."

"Tell me," she demanded.

"Well, have you read the ingredients?"

"No, but everybody makes fun of them."

"In college, I did some research on which combination of nutritional substances could most help me focus my concentration. I tried a lot of different formulas. When I finally found the optimum mix, it included ferrous sulfate, thiamine, riboflavin, soy lecithin, and polysorbate 60. I used to mix it up for myself, but one day after reading a Twinkie label, it dawned on me that all of those ingredients were listed. I did a chemical analysis and found that they were in exactly the right proportions. I figured, why go to the trouble of whipping up a batch of chemicals when I could get it all in a Twinkie. And it tastes good too."

"You're telling me Twinkies are 'brain food'?" Cathy asked.

"Amber Atoms of Aptitude," he assured her.

Meanwhile, the two suits outside were bewildered. They'd seen Nick. They'd seen the crash. Then the cloud of steam interrupted their view, and when they arrived, Nick and Cathy were nowhere to be seen. They had canvassed the dumpster and looked down the hall of the employee entrance. After giving up, they called 911 to get help for Frank. He was slumped unconscious over the steering wheel with a bloody head. They had checked his breathing, saw that he would live, and beat it before the ambulance arrived. They absolutely didn't want to get involved.

Nick and Cathy went out the main entrance on the west side of the hospital and took the long way home.

"So let me get this straight," Cathy said. "You concentrated our way through cracks in the atomic structure of a concrete wall, and when you were finished your brain was so exhausted you needed ten Twinkies to refresh it?"

"I could have used more, but I like to distribute my intake. In fact, I think I'll have a few more now. I'm still not 100 percent."

"And you always eat Twinkies when you think hard?"

"Either before or after. Concentration at high levels takes a lot of focus. A Twinkie is a veritable Condensed Cube of Concentration."

"I find that hard to believe. Have you done this particular thing before?"

"Been attacked by a vicious van? Never."

"No, I mean wiggled through a solid wall. How many times have you done that?"

"Including tonight?"

"Yes."

"Once."

"Once! How did you know it would work?"

"Well, I didn't, but I've considered the exercise before, and at the time, I couldn't think of a reasonable alternative."

"What would have happened if you'd lost your concentration or run out of Twinkie power halfway through?"

"I'm not sure, but I'll bet it would have cemented our relationship."

Cathy swung her purse at him with a smile on her face.

STUDY HALL

Nick grabbed a handful of celery sticks from the fridge and moved to the living room. Tilly was there studying.

"What are you reading?" he asked.

"I'm just looking into the Triassic period when thecodonts evolved into saurischians and ornithischians."

"Dinosaurs always fascinated me too. Have you examined any material on their mass extinction at the end of the Cretaceous?"

"No, what was the cause of it?"

"There was a sudden increase in temperature worldwide that about ninety percent of all existing species couldn't adapt to."

"What caused it?"

"Consensus has it that an asteroid over six miles in diameter entered the atmosphere, split into two pieces, and impacted in Iowa and the Yucatan. A humongous dust cloud covered the earth and the dinosaurs along with many other species died of heatstroke."

"You're the smartest person I know. You seem to have studied and remembered just about every subject in the world," Tilly said.

"You don't know all that many people yet."

"When you were a kid, were you ostracized for your superior intellect?"

"Well, I usually associated with older people, but when I was with kids my own age, I did my best to temper my conversation."

"Did adults get bothered when you knew more than they did?"

"Not really. Most of them thought I was cute, especially the women."

"I worry about showing people up and being unpopular." Tilly sighed.

"I don't think you have to concern yourself with that as long as you're not contumelious."

"There goes another big word even I don't know. What's 'contumelious'?"

"It means opprobrious."

"Now you're messing with me. What's opprobrious?"

"You know, truculent."

"Oh, you mean act like a snobbish brat."

"Yeah, like that. What is your dad like?" Nick asked.

"I haven't seen him since I was four."

"Was he hard to live with?"

"Not hard, just indifferent. When he was there, he mostly just read the paper or watched football games. How about your dad?"

"He left when I was two," Nick said.

"So you don't remember him at all?" Tilly asked.

"Certainly no pleasant memories."

"And your mom?"

"She died just before my dad left."

"So you're an orphan?"

"I guess so, but my aunt, uncle, and cousins are my family."

"Do you wish you had a real dad?"

"Sure," Nick said.

"Me too. He could help me with my homework."

"I can do that."

"He could take me fun places and protect me."

"I can do that too."

"James and Cassy need a father too, and Mom could use a husband."

"You've got me there. I'm probably not going to marry your Mom. But I'll try to help out with you kids."

"I know you will. I just watch those reruns of *Leave It to Beaver* and such, and I think how cool it would be to have a real dad, especially one who cared. Dads who leave just don't care, do they?"

"I'm sure there are exceptions, but dads who really care would want to stay for good. I won't let anyone or anything take me away when I have kids," Nick said.

"I want to marry someone like you, Nick."

"You never know. I might still be available in fifteen years."

"How come you're not married already?" Tilly asked.

"I guess I just haven't found the right one."

"How will you know when you find the right one?" she asked.

"How could I know that if I haven't found her yet?" he responded.

GOOGLING

Press Spurbeck was in her apartment surfing the Internet. She lived on Second Avenue on the third floor of a building called the Cosmopolitan. Her apartment was basically one big open room with ten-foot ceilings and hardwood floors. She loved it. It was spacious and open but private. Press had minimalist decorating tastes. She had modern but modest furniture and a few pieces of inexpensive folk art. Her bedroom consisted of a simple bed (without head or footboards), a night stand, a dresser, and a curtain for privacy. The apartment had one closet at the kitchen end of the room.

As she searched online, she had no idea where to start, so she just typed "Copernicus H. Stringfellow" in the Google search box. The first item that appeared was an advertisement saying, "Buy a book about Copernicus H. Stringfellow on Amazon.com." Then there were tons of references containing Copernicus and people named Stringfellow in the same page. She went back and put quote marks around the name, and the list narrowed to 1,383 results. "1,383," she said aloud. "How many Copernicus H. Stringfellows can there be in the world?" She began to peruse the information.

First was a paper authored sixteen years previous by Copernicus H. Stringfellow, PhD, and several others on the potential of gamma burst radiation reaching earth in lethal quantities.

Second was a fourteen-year-old paper by Copernicus H. Stringfellow, PhD, and several others on the effects of deletion, translocation, and inversion of the 9q34 chromosome on subjects with severe hearing loss.

Third was a nine-year-old paper by Copernicus H. Stringfellow, PhD, and several others on the evolution and differentiation of Japanese from related Altaic languages.

The only conclusion she could draw was that there were multiple Copernicus H. Stringfellows. No one had PhDs in physics, biomedical engineering, and Japanese language. She shook her head violently, trying to clear it for the answer she knew must be somewhere in the cosmos.

Not finding it, she returned to the search results. Next was a paper from ten years ago on a new technique in neurosurgery by Copernicus H Stringfellow, MD, and several others. Dr. Theodore Furney was listed there!

The list went on. There were articles on ophthalmology, psychology, geology, theology, and many other "-ologies." She also found papers on topography, lexicography, geography, and several other "-ographies." She gave up counting all of the "History of" and "Study of" papers. Most of the papers indicated PhD or MD, with other letters signifying a medical specialty.

It was hard to calculate just how many different PhDs there might be, as it was never specified what field the PhD was acquired in, but with the range of different subject matters, it had to be at least fifteen, maybe as high as thirty.

Many of the medical papers also only listed MD, though not having been board certified in a specialty would typically preclude inclusion on such an article. She concluded that there could be up to fifteen specialties represented.

Several other news articles mentioned Copernicus H. Stringfellow, but they were all short and lacked real substance.

She switched targets to CASH Corp A search of SEC, FTC, NYSE, and NASDAQ databases came up with nothing. It was not listed on any of the smaller or international stock exchanges. Finally she found a couple of articles describing it as a closely held private investment group. "Closely held" was undefined.

Press gave up. The portent of all of this information was too fantastic to believe, so she wouldn't. But at least she had some ammunition to take back to Dr. Furney. She would use it to beat a confession out of him.

SCHOLARSHIP

Nick's gang was at lunch the next day, and Press joined them once again. The topic of the hour was musicals as they each recounted their favorite. Still tongue-tied in the presence of Press, Nick was silent till Cathy forced his participation.

"What's your favorite, Nick?" she asked.

"*The Music Man*," he answered.

"I love that one too," Yukiko chimed in. "Don't you think Ron Howard is a doll playing Winthrop?"

"I always liked Buddy Hacket dancing the 'Shipoopi,'" Monty added.

"Who's your favorite character, Nick?" Cathy prodded him, still trying to get him to talk more.

"Rudy Frimmel," Nick answered.

"Rudy Frimmel?" Press asked. "I've seen the movie half a dozen times, and I'm positive there's no character named Rudy Frimmel."

"Sure there is," Nick defended himself. He'd only seen the movie once when he was seven but had enjoyed and remembered it scene by scene and word for word. "Don't you remember when Robert Preston and Shirley Jones were on the footbridge kissing and Buddy Hacket threw a rock to get the music man's attention?"

"Yeah," Press admitted. "So . . . ?"

"Well, as an excuse to break away, he told Miss Marion that he was expecting a telegram from Rudy Frimmel. I've been intrigued ever since wondering just who Rudy Frimmel was."

"I'm sure he just made him up," Press said.

"When interpreting art, one can never be too cavalier in evaluating the nuances for their deeper implications," Nick assured her. "I think there's significance to that name, but I just haven't been able to determine it yet."

"You be sure to let us know when you figure it out, Nick," Yukiko ribbed him. "I've always been curious myself," she said with an exaggerated wink at the rest of the group.

It was time to get back to work, and the gang got up from the table, shaking their heads and snickering. Press sat there alone, the previous night's Googling still on her mind. It confounded her how someone with so much serious education as Nick could pick out meaningless minutia and meditate on it.

After they dumped their trays, Nick followed Monty back to his station. "Monty, are you serious about becoming a doctor?"

"Never more serious about anything. I've applied and been accepted, but I just can't afford it. I've tried to get loans, but I have no credit history, and my mom doesn't own a house or she'd back me with collateral. I'm just going to have to give it up."

"Have you considered applying for a scholarship?"

"I did well enough in school and on the tests to be accepted, but not even close to good enough to get a scholarship. I'm not a minority or deep enough in poverty to get one on special needs. I'll just have to content myself with being a nurse. You enjoy it, don't you?"

"Sure I do. I don't think I'd like the heavy responsibility of being a doctor. But hey, I think I know where you can get a scholarship. In fact, I'm sure of it."

"Don't joke with me, man. This is a touchy subject for me."

"No joke, Monty," Nick assured. "I have a friend in New York—he's an attorney. He works for a corporation that regularly awards scholarships."

"But I told you I'm not the smartest and I don't fit into any special categories."

"That doesn't matter. You can get help from them anyway."

"Then what do they base it on? How do they choose whom they'll help? They don't just give them to everybody, do they?" Monty asked.

"No, they don't give them to everybody. They do it based on personal reference."

"So it's who you know, huh? I don't know anybody."

"You know me."

"And they'd give a scholarship based on your recommendation?"

"I'm sure they would. The owner of the company is a dear friend of mine."

"Really? You've got an in with rich people?"

"Yeah, I've got an in," Nick answered, reaching for his wallet. "Here's the lawyer's card. You give him a call, and I'm positive he'll make all of the arrangements."

"You've got to be kidding me. I can't believe it. I just call this guy and tell him you recommend me, and he'll finance my way through med school?"

"He will."

"I don't know what to say, Nick. I've never had a friend like you," Monty said.

"You should be thankful for that," Nick replied.

BETRAYED

After lunch, Press went to Dr. Furney's office.

"Dr. Spurbeck, welcome. What brings you here?" Theo asked as she rapped on the frame of his open door.

"I need some things clarified," she answered.

"Sit down, doctor. You're just a few months from completing your residency. I figured you'd want to discuss the future before too long."

She shut the door and seated herself. "I'm not here about my future," Press stated in the voice of a third grade teacher about to lay down the law. "I'm here to talk about this Stringfellow fellow."

"You sound perturbed, doctor. Has he done something to offend you?"

"No," she said, hesitating as she considered the tone she'd taken with her superior. "I'm sorry I sounded upset. I'm not offended or annoyed, but somehow I'm greatly bothered."

"What about Nick bothers you so badly?" Theo queried.

"I just have a primal need to know about him."

"That sounds serious. I told you Nick has asked me to keep his affairs and qualifications private."

"I know you told me that, but for reasons I can't explain, even to myself, I have got to know. I've been doing some research, and I just want you to answer a few specific questions. I won't pry beyond that," she said.

"Very well," Theo agreed. "You ask, and if I feel it proper, I'll answer."

"All right then. First of all, I want to know how many Copernicus H. Stringfellows there are."

"You can't be serious. How could there be anyone else with such a name?"

"I'm serious. Have you ever gotten on the web and done a search on 'Copernicus H. Stringfellow'?"

"No, I've never thought to do that," Theo answered.

"I have, and it only added to my confusion. There has to be at least a dozen Copernicus H. Stringfellows. I counted nearly one hundred scholarly papers on anything from neurosurgery to Japanese etymology. I concluded that there must be at least a dozen different PhDs of that name to have generated them. Am I wrong?"

Theo put his face into his hands, which were propped on his desk. He paused and shook his head a couple of times. "I guess if you've gone that far, I'll have to set things straight, but let me warn you, Dr. Spurbeck," he said, turning mockingly serious, "if you ever let Nick know it was me who spilled the beans, I'll do everything in my power to denounce you as the filthy liar you are."

Again he hesitated, drawing a slow, deep breath as if preparing to utter something profound. "There is one and only one Copernicus H. Stringfellow. I doubt there'll ever be another like him. He does have at least a dozen PhDs—I've quit counting. He is also an MD and has passed the qualifying boards in at least seven specialties that I know of, from endocrinology to neurosurgery. I have no idea how many bachelor's and master's degrees he picked up along the way."

Press was speechless. Her jaw hung open several inches. She couldn't begin to phrase any follow-up questions.

"Nick began college at age eleven," Theo continued, unable to stop so soon. "I'm sure he could have begun sooner, but his uncle told me the school district was afraid to allow him free reign.

"I taught at Columbia Medical School, one of Nick's alma maters. I've worked in several hospitals and attended a few universities. Out of all of the intelligent and superintelligent people I've known, Nick Stringfellow is in a class of his own. I'm positive he's the smartest man born in recorded history. Any of the MDs, PhDs, or other scholars that have worked with him that are not totally blinded by their own importance would agree with me."

Dr. Furney paused to let his diatribe soak in to the obviously confounded young resident seated across from him.

After a long, gelatinous silence, Press spoke. "With all of those degrees and the potential for notoriety that could come with them, why is Nick Stringfellow working here as a nurse? And how, by the way, does someone working as a nurse afford to throw the kind of money around that he seems to do?"

Theo paused, thinking. "Listen, Dr. Spurbeck"—he was deliberately formal for effect—"Nick Stringfellow is not only undoubtedly the smartest man in the world, but he is also the kindest, most humble person I've ever known. He doesn't want notoriety. He doesn't want prestige. All he wants is to help people. He thinks he can do that best in obscurity. As for the money," he continued, "Nick wanted to work without pay, but I knew the union wouldn't allow it, so he accepted the minimum. He doesn't need it. He wouldn't need an income for a thousand lifetimes. I don't know exactly how many, but his net worth is in the billions."

"He doesn't dress or act rich. Did he inherit all of that money? He couldn't have earned it going to school," Press pointed out.

"Well, I don't know the source of all of his wealth, but I know he began to accumulate it almost accidentally."

"How could he do that?"

"He just wanted to help somebody. He loves his uncle, who was really a father to him, and though it was always a joke in the family, Nick knew that his uncle was self-conscious about his baldness. Nick would never talk about such a thing, but during his first year in college, he was just eleven, he went to the chemistry lab and whipped up the first minoxidil."

"Rogaine?"

"Yes, Rogaine. He just wanted to help Uncle Stan feel better about himself. The chemistry professor convinced him to patent it, and Nick's first millions began to roll in."

"When he was eleven years old?"

"Yep, and that was just the beginning. When he was sixteen, at Columbia Medical School he pioneered laser eye surgery so his uncle wouldn't have to wear the thick glasses he always needed. He sold the idea to an ophthalmologist there and invested in the guy's laser eye clinics. Which, by the way, he sold out of before the price started to drop. Those are among the most famous of the creations of Copernicus H.

Stringfellow. Oh, I just remembered, you have an iPod, I assume."

"Yes, of course," Press replied.

"That was a gift to his cousins when he was eighteen. And when his aunt complained about wrinkles, he invented Botox."

He went on while Press was trying to digest what she'd heard. "He didn't make all of his money inventing though. He could probably corner the entire stock market if such a thing interested him. He invested heavily in tech stocks and sold them all at their peak in the late '90s just before the bubble burst. Then he sold most of his stocks and his real-estate holdings before the housing crash of '08. He reinvested shortly after and made an immediate killing. I wish he'd warned me it was coming.

"Prescilla," Dr. Furney said, "I really don't know a lot about Nick, though I probably know more than almost anyone else. What I've told you is what I got from our time together at Columbia, where I was his faculty adviser, and from a couple of talks I've had with Uncle Stan and Aunt Lily when they came to visit. You could never get any of it out of Nick. He doesn't want it to be known."

Press sat there for a while, not knowing what to say. Finally, she half staggered to her feet. "Thank you, Dr. Furney. I won't ask you any more. You've told me more than I can process already."

"Listen, Dr. Spurbeck, I've told you a lot more than I wanted to, and if Nick found out what I'd blabbed, he'd be disappointed in me. Anyone else would get mad, but Nick doesn't get mad. His disappointment would hurt me more than I can say. Do you understand?"

"Sure, Dr. Furney, I won't say a word. Nobody would believe me anyway." Press sounded as if she'd been psychologically whipped. "I won't say a word."

SPORTS

Nick's family was devoted to Galena High School sports. When he was younger, his cousin Sally was a cheerleader, and they attended every football and basketball game, home and away. One year, the Galena Bulldogs basketball team was better than usual.

Nick and his family went to a game that would determine whether the team would go to the regional playoffs. The score went back and forth, changing leads several times in the last quarter. With three seconds to go and down by a point, the Bulldogs had the ball out under the opponent's basket. The other team was applying full-court pressure while being careful not to foul. They only needed to slow the Bulldogs down enough to waste three seconds. The ball was passed to the point guard at the opponent's free throw line. He took two dribbles to his right and heaved the ball from about eight feet beyond the half court line.

Nick wasn't really into sports. He enjoyed watching, and he was happy when Galena won because Uncle Stan and the girls were in such foul moods when they didn't. With a few mental geometrical calculations, he could immediately see that the ball was going to fall about 17.6 inches short and 3.23 inches to the right of the hoop. He couldn't see anything wrong with nudging it a bit. It wasn't really a selfish act. He would make everyone in Galena happy with just a minor tweak. He pondered it only momentarily, then went ahead and psychically poked the ball onto the correct course. It swished through the exact center of the net, and the home crowd exploded. They had won by a point. (The three-point shot hadn't been integrated into high school yet.)

Uncle Stan grabbed Nick and hoisted him into the air. "Did you see that? Did you see that shot? I've never seen anything like it. That was one in a million. I didn't know the kid had the strength to get it that far. What a game! What a finish! Did you see that, Nick?"

Nick *had* seen it.

Later that night, after celebrating with the town and the family in the wee hours of the morning, Nick sunk into a deep sleep. He was awakened by the whispered voice of his mother.

"Nick, wake up."

"Hi, Mom. What are you doing here?"

"Nick, you've misused your faculties again."

"What do you mean?"

"Nick, I'm your mother. Don't trifle with me."

"Oh, you mean the basketball game?"

"That's what I mean."

"I didn't do that selfishly. It made hundreds of people happy."

"And what of the hundreds it made sad?" she asked.

"You mean the other team?"

"Yes."

"Well, I don't know any of them," Nick said.

"That doesn't matter. Any time you interfere with nature, you affect people—sometimes positively, sometimes negatively."

"You mean I shouldn't get involved at all with people's affairs?"

"Of course you should, when it's right."

"But how will I know?"

"Do you know right from wrong?"

"Of course . . . basically. But some things don't seem to have a right and wrong."

"Nick, you'll have infinite opportunities to help people in your life, but finite abilities," she said. "You'll have many opportunities to do what seems good for people, when it's not what should be done. You'll have to learn to discern when to get involved and when to leave it be."

"How will I know?"

"The same way you know right from wrong. You'll just know. You'll know if you are prepared to listen."

"How do I prepare?"

"I'm here, Nick. You know that there's a spiritual as well as a physical side of life. You need to tune your spiritual side as though you'd tune a radio. If it's a little bit off, you'll get nothing but static."

"So what's the tuner?"

"You are. Your life is. Think of a path through the jungle. If no one walks it, what will happen?"

"It will get overgrown."

"That's right, and what if it is used constantly?"

"It will broaden."

"Exactly. You use your path constantly, and you'll know what to do and when to do it. Truth is ever present on the spiritual side. Only those mortals who consistently search for it will find it. You must do that, Nick."

"Okay, Mom. I will. You know, I knew all along I shouldn't have done that."

"I know you knew it. Good night, Nick. I love you."

"Good night, Mom. I love you too. When will I see you again?"

"When you need me."

VESHKOV

Press was out for a second date with Cyril Veshkov. It was Saturday, and they were having dinner at Canlis, one of Seattle's most exclusive restaurants. It was perched on the northeast side of Queen Anne Hill overlooking Lake Union. They planned to go to the Seattle Symphony afterward. The symphonic fare was to be Beethoven's 6th followed by his violin concerto, which Press considered the most beautiful composition in the history of earth.

The evening hadn't started off well. Veshkov had been late with no apology. Press figured that was the woman's prerogative. She'd also been poorly impressed with his tone of voice as he ordered the valet to "take it easy" with his new Jaguar XKR.

Press flashed back to conversations at med school as students spoke of luxuries they would acquire once in practice. It always infuriated her that luxury was seemingly their first priority and that the thought of making lives better was seldom discussed.

The maître d' had been polite and certainly seemed to know Dr. Veshkov well as he ushered them to a window table and accepted the fifty-dollar bill slipped into his hand. Press wondered how many dates had accompanied Cyril here previously. It was a sparkling late afternoon, and she could hear the piano from the lounge playing "The Bluest Skies You've Ever Seen in Seattle." She had passed on the offer of escargot as an appetizer. She'd spent long enough in Washington State to want to avoid any cousin of a slug as a nutrient. The clams were fresh and excellent, and the view of Lake Union was entrancing as she watched a sailplane take off for the San Juan Islands. For some reason as she watched, she kept wondering what words of wisdom Copernicus H. Stringfellow would have on each of the items that passed her view.

"Wonderful evening, isn't it?" Cyril asked.

"Yes," Press said. "Do you come here often?"

"Oh, I've been a few times. They know how to take care of you here."

"Really? That's not how you acted with the valet." The incident churned in Press's gut.

"Oh, that. You know those lowlifes get into a hot car and they've just got to see what it'll do. There are people in life you just can't trust."

"Like who?"

"Come on, you're a doctor. Your parents are doctors. You know there's a difference between people with IQ and with no Q. We live, they serve, and if you aren't careful, they'll try to take you for all you've got."

"I thought your parents were common people," Press said.

"Here they are because they're immigrants, but in the mother country they were among the elite. It's proven, you know, that IQ is up to eighty percent hereditary."

"So I've read, but what does that have to do with life?"

"Are you politically naïve? The United States started out trying to be egalitarian, but you can't keep the intellectually superior from rising to the top. The little people don't know what's going on.

"Government evolves to where the elite rule and the peons serve. You have to provide for them—social security, healthcare, whatever— but that only helps keep them satisfied. Only those of us with the potential to lead can and should afford things like this meal or my car. Europe and the rest of the world understand that. Surely you don't believe in that 'of the people, by the people, and for the people' stuff?"

Press was beside herself. She'd been with many an arrogant doctor but had never heard their elitism expressed so blatantly. "So the smartest are the best and the rest are no good?" she asked, barely containing her rage.

"Good? Who said anything about 'good'? You're not going to moralize on me, are you? There's no good or evil. There's no right or wrong.

There's only fact and fantasy. The fact is the intellectual rule the world and the inferior fantasize about it."

Press was furious, and it wasn't like her not to say so, but she had conjured a potential future with Cyril after their first date and she wasn't ready to throw it away until she'd given it good consideration. Against every righteous fiber in her mind, she swallowed a billowing harangue on the virtues of everyday people versus their "intellectual superiors" and coolly changed the subject.

"What's good here?"

"Anything you'd like. The seafood is superb; the beef is the best. What do you feel like?"

Press quickly scanned the menu. "I guess I'll try the salmon. I know every place in town has it, but I never got it growing up in Philly, and it'll give me a good comparison point with other restaurants."

Cyril ordered iced prawns as an appetizer. The conversation for the remainder of dinner was similarly icy—more like business than pleasure.

At the symphony, though polite, Press continued to be frigid. Even the violin concerto didn't quench the seething inside her. By the end of the evening her mind was made up. She had given a future with Cyril Veshkov enough consideration.

TESTING

Mr. Stringfellow, Mama says you're the smartest person she knows. I was wondering if you could help me study for my SATs."

"Sure, James. Call me Nick. Have you taken any practice tests?"

"Yeah, Mama signed me up for some preparatory classes. I've been going for the last four Saturdays. It's not that I need help with math or science or anything. I'm just slow getting through it all. Tilly said she's seen you reading faster that she can turn the pages. Is that something you could teach me?"

"Anyone can multiply their reading speed with practice. When is your test?" Nick asked.

"Saturday."

"That's just three days from now. We'd better get cracking. Let me show you how to increase your reading rate. You'll need to spend a few hours practicing."

"I'll gladly do that."

Nick spent a few minutes with James showing him the beginning speed reading technique of pacing himself with his index finger.

"Just pointing at the words with my finger will make me faster?"

"Yes, if you use that finger to focus your concentration."

"How does the finger help?"

"Most people lose concentration as they read and end up jumping back to the beginning of a paragraph or sentence to start over."

"I hadn't noticed that. Does everyone do it?" James asked.

"Everyone who hasn't trained themselves not to."

"So just using the finger helps you quit retracing what you've read?"

"Yes, if you concentrate. To begin with, go slowly but make sure you follow the finger without slipping. It will take some practice. Try it."

"Wow, that's harder than I thought it would be. My eyes want to keep jumping back."

"That's all right. Everybody does it. It's okay to go real slow in the beginning. If you concentrate, you'll still increase your speed. Try again, slowly."

"I can do it. It's hard, but I can do it. I never would have guessed how much my eyes want to skip backward though. It's hard not to."

"You practice that fifteen minutes at a time, then rest for at least fifteen minutes in between. Try to gradually pick up speed. This is the first step in any of those speed-reading courses they teach."

"Do those courses really work, or do they just teach you what to skip over when you read?"

"They really work, James. You can easily read ten times as fast without missing a word and your comprehension and retention will increase at the same time."

"That's cool. I'll do it," James said.

"If you'll do that an hour a day, pushing yourself to increase speed, you could be twice as fast by Saturday. You'll actually gain comprehension because your mind won't be confused by all of the jumping backward it's used to. With only three days to go though, I think we'll have to resort to more certain measures to improve your concentration. Would it be okay if I picked you up and gave you a ride to the test Saturday morning?"

"Sure, but will that help me do better?"

"I'll guarantee you'll do your best possible. But you'll have to promise you won't tell your Mama."

"You're not going to cheat are you?"

"Heck no. No cheating—just concentration enhancement."

164

DATED

Cyril Veshkov caught up with Press in the hallway.
"Press, how are you? I've tried to call. Is everything okay?"

"Sure, I'm fine."

"So did you get my messages?"

"Yes, I got them."

"Too busy to answer?"

"Yes, too busy," she said coolly.

"Well, I've wanted to talk. You didn't seem yourself when I dropped you off last week."

"I'm nothing but myself."

"You're being rather curt."

"I suppose I am."

"I was going to ask you to the Doctors' Dinner, but you don't seem too friendly."

"That's okay. I have other plans."

"You really should be there. You'll be noticed if you're not," Cyril said.

"My other plans include being there."

"So you have another date?"

"Yes, I do."

"Well, I guess that's it then."

"Yes, that's it."

"I'm sorry to have bothered you."

"I'm sorry too," Press said.

Veshkov looked stunned. Press turned and walked away. She had intended to ignore his calls, hoping he would go away, but she didn't feel bad about shutting him down to his face. His kind of person deserved a good shutdown.

That evening, sitting at home reading *Pride and Prejudice* for the umpteenth time, she set down the book and wondered what was next. She had been relatively friendless at the hospital—busy, not disinterested. She had been having lunch with Nick's group whenever possible for a couple of weeks and felt comfortable there. While on her rounds, if she ran into Cathy or Yukiko or Monty she'd stop and chat.

Lately when she'd run into Nick, she certainly wasn't brusque with him like she'd been in the beginning. She felt badly about her early attitude and had apologized, but Nick would have none of it. She didn't talk a lot when she ran into him. She always left wishing she had spent more time and wondering why she couldn't come up with more conversation. She was always at a loss for words. Was she shy in front of him? Was she attracted to him?

She didn't think so. He wasn't at all handsome. He was kind of gangly. Still, with all she'd learned about him, she was somewhat in awe. He was incredibly smart and incredibly rich, but he never let on at all. No one knew. He preferred to associate with normal people rather than intellectuals or the wealthy. She'd grown up wealthy and intellectual but had never felt as at home as she did with Nick and his gang. She wasn't falling for him. She was sure of that, but she liked him. Why not invite him to the dinner? Would he accept?

He seemed awfully fond of Cathy, but they never acted like lovers. She made up her mind. There was nothing romantic about it. She needed an escort to the dinner, and she just liked being around him. He was a friend, a good friend.

After lunch Press caught up with Nick. "Uh, Nick, could we talk?"

"Sure, Dr. Spurbeck. What about?"

"Will you quit calling me doctor? Everyone else has."

"Sure, doctor . . . I mean, Press, if you want me to."

"Thank you. I, uh . . . well, I was wondering if you and Cathy were, uh, together?" Press asked.

"Well, not right now. She just left."

"I mean, are you *together?*"

"Yeah, we're together at lunch a lot and I walk her home when she works nights."

"I mean, is she your girlfriend?" Press looked frustrated.

"Oh. No. She's a girl though, and we're friends."

"I know she's a girl. I just wondered if you were involved."

"We're both involved, but not always in the same thing."

Press was about ready to give up, but instead blurted, "Nick Stringfellow, would you go to the Doctors' Dinner with me?"

"Sure, but why are you so upset?"

DINNER

At the dinner, Press and Nick were seated at the back, as befitted her resident status. Nick really dressed up quite nicely in a tuxedo; he'd tamed his hair, and the rented tux had been fitted well, unlike his usual attire. Press knew she looked her best in a form-fitting, though otherwise modest, burgundy evening gown. Her hair was down, which it never was at work, and Nick had complimented her on its silkiness.

She smiled to herself, thinking of all of the self-important doctors between them and the dais and what they might think if they knew what she knew about Copernicus H. Stringfellow.

Cyril Veshkov had walked by with a trophy blonde on his arm and failed to hide his disgust as he saw Press seated with Nick, whom he knew to be a nurse. He sat down next to a fellow pediatrician, Dr. Tanner, and immediately asked, "You see that dopey looking guy three tables back?"

"With Dr. Spurbeck?"

"Yeah. You know his name?"

"Uh-huh. He hangs around the nursery a lot. His name is Stringfellow."

"Stringfellow, huh? What's he like?"

"He's a great guy. He's a nurse, but he seems really intelligent. He handles those babies like a new grandmother. He talks to them and cuddles them. You'd think each one was his."

"Sounds like a real sweetheart."

"Yes, he seems to be. Would you like me to introduce you?"

"That's okay. I'll get to know him better."

The meal was pedestrian: a choice of prime rib, chicken, or salmon with a veggie salad for the carnivorously challenged. Nick had gone for the salmon while Press had opted for the beef, which she only indulged in a few times a year.

Press was anxious to get Nick to talk about himself, while hiding the fact that she knew quite a bit about him. "Nick, you never talk about yourself. Where are you from?"

"Galena, Kansas."

"I've never heard of Galena. How big is it?"

"It's not at all big. Actually, in the early 1900s it had a population of over 40,000, but when the demand for lead dried up, so did the town."

"Does your family still live there?"

"Yes, my aunt and uncle do. My cousins are in Joplin and Topeka."

"How about your parents?"

"I don't have any."

"Really?"

"Oh yeah. My mom's dead and my dad ran away."

"I'm sorry. That's so sad." She hesitated. "How long ago did your mother pass away?"

"When I was two."

"So you have no memories of her."

"Oh no, I have two full years."

"Nobody has memories from the day they were born."

"I guess I'm nobody then."

"C'mon, everybody is somebody. Tell me about your first birthday then, if you can remember anything," she challenged him.

"What amount of detail would you like?"

"Tell me about dinner."

"Okay, we had a party at my aunt's house. My dad wasn't there. We had Aunt Lily's fried chicken (they cut mine up for me), with potato salad, green beans (Mom spooned me out twenty-three), rolls, and green Jell-O with pears. Uncle Stan sat at the head of the table. He was wearing one of those cowboy dude shirts with the white peaked flaps over the pockets and on the shoulders."

"Are you kidding me? You can't remember that amount of detail."

"Sure I can. The flaps were white with those fake pearl–covered snaps to keep them shut. Lily was on his left in a Levi skirt with a pink T-shirt that had blue and yellow flowers stitched in. My mom had on her bib overalls and a white blouse with those poofy sleeves; she couldn't afford much of a wardrobe. Sally and Carrie Sue sat on the right. Would you like to know how they were dressed?"

"No, go on."

"I was at the foot of the table. I sat on a volume of Webster's Dictionary and the collected works of Jane Austin. We didn't have a high chair, but I couldn't read those books yet anyway . . ."

"You're making this up," Press scolded him.

"Not one item that isn't the truth, the whole truth, and nothing but the truth," Nick said with a humbly emotionless face. "The tablecloth was red and white checkered, and I had a spoon and a fork. They didn't trust me with a butter knife till a few weeks later. It was on a Tuesday."

"Your birthday was on a Tuesday?"

"No, it was on a Friday, but it was three weeks later on a Tuesday Mom started trusting me to properly use a butter knife. Would you like any details on that event?"

"No, I think I'll pass." She shook her head, still not knowing what to believe. "Let's get to the present. Do you have any hobbies? I hope you don't mind me asking. I just want to get to know you better."

"No problem. I'm basically a boring person though. There are lots more interesting topics than me."

"Indulge me."

"Hobbies . . . I play the piano several times a year."

"I heard you in the cafeteria one day. How long did you take lessons?"

"Twice."

"Okay . . . how long of a period did you take them for each time?"

"Just twice—two lessons."

"Two lessons? You play like a concert pianist. You must have worked on it a lot by yourself."

"I guess so, but music is all mathematical anyway. Once you understand it, there's no reason you can't make it."

"Okay, anything else?" Press asked.

"I read, usually an hour and forty-three minutes a day."

"I'm afraid to ask, but why an hour and forty-three minutes?"

"I've just found that any longer than that and I lose concentrational efficiency. Of course, if I wait for fifty-six minutes and start again, I'll be at my peak, but I seldom have time for more than one session anyway."

"How did you learn to speak Bulgarian?"

"What makes you think I speak Bulgarian?" he asked.

"Mrs. Ivanov told me."

"I just happened to know a few phrases."

"She said you spoke it better than she did."

"I'm sure she exaggerated. I just got lucky in knowing the right words to use during our conversation."

"Well, how did you learn?"

"I told you, I read for an hour and forty-three minutes every day."

"I guess I'm not going to get an answer on that one. What do you do with the rest of your time?"

"I spend time with friends and at the hospital."

"Why do you spend so much time at the hospital?"

"Working at the hospital is replete with endorphic gratification."

As they finished up and the raspberry sorbet was served, Dr. Furney stood and began the program. After a short speech, he started calling on various doctors to stand as he recounted their achievements of the previous year. It was intensely tedious, even for medical minds.

There was a dance following dinner.

"Nick, are you going to ask me to dance?" Press asked.

"I didn't plan on it," he said.

"It's proper to ask your date to dance."

"I'm not really a dancer."

"Well, I'm sure you can learn."

"It's not a matter of learning; I read a book about it. I've just never done it."

"Well, you're about to," she said, standing, grabbing his hand, and pulling him to the dance floor.

The first number was a waltz, which Nick performed admirably, though somewhat stiffly. He did so well, in fact, that Press accused him of cheating. "You dance like an Arthur Murray instructor. You lied to me."

"I didn't lie; I told you I read a book about it."

"And you've never practiced?"

"It's my first waltz," Nick said.

A fast dance came next, and this time Press could believe Nick had only read about dancing. Not that he didn't do things correctly, but his tall thin body just looked like Frankenstein's clumsy cousin gyrating to a fast beat. Next the DJ put on "Do You Wanna Dance" made into a slow number by the Mamas and the Papas.

Still taking the lead, Press pulled Nick close and nuzzled her head into his chest. She'd never danced with anyone nearly this tall, and she found she really liked it. She noticed that, though skinny, Nick wasn't what you'd call bony. He had tightly defined muscles. Her hand and arm around his back could detect the powerful sinews there.

Afterward Nick drove Press home.

"Those doctor dinners tend to be tiresome," she complained.

"I'm sorry. I should have been more stimulating," he said.

"No, I didn't mean you. You're quite intriguing. I just meant the general atmosphere is stuffy."

"We could have sat closer to the ventilation."

"Not that atmosphere—the psychological atmosphere."

"Oh . . . You think I'm intriguing?"

"I think *intriguing* is exactly the right word."

"Like I'm a spy or something?"

"Not a spy, but secretive. I think there's a lot about you that you won't let out."

"Not really. I'm just a regular guy."

"Define regular."

"Regularity can differ from one person to another depending on diet, metabolism, and so on."

"I ought to smack you."

"Oh, did you mean how am I a regular guy?"

"Yes."

"Well, I eat, sleep, and think just like everyone else."

"It's the thinking part I'm asking about," Press said.

"Mostly I just think about my job like anyone else," he said.

"What is your job?"

"I'm a nurse at large."

"What does that mean, in terms of thinking?"

"I guess it means I'm free to think on a wide range of issues."

"Do you think outside of work?"

"Sure."

"About what?"

"Same stuff everyone else does, I suppose."

"You're so informative."

"Thank you."

Just like when Nick picked Press up, he opened her car door, which she was completely unused to. She'd never been out with anyone so quick to jump out and so insistent. Nick walked her up the stairs to her third-floor apartment, and after unlocking the door, Press wheeled around, put her hands on his lofty shoulders, and, on tiptoes, kissed him quickly on the lips. "Good night," she said. "I had an interesting time."

"Me too. Good night." Nick couldn't think of anything else to say. He clomped quickly down the stairs and out to his Impala.

Press was impressed. Copernicus H. Stringfellow wasn't everything he appeared to be. He was much more than the casual observer would never notice. She didn't intend to be a casual observer.

S.A. TWINKIES

Saturday morning Nick picked James up at seven fifteen.

"How did your reading practice go?"

"Great. I think I do read twice as fast, just like you said."

"Good. That should help, but you'll still need assistance thinking faster."

He drove around the corner, out of sight of the Jones's house, and stopped. He reached back, pulled out a ten-pack of Twinkies, and handed it to James. "Here you go. Eat these."

"I thought you said you were going to give me some concentration enhancement."

"That's it."

"If Mama saw me eat ten Twinkies, she'd skin me. She says I'm fat enough without eating junk food."

"Believe me, this is no junk food. You just get those down before we get to the test, and you'll do better than you'd ever imagine."

"You're jiving me."

"No, I'm not. Eat those and you'll see."

"Okay, but if Mama finds out—"

"I know, she'd skin us both. If you don't tell, I won't."

Nick was there to pick James up when test time was over. "How'd it go?" he asked.

"You wouldn't believe it. I finished each section way before anyone

174

else. I had time to go through twice. I've never felt so smart."

"I believe it."

"How do Twinkies make somebody smart?"

"Nothing can make you smart but study and effort."

"How can you say that when you're the one who gave me the Twinkies?"

"Twinkies, or certain ingredients in them, help you to focus on what you already know, but they can't teach you anything. You have to do your own studying. The Twinkies are nothing but Bodacious Baguettes of Brainpower."

"Wow, what a kick of concentration. I'll breeze through college eating Twinkies," James said.

"Listen, you can't just eat Twinkies. In fact, I eat a strict diet of healthy foods and use Twinkies only for special needs."

"You get forty ten-packs a week delivered to your door," James pointed out.

"Well, I happen to have a lot of special needs," he said with a mischievous grin. Then Nick turned serious. "James, you have to swear to me that you'll keep this a secret. This Twinkie thing is far too powerful to end up in the wrong hands. I wouldn't have showed you if I didn't see that you're basically a good human being."

"Sure, Nick. If it's that important, I'll stow it."

"Just understand this: if everyone knew about Twinkie power, you'd be right back to where you were relative to everyone else."

"I hadn't thought of it that way."

"Yes, as long as only a few of us know, a few of us will have an advantage."

"I guess that's true. I won't tell a soul."

"I know I can count on that. Thanks."

JOGGED

Having been impressed with Nick on their first date, Press couldn't stop thinking about him. She was convinced of his intelligence. There was no doubting his credentials, having confirmed them on the Internet and through Dr. Furney. His story of his first birthday had been entertaining and impossible to refute, but still harder to believe.

Nobody could remember his first birthday. She was sure of that. And nobody could dance having just read a book about it, no matter how stiff. She had to figure it out. Besides, she had never run into anyone that seemed so superior to her in every way. In fact, she had kind of always assumed she was as smart as anyone or smarter, though she tried to be humble about it. She decided to meet with him again with home field advantage. She took him aside again after lunch. "Nick, do you run?"

"Sure, if someone's chasing me," he said.

"No, I mean do you jog?"

"Sure, if the person chasing me isn't very fast."

"No, do you jog for exercise?" she asked, exasperated.

"No, I've never done that."

"Good. Will you come running with me tomorrow?"

"Okay, as long as no one chases us."

Press was stoked for this opportunity. She ran five miles three times each week. She figured that she'd get him winded to the point he couldn't talk. Then, when he was near exhaustion, she'd grill him and get into who he really was. Besides, it was a chance to beat him at something. She picked Nick up at six o'clock in the morning.

"Morning," Nick greeted her. "Where are we going?" He was dressed in a cheap dark green velour jogging suit that was three inches too short for his legs and four inches too short for his arms. It looked like he bought it at the Goodwill (which he had).

"I've decided we should jog Alki Park. It's two and a half miles long. We can go up and back."

"*Alki*—that means 'by and by' or 'eventually' in the Chinook language. The first white settlement was there in 1851. They called it New York Alki, meaning it would be a big city someday."

He must have guessed where we were going and studied up, Press thought. *He's trying to impress me.* "We'll run from the point to the Duwamish and back," she said aloud.

"Duwamish was *duwampsh* in Chinook, meaning 'multicolored river.' It must have been polluted even back then."

"Did you study up for this outing?" she asked.

"I've been reading some Northwest history since I moved here. I try to learn about each place I visit."

"Do you speak Chinook?"

"No, it's part of the Penutian family of languages, but it hasn't been spoken since the early 1800s and was never recorded. Most of the known vocabulary is actually part of Chinook jargon, a pidgin trading language used to communicate with other tribes."

"Is this a topic that particularly interests you?" she asked. *Because it doesn't interest me and I can't believe a doctor would spend time learning it*, she thought.

"Not particularly—it's just something I read. I try to learn a bit about everything. You never know when it will be useful."

"Aside from Northwest history, what else have you been reading lately?"

"Since I've moved here, or in the last few days?"

"How about this week?"

"This calendar week or the last seven days?"

"Just since Sunday," she said, a bit perplexed.

"On Sunday I read about the Carnarvon xeric shrublands of western Australia."

"What's a xeric shrubland?"

"It means shrubs that grow with very little moisture. Then I read about the use of the gandaberunda in Hindu architecture."

"What's a gandaberunda?"

"It's a mythological two-headed bird said to possess magical powers. It's the official symbol of the Karnataka government."

"I've never heard of Karnataka."

"It's a state in southern India."

"Have you been there?"

"No, just read about it."

"Anything else interesting?"

"I read a history of cricket in Kenya."

"That sounds fascinating," Press said, trying to disguise the sarcasm in her voice.

"The first noteworthy match was held in Mombasa in December 1899."

"Really?"

"Yeah, and in 1914 they went to Uganda and beat their team at Entebbe by five wickets."

"Five wickets, wow."

"Are you mocking me?"

"Definitely. So that's how you've spent your week?"

"I haven't finished with Sunday."

"Well, we're here. You'll have to continue your listing as we run."

"For Sunday or the whole week?"

"Let's continue with Sunday. Then we'll see how far you can get through the week," Press said, smiling to herself as she leaned against the car stretching her hamstrings. "Aren't you going to stretch?"

"I was stretching as we drove along."

"Really? I didn't see that."

"It was a mental stretch."

"I see," she said, not believing a word of it. "Let's get going then."

Press took off at a modest gait, thinking to pace herself until Nick was winded, then pour it on. "Well, what else did you read on Sunday?"

"I read a treatise on the contrast between generative and interpretive semantics. Of course Noam Chomsky favored the interpretive view."

"Of course." Press sped up slightly. She could feel her pulse rate increase and expected soon to hear some gasping amid Nick's wearisome soliloquy. "What else did you read?"

"I read a book on Tibetan cooking."

"Do you cook?"

"No."

"Why read the book?"

"It sounded interesting."

Press picked up speed, hitting her normal cruising range. Nick kept up, seeming to stroll beside her with long, easy strides. She couldn't see him breathing any more than if he were sitting on a recliner in front of a fire.

"Are you finished with Sunday?" Press huffed.

"No, I usually read more on Sundays than other days. Would you like me to continue?"

"You might as well finish Sunday, and then we'll reconsider."

"I read a comparative macroeconomic analysis between current conditions and the Great Depression."

"Has that altered your investment strategies?"

"What makes you think I have investment strategies?"

"Oh, nothing. I was just joking." Press hoped she had covered her slip on what she knew of Nick's financial dealings. She still didn't notice any appreciable change in his breathing. They were nearing the halfway point and Press was getting desperate. At the turn, she determined to sprint the second half if she had to. She had to wear him down. "Is that it?" she asked.

"For Sunday?"

"Yes, Sunday."

"No, just a few others. I was kind of busy last Sunday."

"What was the next one?"

"It was a comprehensive study of fiber optic communications technology."

"That's the first one I've heard that sounds worthwhile."

"I guess it's okay if we don't share all of our interests."

With an air-stressed voice, Press said, "I guess so."

"Then I read *The Immortal Life of Henrietta Lacks*."

"I read that one too. Her cells are used almost everywhere in the world."

"That's right; we've both used them in med school."

"You went to med school?" she asked, thinking she had caught him.

"Well, nursing is a medical study."

"It's not usually referred to"— she gave a raspy breath—"as med school. Most people call it nursing school."

"My mistake."

"Well, where did you go to nursing school?"

"I never really went to an actual nursing school. I just kind of learned nursing at a school of medicine. But let's get back to Sunday."

Press took an intense, oxygen-engorged breath and quickened her pace. "Okay, please finish Sunday."

"I finished the day with 'A Problem-Solving Approach to Mathematics for Elementary School Teachers.'"

"Do you . . . plan to be an . . . elementary school teacher?" she gasped.

"You never know. The opportunity might arise someday."

Press broke into a full sprint with over a mile left to go. She knew she couldn't sustain the pace but still hadn't heard a puff out of Nick. She was breathing too heavily to talk. Ten seconds passed.

"I'm sorry. That's all for Sunday," Nick spoke pleasantly. "I must have bored you. You haven't commented. I've told you I'm not a very interesting person. I won't say a word about Monday, I promise. Let's talk about you. What do you like to read?"

Press just stared at him incredulously. She pulled up, still three quarters of a mile short of the car. Lungs heaving, she guzzled as much air as she could. She bent over, hands on her thighs.

"Are you all right?" Nick asked. "You seem to have overexerted yourself. Such extreme dyspnea is often symptomatic of interstitial lung disease."

"I don't have a lung disease," Press spat. "I've been running hard."

"I can see that. I thought you did this regularly."

"And I thought," she gasped, "you never did it."

"I don't. I just do a sort of isometric exercise."

"Isometrics don't work aerobically."

"It's a kind of pulmonary isometric exercise."

"I don't believe it." Sweat-drenched and still breathing hard, Press began walking to the car.

"I'm sorry. Have I proven untrustworthy?"

Press gave him a sideways glare, and Nick fell silent. The drive home was silent until Press dropped Nick off curbside. "Thank you for coming."

"I enjoyed it. I'm sorry if I pushed you too hard," Nick apologized. "I hope we can do it again sometime."

"Sure, Nick. See you at work."

"Bye."

LOST

One afternoon, as the gang sat in the cafeteria conversing, Monty's cell chimed his mother's definitive ring. "Hi, Mom," he spouted lightheartedly.

The blood quickly drained from his face. "Uh-huh, uh-huh," he muttered several times. "I'll be right there." Monty rose so quickly, his chair toppled.

"Monty?" Cathy and Yukiko cried simultaneously.

Without bothering to right the chair or answer the girls, he strode for the exit.

Aroused from a contemplation of the life cycle of Toxorhynchites splendens, Nick bolted from his own seat and promptly pursued. Nick overtook Monty in the hallway and asked what the issue was.

"My brother, Matt—he's on a Scout hike and has been lost since yesterday morning."

"Where were they going?" Nick queried.

"His troop was hiking the Pacific Crest Trail from Snoqualmie to Stevens Pass."

Nick had never hiked any part of the Pacific Crest Trail but knew that it had been proposed in the 1930s by Clinton C. Clarke and supported by Ansel Adams, the YMCA, the Boy Scouts, and others. After many proposals, exploration, and lobbying, Lyndon Johnson signed the National Trails System Act in 1968. "The Federal Government is always too hasty," Nick said, grinning to himself. The trail was declared complete from the Mexican border to the Canadian in 1993. The

Snoqualmie-Stevens Pass section is seventy-five miles.

"What are you going to do?" Nick asked.

"They should have completed the hike today. He has to be close to Stevens Pass. I'll go there and hike in," Monty said.

"You won't be able to cover much ground by yourself."

"What else can I do?"

"Let me help. We can cover ground a lot faster from the air."

Nick took out his cell phone and looked for seaplanes in Seattle. He dialed the number for Puget Sound Seaplanes. A receptionist answered.

"Do you have a plane available for immediate charter?" he asked.

"We do. What is your destination?"

"We need it for search and rescue."

"We do that, but only when engaged by a government agency."

"I need it now and I'll pay cash. We'll be there in thirty minutes. Please begin the pre-flight now."

"We'll need to file a flight plan."

"The Pacific Crest Trail near Stevens Pass." Nick hung up.

"Thanks, Nick. You don't have to . . . how can you afford to . . ."

"I have to. I can afford to," Nick said, quieting him. "Let's go." He pushed Monty along, jogging the six blocks to his home.

Monty came willingly but was mute.

It was wet—stronger than mist but less than a shower. The temperature was in the high fifties; the clouds were high, about seven thousand feet.

Nick unlocked the Chevy and half shoved his zombified friend into the passenger seat. He quickly got into the driver's side. "Buckle up," Nick ordered as he turned the ignition. He backed out and in one motion pushed the shift knob into drive and punched the accelerator.

"How long have the Scouts been on the trail?" Nick asked.

"Today would be seven days."

"Did you hear how Matt got separated?"

"No."

"But it was yesterday?"

"Yeah."

Nick drove quickly out to Broadway and agitatedly revved the engine at each stoplight. After the second stop, his impatience got the best of him and he mentally switched the lights green as he approached them. He turned left on Olive Way and went under the freeway.

"Monty, call your mother and get the Scoutmaster's number."

Monty did as he was told. Turning right on Eastlake, Nick pulled to a stop a few blocks later at the REI on Yale Avenue.

"I'll be back in five," he told Monty. Leaving the motor running, he jumped out and headed for the lobby. "Call the Scoutmaster and get the details of when and where Matt was lost."

"Okay."

Nick ran into the store, glancing at the five-story climbing wall to his left. He picked up a featured premium emergency kit. He scanned the fourteen bullets of contents and was satisfied. He hit the escalator, taking two steps at a time, and stopped on the second floor in the mens-wear department.

He was drawn to some warm-looking jackets and grabbed the tag, reading the nine bullets of information. He grabbed an extra large in candy apple red for Monty and an extra-extra large for himself in Amazon green.

Back down in the lobby, he watched the cashier scan the items, pulled out eight hundred-dollar bills, said keep the change, and was soon out the door and into the Chevy.

Pulling back onto Eastlake, he sped north to the junction with Fairview Avenue. Across the street on Lake Union was the Puget Sound Seaplane base.

Monty, somewhat back to himself, had extracted all of the information he could from Matt's Scoutmaster, who was at the trailhead at Steven's Pass. He and a Scout had hiked out for help while the remainder of the troop had been searching for Matt. Search and rescue teams were gathering at the pass, but because it was already late afternoon, they would not begin their efforts until the next morning.

Nick opened the trunk of the Impala and grabbed an oversized sports bag. He unzipped it and stashed the emergency kit on top of numerous ten-packs of Twinkies and a lunch bag full of one hundred dollar bills. Monty came clutching the insulated jackets.

ALOFT

Hustling into the seaplane office, Nick spoke to the receptionist. "I'm Nick. I called to reserve a plane for search and rescue."

The front office consisted of a counter, behind which was a matronly woman looking to be about forty-five. There were four chairs surrounding a glass coffee table covered with aviation and outdoor magazines. The walls were clad with cheap fake-wood paneling. There were various pictures of people standing by seaplanes and of seaplanes in the air and on water. A plastic corn plant sat in a pot in the far corner. There was a hall going off from behind the counter and a door to the outside opposite the door Nick and Monty had entered.

"Yes, sir, we'll require a $2000 deposit," the woman answered. "The rate will be $465 per hour plus fuel. We accept Visa or Master Card."

"I'm sorry I don't carry credit cards. You take cash, I presume."

"I've never been asked about cash. I'll have to speak with the owner." She walked down the hall to an office and disappeared from view. Nick could hear the sounds of a conversation but couldn't make out what was being said.

Returning shortly, she informed Nick that if cash was used she'd require a ten thousand dollar deposit and a copy of his driver's license. Nick supplied the license and, unzipping the bag, pulled out a wad of bills. He counted out one hundred and re-stowed the rest.

"Do you feel comfortable carrying that kind of cash?" the woman asked.

"It's the only kind I've found that works consistently," Nick assured her.

Looking puzzled, the woman picked up a microphone and called, "Brian to the front desk, please. Brian to the front."

Momentarily, a man wearing a "Puget Sound Seaplanes" windbreaker entered through the door opposite Nick. The fellow looked to be in his midfifties and about six feet tall, and he had a stocky frame. "Hi, I'm Brian." He stuck out his hand to Nick, then Monty for a solid shake. "I'll be your pilot."

Nick introduced himself and Monty and, wanting to hurry things along, said "We'd best get going. There are only a few hours of daylight left."

"That's so," Brian agreed. "Right this way." He led them through the door and down the dock to where his plane stood ready. "I've been through preflight, and we can climb aboard and take off." Brian spoke with a slightly slurred voice, looked tired, and seemed to cling to the door as he opened it.

Nick saw that the plane was a Cessna 206 adapted with Peekay 3500 floats. Having once read a Cessna catalogue, he knew that it had a maximum cruise speed of 151-knots, a 989 feet-per-minute climb rate, a 300hp Lycoming Engine, and a McCauley three-blade propeller with polished chrome spinner. He also recalled that it had a certified ceiling of 15,700 feet and airbags for the two front seats. Max payload was 1,359 pounds (Nick estimated the weight of himself, Monty, and Brian plus the bag of Twinkies at about 712 pounds, leaving 647 for the pilot's gear, which he was certain would leave ample margin for weight.) The plane was 28.3 feet long. It had a 36-foot wingspan, was 9.3 feet tall plus, Nick estimated, about 14.3 inches extra for the pontoons.

Nick calculated about a 574.7 nautical mile range. "Brian, you been flying long?"

"I have a little over 12,000 hours."

"That's a lot of experience. Been busy lately?" Nick asked, concerned at the look of fatigue Brian exuded.

"No, not really. I'm well rested and glad for your business."

Having scanned FAA statistics several months prior, Nick recalled that though the Cessna 206 had incurred five accidents in Washington State over the past ten years, none had been fatal. He dismissed his concerns and began to climb aboard.

There were two seats forward and two aft, though Nick knew the plane capable of being configured for six. He climbed in the back, leaving the forward passenger seat for Monty.

As he seated himself, he took note of the Garmin G1000 glass cockpit with synthetic vision technology. It had twin 10.4-inch high resolution active matrix LCDs with digital altitude and heading data, topographic information, and relative terrain mapping.

"Are you familiar with the area around Steven's Pass?" Nick asked as Monty and Brian buckled in.

"Sure. There's no place in this state I'm not familiar with, and you can extend that to most of Oregon and lots of British Columbia and Alaska. I've gotten around. What were your names again?"

"I'm Nick, and that's Monty sitting next to you."

"Great, I'm usually pretty good with names. Have you flown before?"

"Yes," answered Nick, who had a lot of experience.

"No," said Monty. "This is my first time."

Brian fired up the engine and began his takeoff to the north on Lake Union. "Where are we going to start?" he asked Nick.

"Get us to Steven's Pass, and then we'll start south along the Pacific Crest Trail. Do you know the place?"

"Sure do. I hiked that stretch a couple of times myself in my younger days."

It was about a forty-minute flight to the trailhead. "Can we kind of zigzag across the trail as we head south?" Nick asked the pilot.

"Sure can," Brian answered. "And don't worry. I'll stay close enough that we'll be able to see every bend and turn."

"Great," Nick replied while opening a Twinkie. "Monty, you take the right side, I'll take the left, and we'll leave Brian free to fly the plane. Would either of you like one?" he asked, proffering the treat into the front seat.

"Sure," Brian answered.

"No thanks," said Monty.

"Here," Nick said, putting the unwrapped cake into Brian's open hand. "You sure you don't want one, Monty? They may help you see better."

"No thanks," Monty replied in a somewhat surly voice. Nick understood his anxiety and had been sympathetic to his mood from the beginning.

The search began with Brian crisscrossing the trail at about 70 knots, staying 200 to 300 feet above the ground. He paid close attention to the terrain, both visually and on his instruments. With the GPS, he would have ample warning of any mountain wall closing in on him. His head swung from one horizon to the other to the display and back again. Occasionally he shook his head as if clearing the cobwebs.

The ceiling varied from about 7,000 to 8,000 feet, often leaving them close to the top. The drizzle of the city had been replaced with a steady light rain and the air temperature was in the low forties.

Nick regularly replenished his mind with Twinkies, occasionally offering them to Brian, who accepted, and Monty, who declined. There was little conversation other than Brian warning them of a turn in the trail or Nick asking about the terrain.

Nick knew his senses were sharp, and his vision and hearing were as good as possible. He kept his window opened, and Monty did the same on the passenger side.

They passed over Lake Josephine nestled in a horseshoe ridge opened at one end and descended to about 150 feet above it, circling lazily around the perimeter. The lake was mostly surrounded by Douglas firs with an occasional rockslide of granite extending down the mountain slope to the shore. Nick noticed Brian tipping and straining his neck from side to side. Seeing nothing around the lake, Nick asked, "Brian, are you feeling okay?"

"Yeah, I've had a stiff neck since I woke up this morning. Must have slept on it wrong."

Nick noted a slight drawl to his speech that he hadn't noticed earlier.

On the shore were two men and two women setting up a couple of tents. They waved cheerily at the plane as it passed overhead. There would be no help there.

Leaving Lake Josephine, the trail veered to the southwest, coming to Tarn, little more than a pond without surrounding peaks. It had sparse trees and berry bushes on its shores, and moss and water plants proliferating around the brim. The differing shades of verdant foliage were striking, and Nick, other than the bryophyta sphagnopsida, had to restrain himself from attempts at classification to concentrate his optic faculties on the search for Matt.

They sighted a group along the shore that must have been Matt's troop turning in for the night. Brian wiggled the wings of the plane as a signal. The Scouts looked up and cheered but made no sign of having found Matt.

"I haven't seen a thing worth seeing. Have you, Nick?" Monty asked as they flew over the Scout camp.

"Nothing," Nick said.

Dusk was fast approaching as they neared Trap Lake and Slippery Slab Tower. The terrain was severe, and Brian couldn't safely get them within four hundred feet of the water, which was ringed with a few trees and a good amount of granite rockslides down its steep embankments. The tower was as an inverted shark's tooth of jagged stone.

With dark coming on, they traversed the trail from east to west and approached Surprise Lake. "We're going to have to call it a day," Brian warned. "Man, I've got the worst headache I've had in my life," he added.

Nick noted his words, and something gnawed at him. "Let's just circle around the lake once before we give it up," he suggested. Reaching into his bag, he shoved another of the Delightful Dollops of Discernment into his mouth, feeling the need to be more alert.

Surprise Lake, along with Glacier Lake, is wedged between Thunder and Sparkplug Mountains. Nestled among gentle tree-covered slopes, with an easy shoreline, the lake is about 150 yards across at its widest and about 500 yards long. In the center of the lake, it's about 20 yards deep. The trail skirts its eastern reaches while an outlet runs to the steep boulder-strewn Surprise Creek in its northwest corner.

Doing a circle around the lake from north to south and east to west, the plane dipped lower. The sunlight had all but vanished. The showers had turned to steady rain, and the ceiling had dropped to 4900 feet. Nick could see on the dash screen that the lake's elevation was 4628. They were able to cruise at about 100 feet off the surface because of the eased topography around them.

Nick spotted a speck of color on the northeast shore of the lake. "What color would Matt's coat be?" he asked Monty.

"Red, like this one you bought me," Monty shouted back.

"Circle the lake again, Brian. I think I saw something."

"Okay, but then we'll have to go," he said. "It's not getting any lighter." Brian brought the plane about in a tight circle and was passing over the north shore at the center when a searing pain ripped across the back side of his eyes. He saw a blinding light, vomited up a mass of half-digested Twinkies, and slumped over the yoke of the airplane, causing a steep dive.

With catlike reflexes, Nick crossed his arms, grabbed the safety harnesses with each hand, tucked his head into the V created by his arms, and planted his feet straight and flat on the floor. He wished he had time to grab the controls or at least to warn Monty, but given the altitude, airspeed, and payload, he estimated only 2.62 seconds before impact. "Duck!" was all he had time to say.

Nick kicked himself for having been too preoccupied to notice the signs earlier. At least, he *would* have kicked himself had he not been a couple of seconds away from a potential watery grave.

DITCHED

The plane dived at what Nick estimated 68.73 degrees and careened 34.71 degrees to the right, hitting the water at 72.136 miles per hour. He tried to mentally lessen the blow by concentrating on the water surface, but the plane was spinning too fast and the water was too liquidy to push against. The impact caught the right wingtip first and then the nose, causing a half cartwheel and 180-degree flip. The front airbags deployed. The left pontoon was torn from its rigging. The windshield and passenger side window were shattered, leaving the propeller churning and the plane inverted facing north. The engine quickly sputtered and stopped. Waves dashed outward from the plane, and it began to settle.

Nick quickly but calmly unbuckled his harness. He put his left hand down against the roof of the cabin and pressed his feet more solidly up against the floor. He knew that points of reference needed to be maintained—that right was right and left, left—even when upside down.

The water was two inches deep on the inverted ceiling. With his right hand, Nick reached forward, grabbing the pilot by the shirt. Pulling him back against the seat, Nick wrapped his fingers around the neck and felt the carotid artery, hoping for a pulse. As he'd expected, there was none. Nick concluded that Brian had suffered an intracranial aneurysm, causing a subarachnoid hemorrhage, followed by a severe hemorrhagic stroke and immediate death.

The water was now four inches deep on the ceiling. Nick couldn't reach Monty from his current position but knew that Monty's head was facing downward. He turned himself over, until he was right side up. What had been on Nick's left was now on his right. The water on the floor had reached six inches deep.

Monty's harness crossed his body with one strap, like in a car. Being on the passenger side meant the buckle was on his left. Pressing himself against the back of the seat, Nick unlatched Monty's belt and simultaneously grabbed him around the waist to flip his body. Monty's belt got tangled about his neck, and Nick had to let go with his left hand to free it. Once the belt was freed, Monty crumpled to the flooded floor. He coughed into the water, which was eight inches deep.

Righting the young man, Nick found Monty's pulse to be strong. It crossed Nick's mind that the Cessna would be equipped with the 406 MHz emergency beacon, which had been required since February 1, 2009. Being received by geostationary satellites, the new locator saved an average of six hours of search and rescue efforts. It had 5 watt output versus the 0.1 watt output of the old 121.5 MHz unit. It was also accurate to within 100 yards as opposed to the one to three nautical miles the old system could handle, reducing the search area by ninety-seven percent. NASA had estimated that 137 lives per year would be saved. Nick was comforted.

Nick pulled Monty to the back seat. Reaching across to what had been the bottom of the passenger seat, he tripped the latch that allowed the chair to fold down and move forward, making room to move to the front. He jerked on the handle of the door but found that side of the plane crumpled. The water inside was now ten inches deep.

Reaching up, Nick unbuckled the pilot, who fell to the submerged ceiling. He reached across, pulled the handle, and pushed against the door. The door gave grudgingly due to it straining against water and the broken wing. Grabbing Brian's body by the torso, he shoved it out the opening. Reaching across again to what had been the underside of the pilot's seat, he tripped the latch. The seat moved forward while it folded. The water had filled the plane to the halfway point.

Nick estimated the water temperature to be 42.14 degrees. His mind was too preoccupied for a more precise estimate. The lake water was warmed by the sun when not iced over, but he knew that about 3.32

feet below the surface was a thermal cline with what he estimated would be a drop of 6.71 degrees. With his left hand, Nick grabbed Monty by his jacket collar. With his right hand, he stretched toward the back of the plane and grasped at the floating bag of Twinkies. He touched it with the tips of his fingers. It floated just beyond his reach. The plane was within a few inches of submersion. Turning around, Nick set his feet against the ceiling of the cockpit, coiled his body, and with a great thrust pushed him and Monty through the door, just as the plane settled under the water.

There was just enough daylight left for Nick to make out the western shore of the lake about 46.42 yards away. He couldn't count on that estimate as the visibility was so poor. It was raining steadily.

Tucking Monty's neck into the crook of his right elbow and Nick's hand under Monty's armpit, Nick struck for shore. He thrust his left arm out and did a scissor kick with his feet. He thought that while US Coast Guard statistics showed an 88 percent survival rate among plane ditchings, they were already down to 66.67 percent, having lost Brian. He wasn't sure that Brian's death would count against the average, however, seeing that Brian had died prior to the crash.

Nick took another stroke toward shore, tugging Monty along. He knew that humans could survive in 40 degree water for about two hours. In 32 degree water, it was one and a half hours. This water was slightly above 40 degrees at the surface, but was colder 3.32 feet down.

He gave another pull toward shore. Nick tried to calculate survival rate when the water was 42.14 degrees at the surface but only 38.7 degrees from 3.32 feet down. He was 6 feet 7 inches tall with about 10.7 inches protruding above the surface. That would leave 2 feet 8.7 inches below the 3.32-foot thermal cline.

Nick stretched his left arm out and pulled it down, simultaneously kicking with his feet. With 2 feet 8.7 inches in water that was 38.7 degrees while 2 feet 11.6 inches was in 42.14-degree water, he determined that 10.7 inches would be in what he estimated to be 44.2-degree air.

Nick took another pull at the water, and Monty seemed to exert a bit more drag. It suddenly struck Nick that even though he'd approximated the lengths of his body that would be above and below 3.32 feet of water and in the air, he'd never estimated what percentage of body weight was represented by different segments of his body.

Another stroke was a bit weaker. The percentage of body surface was greater in the legs than the torso, while the percentage of body weight would be greater in the torso than in the legs.

Nick couldn't remember whether survival rate depended on the body surface area or the weight. He hadn't yet extrapolated the difference between 40-degree water and water that was 42.14 degrees . . . he hadn't calculated what percentage of his body was above the 3.32 foot level and what percentage was under it. He took another spasmodic stroke.

Nick remembered that having your head under water increased temperature loss by 80 percent, but his head wasn't under water. Monty's head wasn't under water either, so neither of them would lose an extra 80 percent. Nick pulled at the water again.

Boy, he wished he had a Twinkie. Maybe a dozen. He could taste the moist golden cake and the luscious cream-filled center. He fantasized about Savory Snacks of Survival. He took another stroke.

It dawned on Nick that in 50-degree water, a person could swim 0.85 miles before being incapacitated by hypothermia. Activity caused accelerated heat loss over staying still. He took another stroke.

This water wasn't 50 degrees, and he hadn't yet calculated what his heat loss would be staying still with some undetermined percentage of his body below the 3.32-foot level.

With shock, he realized that moving toward shore, he wouldn't be perpendicular in the water, reducing the percentage that was actually below 3.32 feet. That was beneficial to his chances of survival but ruined all of his previous calculations. Nick kicked again but didn't manage much of a stroke with his arm.

If he could just decide whether to determine relative surface area or body weight and adjust for the change in angle due to his forward movement, taking into account the temperature drop below the thermal cline and extrapolating for his activity level and the distance to shore . . . He took another stroke.

If he knew the distance to shore . . . but he couldn't be sure because the visibility was poor. He looked for the shore and, through the twilight, noticed that he'd pulled to the south, probably because of the drag Monty produced. He pulled another stroke, correcting his bearing.

What about Monty? What were his proportions out of the water and in the water and below three feet? Did he lose heat faster because he was unconscious? Or slower because Nick was doing all of the work? He stroked again.

Man, he could sure use a Twinkie. Did he have his backpack on? He couldn't remember. He envisioned the sport bag, bobbing just beyond his reach in the back of the plane. He reached for it. It became another stroke.

The Amazon green jacket was sure heavy. He hadn't had it zipped in the plane and he decided to shed it. He tried to shake it off of his leading left arm but as he did his head and Monty's slipped under water. Monty coughed. Nick remembered that having your head underwater caused 80 percent more heat loss. But 80 percent more heat loss than what?

When he'd slipped under water, what percent had gone beneath the thermal cline? Had Monty gone under by the same amount? He took a stroke.

He took another feeble stroke, then tried again to shake off his insulated jacket. His head went under water. Monty coughed. His feet hit the bottom.

Robotically Nick marched forward, dragging Monty along.

ASHORE

Nick lugged Monty up against the trunk of a cedar tree. He shook off his jacket. He knew that water conducts heat twenty-five times faster than air so he would stop losing temperature as quickly. He remembered that when your core temperature dropped below 89.6 degrees, you would lose consciousness, and at 86 degrees you would die. Of course, once you had lost consciousness, you wouldn't know when you died. Unless, of course, there was life after death, which he was sure there was. Then you would know when you died because you would feel alive again.

Why was he thinking of life after death? Did that mean he was going to die? Was his body temperature at 86 degrees? Of course not. If it was below 89.6 degrees he would be unconscious. Was he unconscious?

He remembered that water conducted heat twenty-five times faster than air. He'd probably be okay now if he kept active. Monty had lost less heat due to inactivity in the water but was still inactive on land. Would he now lose at a faster pace? The water temperature had been 42.14 degrees with the thermal cline at 3.32 feet, but had Monty gone beneath the thermal cline or had he floated parallel to the surface?

Nick knew they needed fire and shelter and to get out of their wet clothes. He couldn't decide what to do first. He was standing there in his hospital blues and sneakers with his jacket on the ground. It was raining steadily.

"Make a fire first," his mother's voiced told him.

"You make it!" he snapped.

"Don't get smart with me!" his mother fired back.

"Sorry, Mom," Nick whispered.

Nick had never been a Boy Scout. He'd started college at eleven. He had read a book about survival skills and put himself on the first page of fire starting. He knew he needed a fireboard, a bow, a drill, tinder, a socket, and fuel for once the tinder was going.

From his jacket pocket, Nick nabbed his key chain and fell to his knees under the thick branches of the cedar tree where he'd deposited Monty. He used his house key to scrape at the soft, dry bark. He gathered a couple of handfuls and deposited them in a pile against the base of the tree.

The polyester filling of their jackets didn't mat as badly in water as a down jacket would, but Nick couldn't remember ever reading actual measurements. How much heat would Monty retain for how long?

Nick stumbled about, looking for dry fuel. He found dead limbs beneath some nearby trees and stacked them next to his tinder pile. He took a minute to check Monty's pulse and found it weak but steady.

Nick's jacket was on the ground. He couldn't stop shivering. Should he put it back on, wet? His clothes were wet. Would putting a wet jacket on top of wet clothes make him double wet? If he only had a Twinkie, he knew he could figure it out. Where were his Twinkies?

He remembered the tools prescribed by the survival book. He'd collected the tinder. He needed a fireboard. Cottonwood was one of the suggested species. He'd seen a cottonwood log rotting a few yards from the cedar tree, but which direction was it? His vision was clouded. He turned to his left and saw the log. "Do you know what I saw?" he muttered, remembering the old riddle. "What?" the other kids would respond. "Logs," was the reply. "I saw logs." Nick laughed. He'd used the joke since he was two.

He stumbled to the cottonwood log. He reached around inside the hollow end and broke off a dry piece about 10.2 inches long and 2.74 inches wide. He carried it back to the cedar tree.

He trembled uncontrollably. He needed a bow. Nick remembered seeing the movie *Robin Hood*. He liked Errol Flynn best. There was also Kevin what's–his–name. "I don't forget names," Nick puzzled. "If I had a Twinkie, those Magnificent Morsels of Memory, I could remember what's-his-name. He had a bow. I need a bow." Nick juddered. He broke off a limb about 23.6 inches long and .66 inches in diameter. He wasn't confident of the diameter estimate. His fingers were cold, and it was hazy in the dark. The limb had a fork at one end.

Tinder, bow, fireboard . . . He knew there were other things he needed. A round thing with a pointy end . . . "A drill," he shouted. He went back to the cottonwood log and fished till he had a limb piece .48 inches in diameter and 6.72 inches long. He was proud of his discovery. Where were his Twinkies? He deserved a Nummy Nugget of Knowledge.

A socket. Nick needed a socket for the top of the drill. There were a number of small stones around the tree, and he found one with a rounded top and a depression underneath. He reviewed his list. A fireboard, a bow, a drill, tinder, a socket, and fuel for once the tinder was going. What came next? *A notch*, he thought. Fumbling in his pocket, he extracted his keys and whittled a notch into the edge of the fireboard.

He felt Monty's pulse. It seemed weaker but was still ticking. What was the pulse rate? Nick couldn't estimate time. If he couldn't estimate time, how could he estimate survival? Would they survive? What was the air temperature? Was it warmer inside Monty's jacket? If he had a Twinkie he could figure it out. If he had two Twinkies, he could shove one in Monty's mouth. Could Monty chew?

"Start the fire!" a female voice shouted. "Yeah, the fire," Nick repeated. He had what he needed. He could make the fire! He got down on one knee and placed one foot on the fireboard to hold it steady. He picked up the drill and the bow.

"The bow needs a string!" the voice shouted again.

Oh yeah, Nick thought. He took off the shoe that was holding the fireboard and extracted the shoestring. He tied one end around the fork on the bow.

Holding the socket atop the drill with his left hand, Nick wrapped the shoestring around the bow and held the other end in his right hand. Forward and back, he stroked, getting gradually faster till whiffs of smoke curled up from the fireboard. *Almost there*, he thought and stroked faster. *What about the tinder?* He'd forgotten the tinder. "If I had a Twinkie, I wouldn't have forgotten," he said to himself. Digging a small hole, he filled it with tinder, placed the fireboard over it, and started again.

The spark from the drill dropped into the tinder below. Nick lifted the fireboard, bent low, and blew on the nest. As he leaned over, drops of water from his soaked hair fell into the tinder and extinguished the spark.

Unable to master the shaking of his body, he threw the tinder away and started over. This time, without bending over, he raised the tinder to his lips and gently puffed until a flame burst out. He seated the flame in the depression in the ground and grabbed for some kindling. It wasn't there!

He wagged his head to clear his vision, and he saw that the kindling was there. He snapped up a few pieces and stoked the flame. In a few seconds, the fire crackled to life. Nick took a deep breath, shuddering as he straightened up. His head hit the overhanging branches. He lay wood on the fire, knowing he must quickly create some kind of shelter.

Getting the fire started had somewhat cleared Nick's head. He still wished for a Twinkie, but his thoughts turned to what he needed to accomplish. Going to the nearest tree, he struggled to break off limbs that would be long enough to reach from the ground to the lower branches of his home tree. He gathered nine and decided it would suffice. Returning, he stood them up in a semicircle around the trunk, with Monty in the center.

Nick checked Monty's pulse, which was barely discernible. He quickly stripped Monty to his briefs and hung his jacket and his hospital blues on the overhanging limbs. Leaning Monty against the trunk, he shook him and began slapping and rubbing his skin. The clothing began to shoot great clouds of steam, and Nick stripped himself to his drawers and hung his own clothes.

Nick snuggled up with Monty with his back to the trunk and closed his eyes. He snapped awake six minutes later and saw that the fire had dwindled. Shaking the cobwebs away, he threw more wood on the fire. He checked Monty, who seemed to have stabilized, and rearranged the clothing to dry the backside.

Clutching Monty gently by the face, Nick shook him. Monty coughed and his eyes fluttered. "Monty, wake up," he said. "Monty, wake up." Monty groaned and forced his eyes open.

"Monty, we've got to get you some exercise," Nick said.

"What?"

"We need to get your blood circulating so you don't lose your fingers and toes."

"Fingers and toes?" Monty slurred.

"Yes, fingers and toes. Let me help."

Nick grasped Monty's right foot and bent the knee to Monty's chest. He repeated it several times and then switched to the left. He then continued with the arms and began the process over again. Nick's own mind was still a bit cloudy, and he wished for a Twinkie, but he continued Monty's exercise regimen several times. All of a sudden, it dawned on him. "Matt," he muttered.

MATT

Where's Matt?" Monty asked.

"He's nearby. I'm going to get him."

"Get Matt," Monty repeated.

"Let's get dressed first." Nick quickly pulled down their T-shirts, blue pants, and tops, which were dry and pleasantly warm. He dressed Monty first, then himself. Their socks were dry, so he pulled them on.

"Warm," Monty said, dozing off.

"Warm," Nick repeated and pulled on his still, wet sneakers. The jackets weren't yet dry, but Nick decided he'd be better off wearing his when he left the shelter. He threw most of what was left of the wood on the fire and stood outside the cover of the branches to get his bearings.

He could see the lake a few yards away on his right and calculated that he'd seen Matt's red jacket at the northwest corner of the lake. He reckoned it had been about 10.32 yards west into the trees. Nick struck out along the shoreline, wishing he could calculate the distance from his location to the corner of the lake, but not knowing the speed of the plane nor its exact heading upon impact, he decided calculation was meaningless. He couldn't see the end of the lake and could barely see the terrain in front of him. The rain was falling steadily.

He figured he couldn't have been more than halfway down the lake or about 250 yards from Matt's assumed position. What worried him was where to turn 10.32 yards to the west. Walking too carelessly, Nick tripped on a snag and tumbled into a small gulf about a foot deep. His face and the front of his jacket were covered with muck, his pants were soaked, and a fair amount seeped up into his chest.

"Dang it!" he swore, using the strongest expletive in his repertoire. He did a push-up and brought his feet forward till he was standing in the shin-deep water. Losing his balance, he slipped again in the muck, catching himself on the shallow bank. He climbed the shore and pressed forward.

Nick's chest and legs felt the chill of a breeze across their soaked exterior, and the rain had newly soaked his matted hair. A frigid shudder quaked through his entire body. He knew that, sopping wet, hypothermia would attack him again. He picked up a dead bough and, using it like a blind man's cane, quickened his pace.

There were more puddles, fallen logs, and branches clawing at him. Nick made his way as quickly as possible along the lakeside. He trembled with every footstep. *Why did I lost those Twinkies?* he wondered. Vague memories of the crash wound through his muddled consciousness. He was oblivious to the scraping of the undergrowth until it dawned on him that he was no longer following the shoreline. The terrain had begun to slope downward. He had continued on when the lake had ended.

Nick shook his head. He had to retrace his steps and find the lake shore. How long had it been? His shivering was violent now. He needed to get back to the fire quickly. He mustered his remaining brain power and turned around. The lake should be to his left if he was successful.

"I've got sunshine on a cloudy day. When it's cold outside, I've got the month of May. I guess you'd say, what could make me feel this way? My girl . . ." Would Press ever be his girl?

He began to count his steps, not that he could calculate anything, but to occupy his mind and keep it awake. At seventy-three, he sidestepped a tree, and there was a body wrapped in red.

Instinctively, because there wasn't much cognizance left in his head, Nick reached for the carotid artery. Pushing hard, he felt life. Nick dropped to his knees. *I think I'll just rest for a minute,* he thought.

"Pick him up!" a voice chided him.

"But I'm tired. Just give me a minute."

"Pick him up!"

"Okay, okay, I'll do it."

Nick grabbed the corpse-like body by the shoulders and yanked it onto his back. He struggled to his feet.

He slipped on some grass and fell. He re-shouldered the boy, got to his knees, and then stood.

The shoreline would be to his left, he knew. He began to walk. With his right hand holding Matt's legs, he counted fifteen paces to the shore. Turning right, he continued to slog forward. Where was he? He remembered seventy-three and fifteen. He was sure that made eighty-eight paces, but he didn't know how many to count for the time he'd spent on his knees.

Three more paces, and he tried to calculate again. If he'd taken eighty-eight, plus three more, that was ninety-one, but did the time on his knees count? Ninety-two, ninety-three . . . he passed one hundred. Then he dropped the hundred and began again at one. At nineteen, he couldn't remember if he'd gone past one hundred or two hundred. How would he know where he was if he couldn't keep track?

"I'd be safe and warm if I was in LA." The tune wafted through his mind.

He didn't feel cold anymore. The cadaver on his shoulder didn't feel heavy anymore. He felt better than he ever remembered feeling. Thirty-seven—was that 137 or 237? It struck him that if he couldn't remember he'd never know when he arrived. Then it hit him that he wouldn't know anyway. He didn't know where he'd started.

Forty-eight, forty-nine . . . there was a glimmer of light ahead. Fifty-two, fifty-three . . . if he could just sleep for a few minutes, he knew he could make it. He dropped to his knees, and Matt's body flopped forward through the underbrush. "Nick, is that you?"

Monty clambered through the back of his shelter and found Matt and Nick lying in a heap. He drug Matt to the fire and returned for Nick. Monty had been dozing but was somewhat recovered. He knew he had to act quickly. He stripped Matt and Nick to their shorts.

His jacket was dry. He laid it under them and placed them front to back. He lay on top, rubbing his hands up and down their torsos as fast as he could. He kept at it until he was exhausted. Then he got off, took off his blues, and put them atop the two men. He checked their pulses—still beating. Nick's was better than Matt's. He rubbed their feet, one at a time. He knew he was losing ground.

"Nick!" he yelled. "Get up! I can't do this alone! Nick!" Monty grabbed Nick by the hand and pulled him up to a sitting position.

"Nick!" Monty slapped him and slapped him again. "Nick, wake up!"

Nick heard his name through a fog in the forest. *Thirty-eight, thirty-nine.* Was it one hundred or two hundred? He couldn't recall.

"Nick, wake up!"

Forty, forty-one. It was one hundred, he was almost sure of it.

"Nick, Nick!"

It was Monty. Monty. Had he made it back to Monty? Was Monty okay? "Monty?" he mumbled.

"Nick! Nick! Wake up!"

"Monty, you okay?"

"I'm okay. Nick, get up. Matt—he's here. Help me."

"Okay, let me rest a minute."

"Nick! Get up! Now!" Monty grabbed him by the hand and pulled him to his feet. "Nick, you've got to move around. I've got to help Matt. I can't help both of you."

"What should I do, Monty?"

"Dance, Nick, dance."

"What kind of dance, Monty?"

"A jig, Nick. Can you do a jig?" Monty was rubbing his brother all over and moving his limbs in and out.

"Sure, I read about it. Is this okay, Monty? Am I dancing, okay?"

"You're doing great, Nick. Don't stop."

"I'm tired, Monty."

"You've got to keep it up."

"How long?"

"Till I say stop."

"It's hard, Monty. I have to bend over while I dance."

"Do it anyway."

"Do you have any Twinkies?"

"No Twinkies, Nick." Monty kept working with Matt. "Why the Twinkies, Nick?"

"I like Twinkies. They make me smart."

"Sure, Nick. Twinkies make you smart."

"You know that too?"

"Sure, Nick. Everybody knows Twinkies make you smart. Keep dancing."

"I'm tired, Monty."

"Keep dancing, Nick."

After a few minutes of dancing, something popped in Nick's head. "Monty, how's Matt? Have you checked his pulse? Never mind, I'll do it. You keep rubbing." Nick checked the pulse, which was weak but steady. He checked the clothes. His blues were warm and dry. He pulled them down and wrapped them around Matt. "I've got to get more wood."

"You're nearly naked. You work with Matt. I'll look for wood. It's good to have you back."

"It's good to be back." Nick began rubbing Matt through the warm clothing that had been laid atop him.

In a few minutes, Monty was back with an armload of wood. "How's Matt?"

"He's coming along fine. I'll just turn him over and let him brown on the other side."

"Your humor is back. He must be okay."

"We're all going to be okay," Nick assured.

"Will we be able to hike out in the morning?" Monty asked.

"I'm sure we won't need to. The plane has a transponder."

"How about Matt's extremities?"

"I don't think he'll lose any fingers or toes. They may be painful for a while."

"Nick, you saved my life. Thank you."

"You saved mine, so we're even."

"You saved Matt's too, so I'm in debt."

"It's not polite to try to get even with people. Forget it."

"I'll never forget it, Nick. You're family."

"That's all the thanks I need."

Nick and Monty sat against the tree with Matt sandwiched between them. The fire was warm, their clothes were dry, and they dozed. By morning, the fire was a few glowing embers. Nick arose and stoked it, blowing the coals to light. Before the others woke, but not before Nick craved a hot breakfast, the rescue party arrived.

Nick roused Monty and Matt. Matt had not fully regained consciousness before that and was confused at the situation. With all three of them stiff and trembling, it was decided that leaving by a mountain trail would be too arduous. Without any Twinkies, Nick agreed. A medivac helicopter landed on the lake to evacuate them.

The pilot's corpse had floated ashore and was carried home on a second trip. Nick and Monty were treated and released. Matt stayed at Harborview overnight. All three were victims of giant hugs from Monty's mother.

FERRY

The next day, Nick ran into Press in a hallway.

"Nick, I heard you and Monty almost died night before last."

"I wouldn't put it that way, but we did experience a particularly perilous period."

"I was told you lost consciousness due to hypothermia."

"I merely took repose to replenish my cognitive powers."

"Monty said you saved his life and his brother's."

"I did my best to help."

"He also said you nearly died doing it."

"If that was the case, then he saved my life," Nick said. "By the way, would you be willing to go out with me Saturday?" He tried to throw the question in casually to hide his anxiety.

"Are you asking me for a date?"

"No, I'm aware that Saturday is the eighteenth."

"I won't get caught in that circle . . . I'd be happy to accompany you Saturday. But tell me more about your rescue."

"It was nothing really. You must have talked to Monty or someone?"

"Yeah, Cathy got the whole story from Monty."

"Then there's no need to discuss it further."

"I guess, if you don't want to. So Saturday . . . where will we go and when would you like to pick me up?"

"If you're available for the entire day, I'd like to ride the ferry to British Columbia and back."

"I'd like that. When will we leave?"

"I'll need to pick you up about five thirty."

"That's awfully early, but it sounds like fun," Press said.

"Great. I'll see you Saturday."

They made a day of it, leaving early Saturday morning, driving to Anacortes, walking onto the ferry, and riding to Sidney, BC. The trip took them up and back through the San Juan Islands. They stood on the stern's upper deck to watch the departure. The diesels roared and the propellers churned the water to foam.

"Isn't it great the way the gulls congregate and then launch themselves to wish us good-bye?" Press asked, leaning on the rail.

"Perhaps they're just hoping a passenger will provide them a hot meal over the side."

"I hadn't yet seen your crass side, Mr. Stringfellow."

"How many sides have you seen?"

"How many do you have?"

"Front, back, left, and right."

"I think it's many more than that."

It was a beautiful day, but chilly. They moved to the bow and let the wind scour their faces. The water was a deep blue-green that turned white when the bow plowed a vast furrow in the fertile deep. The trough between the Decatur and Blakely Islands was like a verdant valley between more abundant mounds of vegetation. There was scarcely a parting line between sea-green and tree-green. The sweet salt spray added aromatherapy to the visual feast.

"It's magnificent," Nick opined.

"Your first time?" Press whispered.

"I'd read about it, but words betrayed the author's feeble attempt at description."

Press looked into his eyes, which shone like a little boy watching a rocket launch. She snuggled into him for warmth and to treasure the first time she'd heard Nick admit that books couldn't always compare with firsthand experience. They stood in silence for several sumptuous seconds.

"So you grew up in Philadelphia?" Nick asked, breaking the spell.

"Yes, Chestnut Hill."

"That's an upscale neighborhood, right?" Nick asked.

"Sure, I guess so."

"I'll bet you never met James Bond."

"What does James Bond have to do with anything?"

"He lived in Chestnut Hill before you were born."

"Nick, he's a fictional character."

"He was fictionalized, but he was real."

"You're jerking my chain."

"It's totally true trivia. Ian Flemming used the name of James Bond from Chestnut Hill for his stories, with James's permission of course."

"And how did Ian know James?"

"Ian lived in the West Indies and was an amateur ornithologist. James wrote *Birds of the West Indies*. Have you read it?"

"No, have you?"

"Yes, it's kind of boring, but the pictures are nice. Anyway, Ian wanted a simple but masculine name for his novel, and the rest is history. But enough of trivia, what does your father do?" Nick asked innocently.

"He *and* Mom are doctors at the University of Pennsylvania," Press answered, emphasizing "and."

"Is that where you went to school?"

"To medical school, yes. I did my undergrad at Bryn Mawr. Where did you go to school?" Press was trying to turn it around.

"Missouri Southern State University and some others."

"Where did you study nursing?" Press asked, assuming Nick wouldn't lie.

"I didn't exactly go to nursing school," he admitted.

"So what exactly did you study that qualified you as a 'nurse at large'?"

"Several things I've talked with Dr. Furney about. It's getting kind of cool. Can we go inside for some hot chocolate?"

"Sure."

Inside, Nick turned the tide.

"So you grew up a spoiled rich kid?"

"Yes, I never lacked for anything, but neither did any of my friends."

"So what do rich kids do for fun?"

"Same as poor kids, but the ambience is more opulent."

"Did you always want to be a doctor?" he asked.

"I guess so. Mom and Dad seemed to enjoy it," she answered.

"How did you picture life as a doctor?"

"I saw it as a way to help people and society."

"Not for the money?"

"I never thought about the money. Do I seem like I care about the money?" she asked, a bit peeved.

"No, I was just wondering. I grew up without money and just don't know how the other half thinks."

"Well, I'm sure I don't think any differently than you do!"

"So not even your muliebrity makes a difference?"

"I do believe men and women are different. I never needed a study to prove it. Nevertheless, my mother showed me that women are just as capable intellectually as men."

"Do your parents get along well?" Nick asked.

"They love each other," she replied.

"How do you know?"

"I've always known. They hold hands, they kiss, and when they think I'm not looking, they even pinch."

"Have you ever been in love?"

"Many times, but not like they are."

"What's the difference?"

"Some of it I won't understand until I've been in love as long as they have. But it has to do with mutual respect and having survived life's trials together."

"And your love affairs, how were they different?"

"I guess they all ended when I lost respect for the guy."

"How did that happen?"

"I discovered their outlook on life was warped."

"What outlook are you out looking for?"

"Very glib," she said, smiling. "I'm just hoping for someone sincere, real, and spiritual as well as intellectual."

"Are you religious then?"

"I wouldn't say that. We went to church occasionally, but I do believe there's more to life than the physical and the intellectual. It's the intangible inner fiber that makes someone care. It's goodness and virtue, or the lack thereof."

"How do you judge those things in a person?"

"There's no test. You just watch and listen for the way they see their fellow men *and women.*"

"Give me a for instance."

"For instance, Cyril Veshkov thinks poor people are supposed to be subservient to rich people."

"You were in love with Cyril Veshkov?"

"No! But I did date him a couple of times."

"How about me?" Nick asked.

"Huh?"

"Now you've dated me a couple of times, will you dump me?"

"If you keep asking annoying questions, I will."

That shut Nick up for a moment as the ferry docked at Sidney. They had fish and chips with clam chowder for lunch.

Seated on the ferry for the return trip, Press got to what was really vexing her. "What do you do when you visit patients?"

"I do whatever I can to help them medically, but I'm just a nurse. Mostly I try to cheer them up, make them feel comfortable."

"I remember snapping at you the first few times I saw you with patients. I'm really sorry, but—"

"Oh, forget about it. I have."

"I can't believe that someone who remembers their first birthday can forget being insulted a few months ago."

"Well, I haven't really forgotten, but I've definitely forgiven."

"I appreciate that, but back to the patients. After about the third time, I noticed a pattern that has to be more than coincidence." She breathed deeply. "The patients you visited all had miraculous recoveries."

Nick smirked. "I guess I just know how to pick 'em."

"Don't patronize me. All doctors realize that people heal sometimes with no discernible medical reason. Miracles do happen, but not one after the other in every room that a certain nurse might drop in on. I think you must have some medical knowledge you haven't shared with me."

"I told you. I read a lot."

"There's more, isn't there? A whole bunch more," Press insisted.

"Well, I guess I could tell you, but then I'd have to decapitate you."

"If you don't square with me, I'll never speak to you again!"

"Really?" he said, pausing. "I don't think I'd like that."

"I'm serious. I've got to know."

"Why?"

"I'm a doctor. I was curious from the first time I saw you. I do know that the frustration of unresolved curiosity is part of what made me treat you superciliously. I feel bad about my behavior, but I was driven to figure you out."

"There's not much to figure."

"Don't interrupt! I'm in the middle of true confessions. I pulled strings in Human Resources. I pestered Dr. Furney. I got to know Cathy and Yukiko and Monty just to get information about you. I even went to your house when I knew you were at work and talked to Jemima and the others."

"Wow. You wanted to know me that badly?"

"Hush! If I don't come clean, I'll explode."

"I'm sorry. I'll keep quiet. What else did you want to say?"

"Uh . . ." She took a deep breath. "Nothing. I guess I'm finished."

"Okay." Nick pondered this relationship. "If you're that insistent, I'm going to tell you something I don't want anyone to know. Will you keep my secret?"

"Cross my heart and hope to spit purple peanuts."

"I'm not sure that qualifies as a promise."

"Well, it is."

"Okay . . . I'm not just a nurse. I'm also a doctor."

"That's your big secret?"

"Yep. Are you disappointed?"

"Give me a break. You're not just a doctor either, are you?" Press asked.

"What do you mean? In medicine, what can you be that's higher than a doctor?"

"Nick, you don't talk about yourself, but you can't hide your talents from an inquiring mind with access to the World Wide Web."

"You mean you Googled me?"

"Yes."

"I can forgive all those other things, but that's insidious. I don't know if I'll tell you anything now."

"Come on, Nick. Fess up."

"Did you learn a lot from the Web?"

"Well, I didn't take the time to read all 1,383 items, but yeah, I know quite a bit about you."

"That must have been between thirty-two and thirty-seven days ago."

"How do you know that?"

"Well, that was the only period with 1,383 items. There are 1,391, as of this morning. Anyway, what do you think you know?"

"My preliminary count says you are board certified in at least seven specialties and have at least seventeen PhDs. Is that right?"

"Yeah. I guess so."

"Well, how many is it?" Press asked.

"At least seven and seventeen," Nick answered.

"You don't know how many?"

"Sure, I know exactly how many, but no one else needs to."

"Why so secretive? Don't you realize what you could accomplish if people knew your impressive credentials? I would never have dared given you a hard time if I'd known."

"And how would you have treated me if you'd known my credentials?"

"With respect and deference," Press stated promptly.

"You would have treated me respectfully if you'd known I was accomplished. How do you treat people who aren't accomplished?"

"Well I, uh . . . I, uh . . . always try to respect everybody, but . . ."

"Do you realize how notoriety ruins opportunities to make a difference in people's lives? Do you think I could go about doing good with groupies hanging around and wannabees and jealous haters interfering? Have you ever noticed that charity from a celebrity breeds nothing but publicity? I have no desire to be renowned or even known."

"Okay, I'll grant you that, and you've caught me in the hypocrisy of treating some people with more respect than others, but back to my original question. How is it that patients you spend time with seem to miraculously recover?"

"I think you're exaggerating."

"I'm not! Now tell me!" Press demanded.

"All right . . . I do know some techniques that aid in the healing process."

"You know miraculous cures, and you don't share them with the world? That's the most selfish thing I've ever heard."

"I can't."

"You can't share or you won't?"

"I could, but it wouldn't do any good."

"Why?"

"'Cause even if they knew what to do they wouldn't have the means to do it."

"Are you saying that you know medical techniques that only you can apply?"

"Yes."

"Why?"

"I can't say."

"You can't say or you won't?"

"I can't tell you. Not yet anyway . . . Maybe if things progress."

"What do you mean 'progress'? What things?" she asked.

"You know, *things*. Things between you and me," he said.

Press shyly averted her eyes, pausing. "Do you want those *things* to progress?"

"I do," was all Nick said. The ferry docked, and they walked silently hand in hand back to the Impala. Two men in dark suits followed them, not holding hands but trying to look casual.

This time at the top of the stairs, the kiss was not so quick. When he left, Press danced around the room like she hadn't done since she was nine years old.

NUMBER 3

Angie Phillips was thirteen years old. Her single
mother worked swing shift. Each weeknight Angie would stay at
her girlfriend's house until eleven and return before her mother got
home at midnight.

Angie lived a couple of blocks east of the Beacon Hill playground.
Getting home from her boyfriend's house involved walking three blocks
south, then around a half block to a single-story apartment. The half
block could be saved by walking through a dirt road alleyway, which she
invariably did.

Angie had never been a fearful child. Her confidence bordered on
recklessness. She even fancied herself the physical equal of any man. She
had seen all of the tough women movies. The alley held no dread for
Angie.

This particular evening the darkness held an ominous portent even
for the usually foolhardy child.

She entered the north end with a prickly sensation in her spine. It
was a moonless night, as most in Seattle are. Her eyes darted from side
to side, searching the gloom of the backyards she passed. Even the lights
in the windows seemed dim. The length of the lane was unlit, and the
house on the southeast corner had a grove of thick bushes bordering it.

For the preceding four nights, a white van had been parked at the
intersection. Tonight the side door stood open.

BUSTED

Cathy and Monty were getting off shift at eleven thirty at night. Nick didn't really have a shift, and Press was on night duty. Cathy and Monty rounded the corner to the back entrance hallway just as Press, who'd arrived a few minutes earlier, was giving Nick a parting kiss.

"Hi, guys!" Press greeted them cheerily. "Got to be off. See you."

Cathy stood there, shocked. Finally she blurted out, "You've never kissed me like that, Copernicus H. Stringfellow."

"I thought we were just friends," Nick protested.

" 'Were' is the correct tense . . . Monty, will you walk me home?"

"Uh, sure," he said sheepishly, averting his eyes from Nick.

The door slammed as Cathy and Monty walked out.

Nick was stupefied.

The next day at lunch, Cathy didn't show up. "Where's Cathy?" Nick asked as Monty took a seat.

"I don't know. I haven't seen her this morning."

"Well, what did she say last night . . . about me, I mean?"

"She didn't say a word about you. As soon as we walked out the door, she acted as though I was the most interesting person in the world. She had me telling half of my life story by the time I got her home. Then she just said 'Thanks' and went in."

"Well, do you think she was mad?"

"No, I don't *think* so," Monty answered.

"You don't?"

"I don't *think* so. I know so."

"How do you know if she didn't say anything about it?"

"Do you know anything about a woman's psyche?"

"I've read a number of books about it, but none of them made any sense," Nick said.

"That's true, but you can know when they're really mad."

"How do you know?"

"Because they don't mention it."

"Well, what was she mad about?"

"I'd guess it had something to do with you kissing Dr. Spurbeck," Monty said.

"Why would that upset her?"

"If you don't know that, you'd better read those female books again."

"Do you mean she has romantic interests in me?"

"Anyone who doesn't know that hasn't looked in her eyes."

"I've looked in her eyes. Her corneas and retinas are sound."

"For such a smart fellow, you're pretty dim."

"Oh . . . you think she's ogling me? What should I do? I feel terrible."

"You should try flowers."

"Why? They won't make me feel any better."

"Not for you, Nick. For Cathy."

"Oh, women like flowers, don't they?"

"Yeah, they do."

"Thanks, Monty. I'll try it."

That night Cathy again asked Monty to walk her home. As they were standing in the doorway opening an umbrella, Nick approached. "Cathy!" he shouted as he rounded the corner.

Seeing Nick, Cathy grabbed Monty by the shoulders and kissed him passionately. Then ignoring Nick, she pushed Monty out the door and followed him into the rain.

Nick stood there in surprise for a moment, then shoved through the door, yelling, "Cathy, just a minute!" Seeing it was useless, he tromped back inside.

"What was that for?" Monty asked.

"Just for being a good friend," Cathy answered.

"I don't want to be your retaliation against Nick."

"You're not. I just realized that he'll never be what I want."

"What's that?"

"Someone I can count on in every way."

"Nick's a great guy. None better."

"Yes, he is a great guy, but I realize I want more than a guy."

"You think of me as more than a guy?" Monty asked, surprised.

"I think you could be a lot more," she answered.

They walked in silence to her place, and, on the steps, her kiss was reciprocated.

"So you're out there sucking face with your man," Cathy's dad said as she walked through the door. "From the size of these flowers, I'd say he wants a lot more than a smooch."

"Whoa!" Cathy exclaimed, looking around the living room at eight stands of flowers six feet high. "I guess Nick really is sorry."

"So Nick's your guy, huh?"

"No, Nick used to walk me home, but that's over with. Monty walked me home."

"Monty, huh? You're on to a new one now?"

"Yes, Monty has been a friend for a while. Now maybe he'll be more than a friend."

"You should go back to the other one. Anybody that can afford to throw that much away on flowers would be a better mark. What a waste on a twig like you!"

THE HOOD

Nick knocked on the neighbor's door. The house had once been painted a cheery yellow, but that had been years ago. Half of the siding on the south-facing front was a light gray sun-dried cedar. The rest was in various stages of peeled yellow or white undercoating. The yard was mostly dead brown grass with occasional golden weeds as high as four feet. A side window was boarded over, and the drawn shades were stained variations of brown. The roof on the front was old though fairly moss free, but the north side was thick with the shade-loving vegetation. Nick had been careful mounting the steps because they looked as though their hold on life was tenuous.

Nick heard the sandpaper-like shuffling of feet across a worn linoleum floor, and the door was eventually opened by a short, thin woman in a tattered floral house robe. Abby Pendergraft was seventy-two years old and looked every year of it. She was barely discernible from her ninety-four-year-old mother, Leah, who was craning her neck to see who was at the door. She was perched on an old-fashioned dark brown rocking chair covered in weathered pink padding. "Who is it?" she demanded in a high-pitched, crackly voice. "We don't want any!"

"Nick Stringfellow, madam. I'm your next-door neighbor!" Nick bellowed.

"Well, you don't have to shout, sonny. Let him in, Abby. He's too funny lookin' to be one of them bill collectors."

"Thank you, ladies," Nick said as he strode through the door. "May I be seated?"

"Make yourself at home. If you don't, you oughta be," Leah Pendergraft said, still taking command of the conversation. "What kind of neighborliness did you have in mind?"

"Well, I hope you don't consider me overly snoopy, but I found out that you ladies were a bit behind on your mortgage."

"Our mortgage and our garbage and our cribbage neighbor. Social security don't go as far as it used to, but why should you care?"

"Well, I. . . that is, the corporation I work for has purchased your mortgage, and we'd like to make it a present to you, but only if you're willing to accept certain conditions."

"Did you say your name was Snidely Whiplash?"

"No, ma'am, it's Nick Stringfellow."

"Might rather be Strangefellow, sonny. Why'd you buy our mortgage and why'd you want to be givin' it away?"

"Just wanting to be neighborly, Mrs. Pendergraft."

"Sure, and I'm Reese Witherspoon without my makeup on. What kind of conditions?"

"Only that you let us maintain it, and if you die without heirs that it reverts back to the corporation."

"Not likely to have heirs unless Abby goes out cavorting with wild men. You gonna do that, Abby?"

"No, Mama."

"Didn't think so. Now, Mr. Stringfellow, I wasn't born yesterday or the day before that. What's the catch?" Mrs. Pendergraft asked.

"No catch, ma'am. I just moved in, and I like to do what I can to improve the neighborhood I live in," Nick said.

"You must be richer than plum pudding."

"I do have more than I need, but I work for someone that believes in sharing the wealth. I've had the papers drawn up, and if you'd like to have a lawyer check them out, I'd be happy to oblige," Nick said as he withdrew a single sheet of paper from a manila folder he'd been carrying.

"Just give me the paper," Leah commanded and reached for her spectacles on the table next to her rocker.

The sheet listed the address and the property's abbreviated legal description. Then it read:

"CASH Corp hereby releases all interest in said property provided Leah and Abigail Pendergraft agree to have the property maintained by

CASH Corp or its assignees and to restore ownership of the property to CASH Corp in the event that no heirs exist upon their deaths."

"That's it?"

"That's it!"

"Don't need no lawyer to read that. It's in plain American."

"That's right, ma'am. No tricks. No loopholes. The house is yours."

"We'll sign it won't we, Abby?"

"Yes, Mama."

Nick called an emergency meeting of CASH Corp employees that evening. Jemima, Russ, Lisa, and Mr. Ishikawa were in attendance.

"I want you all to know that CASH Corp has purchased the house next door on the left."

"The yellow one?" Jemima asked.

"Yes."

"That one's in almost as bad of shape as this one was."

"That's right, and that's what we're here to talk about. If you are all willing, we'd like you to do the same for the yellow house as you've done for this one. The interior design will be subject to the occupants' consent. The structure and the exterior will be brought to our standards."

"What are the occupants like?" Lisa asked.

"Mrs. Pendergraft is ninety-four and sharp as a new scalpel. Her daughter is seventy-two and looks just like her mother."

"Are they okay with this?" Jemima asked.

"I cleared it with them. They're happy to have us come in and fix things up."

"How about if they get old and need special help?"

"They're reasonably old already, Jemima, but when it's time, CASH Corp will hire a nurse to help out. At this point, some deep cleaning and an occasional meal would be sufficient. Ishikawa-san, your and Jemima's salary will be doubled, Russ and Lisa the same as long, as your services are required."

"How long might that be?"

"CASH Corp is planning to buy the entire block and perhaps more. You may never run out of work," Nick said.

"I'm going to quit working at the hospital," Jemima said. "This sounds much better, and I know it pays better."

"Any of you that require extra help will be able to hire and direct it yourselves."

"Whoa . . ." Russ breathed out.

Whoa . . . everyone thought.

BRUNK BACK

Frank Brunk returned from a month of medical leave. He'd been treated at the Harborview emergency room and released to his mother's care. He'd had a sprained wrist, a stitched-up head, and a concussion. His leave had been as much psychological as physical. He was embarrassed and mad that he'd botched his murder attempt. He'd extended his leave to contemplate his life. His contemplative skills approached those of an aardvark. He decided it was him or Nick Stringfellow.

He'd returned to work to plan his plot. His entire month of hatred was shattered on his first day back. From the far side of the cafeteria, he watched Nick's gang gather. Yukiko was there first, followed by Jemima—then Nick walked in hand in hand with Dr. Spurbeck! Shortly thereafter came Monty, his arm around Cathy.

Frank was as frustrated as a toothless tiger in a butcher shop. He hadn't built up any hate for Monty. He didn't even know his name.

Nick took notice of Frank seated in the corner. It came to his mind that Cathy and Monty might not be safe until he had solved the Brunk problem. A cure occurred to him immediately. He'd find Frank on duty as soon as possible.

Meanwhile, as Frank fumed, his coffee cup slipped off the table, scalding his lap.

"Sorry, Mom," Nick said as he smiled to himself.

LOUNGE LIZARDS

Cyril Veshkov sauntered into the doctors' lounge at his usual "too cool to hurry" pace. He drew himself a twelve-ouncer from the Espresso machine and eased himself into an overstuffed recliner. Among doctors there is a pecking order, and any kind of surgeon outranked a pediatrician like Veshkov. He didn't usually involve himself in conversations in the lounge, but on the couch beside him were two radiologists conducting a convulsive dialogue. Radiologists aren't surgeons—they just look at pictures—but in their own mind they're atop the physicians' pyramid.

Drosdick was conversing with a fellow radiologist. "I tell you, this guy is a menace to the health of the entire hospital."

"I've seen him in the lab, but he's never been involved in any wrong-doing that I'm aware of," the other radiologist said.

"I tell you, he re-diagnosed a patient of mine and he's nothing but a nurse. He could bring lawsuits that just wouldn't quit."

"If it's that serious, why don't you take it up the ladder?"

"I tried. I grabbed him by the scruff of the neck and drug him to Furney's office."

"Furney's a straight shooter. What did he do?"

"The joker was some kind of friend of Furney's. He shooed me away, brushed me off, and spit me out."

"And this guy is some kind of nurse?"

"'Nurse at large.' I went to HR, and they said Furney made up the title just for him and waived the requirement for qualification investigation."

"What did you say his name was?"

"Stringfellow."

Veshkov cleared his throat. "Excuse me, did you say Stringfellow?"

"Yes, do you know him?"

"In fact I do, indirectly. I'm Cyril Veshkov, and you?"

"Sidney Drosdick."

"You say Stringfellow has been sticking his nose where it doesn't belong?"

"Definitely. Twice I've caught him interpreting images he had no business looking at."

"He's been messing in my business too. You say Furney's a friend of his?"

"Bosom buddy."

"Well, if we can't get him that way, there are other avenues: the state medical board, the nursing board, and the nurses' union. If those don't work, we could always take it public."

"To the press?"

"Sure, there's always some correspondent eager to expose medical malfeasance or incompetence at the hospital."

"I wouldn't want to hurt the hospital."

"Of course I wouldn't either, but idiots can't be allowed to run wild, no matter whose friends they are. Listen, the president of the nurse's local is the father of a couple of my patients. I'll get hold of him and see if we can't get the union to investigate. What do you know about him so far?"

"Nothing but his name—Copernicus H. Stringfellow."

"No one with a name like that could be for real."

"He's real all right, a real pain in the posterior."

"Has he messed with any of the other docs that you know of?"

"I haven't found anyone yet, but I'm looking for allies."

"You've got one now. With both of us keeping an eye on him, I'm sure he'll hang himself sooner or later."

"He'll sure do that. He's an ungainly oaf."

"Leave it to me, Drosdick. I'll expose this charlatan for the fake he obviously is."

SCHOOLWORK

Thurgood Marshall Elementary School was very modern compared to most in the Seattle Public School System. It was located at the south end of the Central District, and its playground sat square atop the I-90 tunnel as it entered Seattle from Mercer Island. It didn't really mesh with its surroundings of century-old homes on the north but looked good in the park-like surrounds to the south. It was built in 1990 and had distinguished itself for greatly improving inner-city students' test scores through innovations such as school uniforms and single-sex classrooms.

Nick sat in his Impala at the corner of 24th South and Irving Street, watching a classroom of girls at PE on the outdoor basketball court. It was a semi-sunny day of about 60 degrees, and the kids seemed to be enjoying the outdoor exercise as only those in a typically cool, wet climate can enjoy good weather.

As he watched, Nick was deep in thought. Everything he did in his life was with good intentions. He followed his instincts in an attempt to always be in the right place at the right time, to meet his mother's expectations of fulfilling his mission in life. Right now, he knew Seattle was the right place for this time.

He'd met Cathy, who had become a close friend. He wasn't sure where the relationship was supposed to go, but he'd shared with her things about himself that he'd never shared before. Letting her know of some of his special abilities was right—he felt it. Still, her recent hostility worried him.

Monty was a great guy. Helping find Matt was a real joy. Getting Monty a scholarship felt great too. Those two and their mother were now like family to Nick.

He hoped Dr. Prescilla Spurbeck was a big part of coming here. His feelings for her were already at a level he'd never experienced. She was always on his mind at work or home, and for the first time in his life, he was seriously considering a lifetime commitment. Press alone would make living in Seattle his greatest adventure yet.

He was also certain that Matilda Jones—Tilly—was part of the reason he was here. Having spent time with her, he could tell she was special and intelligent, but not just that—she was good, good to the core. He was positive Tilly was going to be someone someday, not necessarily someone famous, but someone virtuous. He'd parked next to her school to watch her, hoping he could ferret out a clue as to how he was to help her.

He was contemplating what he knew of Tilly and Jemima, their family, and their circumstances while The Lovin' Spoonful crooned, "Younger girl keeps a-rollin' 'cross my mind." He felt accepted, almost like a father to the kids. Though Jemima technically worked for him, she treated him like a fourth child. As he sat staring across the playground, deep in thought, a sharp rap on his window startled him. He snapped back to reality and looked up to see a plain-clothes police officer brandishing his badge and beckoning him to get out of the car.

Nick rolled down the window. "Can I help you, officer?"

"Would you step out of the car, please?" Detective Kimura asked.

"Certainly. Is something wrong?"

Terry looked up at Nick, who was nearly a foot taller. "You tell me. Do you spend a lot of time staring at young school girls?"

"What? Oh, I, uh no. It's not what you think. I'm not that kind of guy."

"What kind of guy are you?"

"Well, I'm just kind of keeping an eye on Tilly Jones. Her mother works for me. We're friends."

"I see. Tilly Jones, is she one of the girls on the playground?"

"Yeah, the one over there, in the uniform."

"Right." He answered, glancing at twenty-five girls, all in uniform. "May I see your driver's license and registration, please?"

"Certainly, officer," Nick said, reaching into the car for the registration and fishing his license out of his wallet.

"Copernicus H. Stringfellow," he read. "Is that your real name?"

"Yes, sir. I'm called Nick."

"Well, Nick, are you aware of what's been happening to young girls in this neighborhood recently?"

"No, sir. Is it something bad?"

"Look, Mr. Stringfellow, I've called in your license plates, and they match with the info on your registration. You have no wants or warrants, no criminal record, and there's nothing I can hold you for, but I suggest you quit hanging around elementary schools watching young girls. I'd like to check things out further. Can you tell me how to get a hold of the girl's mother, or do I have to work through the school?"

"No, officer, I'm glad to help. Tilly and her mother will both be at my place tonight between six and nine. You're welcome to come. I really have no evil intentions. Please come and talk with them."

"I'll be there," he said, making a note of Nick's address.

"Thank you, sir," Nick said, thoroughly embarrassed. "I'll be leaving." He started the Impala.

"I'll be seeing you again," Detective Kimura said as Nick pulled away.

BARBECUE

That evening, there was a barbecue at Nick's place. The living room had been renovated and furnished. The hardwood floors were removed and replaced with Australian cypress, which brightened the atmosphere. The décor was early American, including the only piece of furniture on which Nick had insisted: a beautifully crafted 1890s upright piano. The large kitchen had been spruced up with earthy, red ceramic tile floors and black marble countertops. The dining room had a small chandelier and a custom-made dining set that spoke of understated wealth.

Press was there talking with Yukiko and attempting to get to know the older Ishikawas. Grandma Ishikawa's English was quite a bit better than her husband's, and she was telling Press their immigration story from the early '50s.

Cathy and Monty were discussing the state of hospital maintenance with Jaime Beltran while his wife was helping Jemima in the kitchen. Cass and Tilly had taken the Beltran and Schaff children upstairs for a spirited game of hide-and-seek among the as yet not refurbished bedrooms. James, who was there nearly every evening with his mom and sisters, made himself at home on the couch and was questioning Russ Pauley and Lisa Schaff on the merits of a career in construction management.

Terry Kimura knocked on the screen door and was greeted immediately by Nick. "Officer Kimura, come in. Have you eaten?"

"No, but no thanks. Are the Joneses in?"

"Sure, come to the kitchen . . . Jemima, you have a visitor. Jemima Jones, Detective Kimura. Detective Kimura, this is Jemima Jones, and this is Señora Beltran."

"Detective? Are we playing a game of clue? The cook is never the one that 'done it.'"

"He's here to talk to you about me, Jemima."

"What can he tell me about you I don't already know?"

"No, he wants *you* to tell *him* about *me*."

"Oh, I can sure do that. What would you like to know?"

"I'll leave you two to talk. Señora," he addressed Jaime's wife, "would you come with me?"

"Sí."

"What exactly is your relationship with Mr. Stringfellow?" Detective Kimura asked.

"I work for him, but I'm the boss," Jemima said.

"What does that mean?"

"He gives me the paycheck, but he does what I tell him to do."

"What do you do for him?"

"I run the house. I cook and clean and set down the rules."

"Do you have children?"

"Yes sir. A boy and two girls."

"And their names?"

"James, Cass, and Tilly."

"Tell me about Tilly. How old is she?"

"Nine."

"What kind of relationship does she have with Mr. Stringfellow?"

"I think he's the best friend she ever had."

"Do you trust him with her?"

"Like my mama with a skillet."

"You feel safe with her alone with him?"

"Absolutely. Why are you asking those kinds of questions?"

"You've heard of the kidnappings recently?"

"Yes, sir."

"I just found Mr. Stringfellow by Tilly's school and wanted to check up."

"If he was there, it was to help her out, not to do any harm."

"Are you sure of that?"

"Sure as a dog has fleas. Now, why don't you forget that baloney and come out to the dining room? There's some of your own kind out there. You're Japanese, aren't you?"

"Japanese-American, yes."

"I knew the American part. We're all that." She grabbed him by the arm, dragged him to the dining room, and set him down by the Ishikawas. "Ishikawa-sans, this is Detective Kimura. He wants to get to know you." Jemima went back to the kitchen to work on the food.

"Ah, nihonjin desu ka?" the senior Ishikawa asked.

"So desu . . ." he answered, "but I really don't speak Japanese. My great-grandparents did."

The woman next to Mr. Ishikawa extended her hand. "These are my grandparents. I'm Yukiko," she said.

"Detective . . . Terry Kimura. Glad to meet you."

By the end of the night, Terry Kimura was part of the gang. He was conversing with the Ishikawas. His Japanese was sketchy, but he enjoyed having Yukiko translate for him.

HARDBALL

Nick and Press had gone to a Mariners game. Nick always preferred going somewhere they could talk instead of to a movie or play. The Mariners were particularly bad that year, and there was no one within fifteen feet of them in the outfield bleachers. Nick had apologized for the cheap seats, mumbling something about a nurse's salary. Press had assured him that residents didn't make much either and stifled a hilarious grin thinking about Nick's billions.

She hadn't told him she knew and, despite several attempts, had never gotten him to admit to being disgustingly wealthy. Since their first date, Nick's honesty and humility had shown through in all of their conversations. Though he could be a terrible tease, he couldn't play the kind of games many men played while trying to influence a girl. Press felt completely at ease and marshmallow comfortable when she was with Nick.

"Nick, has our relationship progressed to the point where you can tell me about your healing techniques?" Press asked.

"Almost. I'd say we're just a date or two away from full disclosure."

"You sound as if there were some measurable accounting going on."

"You can't measure love and you can't measure trust, but you know when they arrive."

"So where is your love and your trust?" she asked, trying to push him to open up.

"Too many people fall in love before they really trust each other."

"What does that mean?"

"You know how people say 'you can't choose who you fall in love with'?"

"Yes."

"Well, of course it's not true. You can choose who you associate with and you certainly won't fall in love with someone you don't see, but it should be built on more than association."

"Yes . . ."

"I've always felt you should hold on to your love until you know your lover is the one you want to spend your life with. Then you can pull the plug and let it flow," Nick explained.

"Are we talking about love or plumbing?"

"I wouldn't venture into plumbing in a circumstance like this."

"Love then," she said, smiling. "How do you know when you're ready?"

"You have to share your deepest feelings. You have to discuss what's most important to each of you. You have to know you have common goals and desires. If not, you can't let yourself fall into that burning ring of fire." Nick paused.

After a moment laden with ponderous silence, Press asked, "So what do you need to know about me?"

"I—"

The crowd roared, and Nick looked up just as a ball passed right between Press and him. It smacked against the bleachers in the next row and careened off to an eager bunch of kids to the left and behind them. Their picture was flashed on the big screen, and the crowd, though sparse, had a good laugh at the couple so engrossed that they'd nearly been beaned.

"I guess we'd better pay attention," he said as the "so rare it was nearly extinct" phenomenon of turning red embraced his face.

"You're not getting off that easy, Copernicus H. Stringfellow," Press said, grabbing his face, looking him directly in the eyes, and demanding that he do likewise. "You tell me what you need to know to trust me totally, or I'll bean you myself."

Nick paused, obviously reluctant to proceed. "Well, I really love my Mom."

"And I love mine. So . . . ?"

"Well, I really miss her."

"I know you do. So?"

"Well, I want to have a family."

"Me too. So?"

"Well, you seem so focused on your career."

"Of course I do. I've spent a lifetime preparing for it," she said with a hint of defensiveness in her voice.

"Well, I'm not certain of your priorities."

"Nick Stringfellow, are you saying you want me to give up my career for a family? You want me to throw away years of training to be barefoot and pregnant?"

"That's not what I mean at all. I just want us . . . *you* to use your training differently than you've planned. I want my kids to have full-time parents."

"You *do* want me to throw away my career! You want me to stay at home."

"No, that's not it. Let me explain."

"I've heard enough. I can't believe you," Press fired out, not wanting to give him the chance to say any more. "You'd better find someone else to cook and clean and keep your house for you. Why don't you go back to Cathy? I'm sure she'd be happy being everything you want." She turned her back and stomped down the row to the aisle.

"Press, wait. Let's talk," Nick said, walking after her.

"Forget it. I'll take a cab home," she spat back at him and turned again quickly, clomping up the steps to put as much distance as possible between them.

"Press," she heard him call. "Remember the ferry to the San Juan Islands? Isle of View!"

Press pretended not to hear and hurried to escape.

Nick collapsed onto the bench with his head in his hands. He'd never had the feeling of having blown something this badly.

SHADOWING

Nick wandered in to the emergency room. It was in the early morning hours, and there had been a high-speed multiple-vehicle crash on I-5 just a few blocks from the hospital. Several patients had arrived, and though it was not of the scale to bring in extra help, the doctors on shift were as busy as could be.

A young man in his twenties was lying unconscious on a gurney just inside the restricted area.

Nick arrived after the wave of casualties had been triaged and assigned. He was drawn to the unconscious young man on the gurney. A quick look at the chart showed that the patient had been diagnosed as having received blunt trauma to the head. The bleeding had been stopped, and he had been strapped in to prevent movement should he come to. No other problems had been noted.

Nick noticed shallow breathing, and the victim's skin was cool to the touch. Nick didn't need a sphygmomanometer to tell him that the man's blood pressure was low. By touch, he estimated Systolic pressure at about 74.67 and diastolic around 49.74. The pulse was weak but rapid. Nick pushed up an eyelid and noted a greatly dilated pupil.

The man coughed, and Nick quickly turned the head to the side as a mixture of both bright red and dark coffee ground–like blood was expelled from his mouth.

The man was no doubt in a state of hypovolemic shock and experiencing internal bleeding. Nick adjusted the gurney to raise his legs, though he knew that shock was a symptom, not the cause.

Nick undid the patient's trousers and pulled up his shirt. He quickly detected Cullen's sign around the umbilicus. Touching the skin caused the man to groan even though unconscious. The skin was rigid, and Nick deduced that the internal bleeding had spilled into the peritoneum.

Angiography would typically be used to ascertain the location of the rupture, but no ultrasound machine was at hand. Nick put his fingers on the distended abdomen and concentrated. Tracing the vascular system, Nick's focus was drawn to a section of the renal artery where a perforation was leeching life's liquid into the abdominal cavity.

Nick needed a quick Twinkie break. He unzipped his fanny pack and withdrew four Leavened Loaves of Logic. Refocused, Nick went back to work.

Popeye wouldn't have this problem, he posited as he considered the vitamin K levels present in spinach that would facilitate the patient's clotting. He quickly moved to the large intestine, where he stimulated the vitamin's creation by bacteria present there.

He then moved on to the generation of other agents required to produce the coagulation cascade necessary for the man's survival. He needed no refresher on the factors involved. He zoned in on the subendothelial cells of the vessel wall. Locating the von Willebrand factor, he stimulated the sinusoidal cells of the liver and increased production of factor VII to bind with it.

While in the liver he snatched a load of prothrombin, which in the presence of vitamin K converted to gamma-carboxyglutamic acid (G1a). Mixed with calcium, the G1a became thrombin when activated by Factor X and enhanced by Factor V. The thrombin then combined with Factors X, XI, and XIII to produce more thrombin.

The flood of thrombin combined with other factors to produce fibrin and promoted the activation and aggregation of the platelets. The platelet and fibrin combination quickly formed a clot to stop the bleeding and begin repair of the vessel wall.

Nick needed refreshment and again reached into his pack. After six more Allotments of Abundant Acumen, he was ready to go back to work.

All that was necessary now was to allow rehydration via intravenous injection of a sodium chloride solution. He grabbed a bag of the fluid and hooked it on a wheeled pole. He inserted a 14-gauge cannula into the median cubital vein near the man's right elbow and stood back, surveying the patient. His assessment was that everything critical had been addressed. He filled out the chart and walked away, leaving the man to the care of the hospital staff.

Dr. Veshkov arrived at the hospital and entered through the emergency room door. He noticed Nick leave the area while munching a Twinkie. He was in no rush and decided to poke around. He approached a female nurse standing nearby.

"Hey, I'm Dr. Veshkov. I see nurse Stringfellow was just here. Does he work here regularly?"

"Not on my shift."

"Well, does he work here on some other shift?"

"He doesn't seem to work any shift at all. He comes and goes as he pleases."

"I guess that's because he's a 'nurse at large.'"

"Nurse at large. What's that?"

"It must mean he gets to go wherever and do whatever he wants."

"Who made him that?"

"I heard it was Dr. Furney."

"That's a load of tripe. I've been wanting to get off graveyard for a year, and I'd much rather work in maternity or orthopedics or any number of places but emergency. We get a lot of tough cases down here, and I'm not talking medically."

"I think he must have some special qualifications."

"I have all the qualifications a nurse can get."

"Maybe he has seniority?"

"How long has he worked here?"

"Several months."

"I've been here seven years."

"Well, I don't know. There must be some reason he's special."

"I gotta talk to HR about this."

"It won't do any good. He's a friend of Dr. Furney's."

"Somebody's got to do something."

"Maybe you could talk to the union."

"Absolutely. This is an outrage."

"I'll drop by again to see how it goes."

"Why do you care?"

"Oh, he's been sticking his nose in all kinds of places where it ought to get snipped off. See you later?"

"Yeah, we need to do something."

HOME TO MAMA

I don't know what to do, Mom. He made me so mad I never want to see him again," Press said.

"So never see him again."

"I can't do that. I miss him already. I love him."

Mother and daughter faced each other, each on an overstuffed brown leather couch. It was late evening, and the ambient lighting was confined to the space between them.

"Well, if you really love him, let's talk about it. You call and say you need to see me right away. I fly out here, and you're as confused as a dog in a hydrant factory. You wouldn't tell me anything about him on the phone. You'd better explain things now. You hate this guy and you love him. We've got to sort this out. What are his good points? What are his bad? Let's start at first base. Is he handsome?"

"No, you definitely wouldn't say that."

"Well, are you attracted to him?"

"Absolutely. I've never felt more drawn to a person."

"Then what is it that attracts you? Is he intelligent?"

"I doubt if there has ever been anyone more intelligent."

"That's hard to believe. You must be love-blind biased. You're not usually so gullible. What convinced you of that?"

"Well, he has at least seventeen PhDs. He medically specialized in at least seven disciplines. He started college at eleven."

"Okay, okay. Get real. Quit exaggerating."

"Mom, I'm not exaggerating. He has at least seventeen PhDs and

239

seven medical specialties—he won't tell me exactly how many. And he started college at eleven. I was told his guardians wouldn't let him go earlier than that."

"Okay, I'll play along. Let's assume he's Einstein's smarter brother, but eggheadedness doesn't necessarily translate to social aptitude. Does he seem intelligent when you talk to him?"

"Well, you'd have to talk for a while. He doesn't say that much in social situations, but he can expound on any subject from musicals to geology, if you ask him."

"Does he make people around him feel stupid?"

"He's the nicest, sweetest, most considerate person I've ever known. You'd have to be a creep to be offended by Nick."

"Let's go on then. I hardly believe he could be the smartest and the nicest person in the history of the world, and I'm surprised to hear my usually levelheaded little girl so carried away by a man that she'd make such claims. Anyway, we'll say that you enjoy being around him and that he'd challenge you intellectually. Let's get on to more practical matters. Does he make enough money to make you comfortable?"

"He's probably in the top one hundred richest men in the world."

"Press, get a grip. You've got to be out of your mind. He's the smartest, the nicest, and one of the richest people in the world? Give me a break. Where did he get his money? Why isn't he famous?"

"He invented Rogaine and laser eye surgery and iPods and who knows what else, and he's invested wisely in the stock market."

"You mean he started with nothing?"

"He doesn't even have parents, and the aunt and uncle that raised him lived in a trailer."

"And he's worth how much?"

"Well, I don't know exactly, but it's in the billions."

"I knew I never should have read you Cinderella. You're spinning a fantastic yarn, and I can hardly believe any of it, but I'll play along. Let's say it's all true. What was your original question?" her mom asked.

"Well, I don't know what to do about him."

"Has he asked you to marry him?"

"No, not exactly. In fact he kind of said we wouldn't work out together."

"Why was that? Doesn't he like you?"

"He admitted he liked me but was hesitant to get involved any deeper."

"What's holding him back?"

"Well, his father murdered his mother when he was two."

"That's horrendous. It's a good thing he was so young or he'd be permanently scarred."

"Actually he remembers it in great detail, and he said he couldn't bear the thought of his own children growing up without a full-time mother. He also said that if he were married, having a settled medical career would be out of the question."

"So he basically said he wouldn't marry you if you were a practicing physician."

"Basically, yes," she said, hesitating. "At least I think that's what he said." There was a several second pause in the conversation while Press contemplated her own life. "You and Dad are both doctors, and you met in medical school. If he'd demanded that you give up your career to marry him, would you have?"

"No way."

"See, that's where I am."

"What I mean is, there was no way I would have given up my career at the time, but knowing what I know now, I'd drop it in a minute. Being married to your father and being your mother has been much better than anything I could have done with my career. Giving up your father would have been the biggest mistake I could have made. Nothing could have made me happier than his love and yours."

"But what of all of the women you've helped and all of the babies you've delivered?"

"It all has been wonderful and very rewarding, but if I hadn't done it, some other doctor would have. Being your dad's wife and your mother are things I'd never want for anyone but myself."

"Wow. I never would have guessed you'd say that. You seem so dedicated to your work."

"I hope you don't mean I'm not dedicated to my family."

"Of course not. I just never compared the two."

"Well, I'd hope it would be obvious. I can tell you for sure that what you do with your life is much less important than who you do it with."

Silence fell again as Anna and Press both felt the gravity of what had just been said.

"Now back to your problem," Anna began after a couple of minutes. "Let's see . . . he's not handsome but is attractive. He's smarter than Einstein. He's rich enough to be next-door neighbors with Bill Gates. He's kind, polite, humble, and you don't know what to do about him." She looked at Press with a sardonic grin. "Has he mentioned a pre-nuptial agreement?"

Press looked shocked. "No, I'm sure he'd never do that. He's much too genuine. He'd be offended by the thought of it."

Anna smiled in mock slyness. "So if it didn't work out, you'd get half of his billions?"

"I guess so," Press answered innocently.

"And what was your problem again?"

"Mom, don't be so mercenary."

"Well, he's rich, intelligent, trustworthy, loyal, brave, clean, and reverent. What are you waiting for?"

"You make it sound so simple."

"It's not?"

"I don't know." She pouted. "Anyway, I really teed off on him last time we were together. I'm not even sure he wants me anymore. It's probably a moot point. I may have blown it entirely."

"What exactly was the last thing he said to you?"

"He shouted something about the ferry ride we took and said some strange thing about the 'Isle of View.' I'm going to take a shower. I need to think."

Anna Spurbeck smiled to herself. "Isle of View," she chuckled. "Isle of View!"

Press took a long, hot shower. As she was drying off, she felt rather than heard strong musical vibrations. She put a towel on her hair, tied on her robe, and opened the bathroom door. Her mother was hanging out an open front window, and a familiar tune was dominating the air. She hurried to the sill and leaned out beside her mother. The sight below took a moment to register.

A large truck was parked at the curb with four six-foot high speakers. There was a drummer, a bass, and a guitarist. In front of it all was an old-fashioned upright piano with the top open and a microphone pointing directly at the voice of the standing pianist. It was as grand as the Beatles in concert.

After a brief interlude of honky-tonk piano, the words "and in your dreams whatever they be, dream a little dream of me" floated out not so beautifully but not off-key from the throat of one Copernicus H. Stringfellow.

"I think he's still interested," Dr. Anna Spurbeck shouted above the din, elbowing her daughter. "I think you should go talk about it."

Barefoot and toweled, Press bolted through the door and down the stairs. Her mom just smiled as she watched Press jump into a bear hug with a tall, skinny, somewhat funny-looking guy that would soon be her son-in-law.

POT STIRRING

Dr. Drosdick saw Nick walking away from a room with a Twinkie in his mouth. Another doctor was examining a chart near the door.

He extended his hand. "Sidney Drosdick."

"Gordon Davis. Glad to meet you."

"Were you just talking with that nurse Stringfellow?"

"That guy was a nurse?"

"His badge calls him a 'nurse at large.'"

"I thought he was a doctor. What's a 'nurse at large'?"

"Apparently a new classification made especially for him."

"He talked like he was a doctor, and he amended the prognosis for this patient. Nurses can't do that."

"Exactly. The guy reversed a diagnosis on one of my patients."

"That's unconscionable."

"It sure is. I've approached Dr. Furney about him, but apparently he's a friend of Furney's," Dr. Drosdick said.

"Furney's letting some nurse run wild overriding doctors' opinions?"

"That's right."

"Someone's got to do something about that."

"A group of us is working on that. Will you join us?"

"What are you doing?"

"We're working through the nurses' union, and we're state medical board. Can we count on you?"

"You sure can. Let me know what you need from me."

"Great. I'll be in touch."

MEDIUM RARE

Nick found Frank cleaning the sterilization room at about nine o'clock at night. He slipped through the double doors. This room was central to four operating rooms and was fairly large, with sinks for washing, autoclaves for instrument sterilization, and cabinets and drawers with disposable and reusable instruments and protective gear. It was painted a sterile white and had a white tile floor.

"Pssst, Frank."

"What the . . ? What are you doing here?"

"Frank, I need to talk to you."

"Why?"

"I'm concerned for your safety," Nick said.

"Huh? You're concerned for me?" Frank asked.

"Yeah, Frank. We gotta talk. Sit down." Nick pulled up a wheeled stool for himself and pushed one across the room to Frank.

"What do you want with me?"

"Just sit down, Frank. I told you I'm concerned for your safety."

"Why?"

"Listen, have you noticed some strange things happening?"

"Like what?"

"Remember when we first met. You tried to push me around the locker room and got flung back across the bench."

"Yeah?"

"Well, didn't that seem odd to you?" Nick asked.

"Yeah."

"Then remember when you tried to run Cathy and me down with your van?"

"Yeah."

"You ran into the hospital wall, but what happened to us?"

"Yeah, what *happened* to you?"

"Well, that's what I'm talking about, Frank. Doesn't that seem strange?"

"Yeah, it does. So what happened?"

"Well, I've been wondering that myself. Last night Cathy and I and some others went to see a medium."

"A medium what?"

"A medium. You know, we went to a séance."

"Say what?"

"A séance. You know, where dead people come to talk to the living."

"Yeah, a séance. I've seen those on TV."

"Anyway, Frank, we were at this séance when the medium began channeling Cathy's grandfather."

"Like a TV channel?"

"Yeah, Frank. The spirit uses the medium like a TV channel to talk to people. So Cathy's grandfather starts telling us how he's seen people trying to harm Cathy and her friends and that he would use all of his powers to protect them."

"Come on, you expect me to believe in that ghost stuff?" Frank asked.

"I don't know, Frank. I wouldn't have believed it myself if I hadn't been there in person."

"Are you trying to scare me? 'Cause I don't scare easy."

Nick lowered his voice to a whisper. "Frank, I'm telling you, I didn't believe in any of this either until those strange things started happening. Then the séance seemed to tie it all together."

Frank raised a fat finger. "If you think I'm gonna fall for this—"

Just then there were two distinct clicks as the doors on both sides of the room locked themselves.

"Who's that?" Frank asked.

There was a loud screech as the curtains were dragged shut on their metal rollers.

"You—"

Frank was shoved across the room and crashed back to the wall. His eyes popped wide as a stainless steel drawer sprung open. Half a dozen scalpels levitated, hung in space, then flung themselves simultaneously into the wall around Frank's head.

What would have been a scream from any other person escaped as a prolonged guttural grunt from Frank's throat. He erupted through the locked doors and escaped the hospital without punching the time clock.

"Sorry, Mom," Nick said softly.

THE KNOT

Nick flew into Joplin in a Learjet. Press would be arriving the next morning by commercial airline with her parents. Reverend Duck was to perform the ceremony at noon, after which they would fly together with Stan, Lily, and Nick's cousins' families to Philadelphia for an evening reception. Nick and Press would then be off in the company plane for a four-week honeymoon in Japan.

Reverend Duck was there to meet Nick, who would be staying in the reverend's spare bedroom for the night. After a huge hug that only a man as tall as Nick and close to twice the weight could give, the reverend held Nick at arm's length and bellowed, "So, Nick, you're going to finally tie the knot. Tell me about this girl. Is she worthy of the pride of Galena?"

"She's great, Reverend Duck."

"That's not very descriptive, Nick. Is she the kind of girl you always dreamed of?" They were walking out to the car. Reverend Duck carried Nick's suitcase while Nick toted the one filled with cash and Twinkies.

"I don't know. I've never really read any books about choosing a wife. I've read about love and the chemicals involved, and I've read about women biologically, but none about marriage. I guess I've dreamed about a wife mostly based on my mother."

"Is she like your mother then?"

"Well, she's pretty, she's smart, and she's female," Nick replied.

"I guess that's close enough." He laughed. "Does she know what she's getting into? Does she know who you are, what you do, what your life's mission is?"

"She knows a lot. She knows I can heal people. She knows I like to help people."

"Does she know you're special?" Duck asked as he started the car.

"She treats me special, but I'm just an ordinary guy trying to do the best I can like everyone else."

"You're not like everyone else, Nick. You've got more abilities, and believe me, not everyone else is trying to do the best they can." He paused, switching gears mentally. "Would you like an accounting of the foundation's expenditures?"

"Not especially."

"Nick, you've given me over a billion dollars, and you don't want an accounting?"

"Reverend Duck, I'm thrilled to have given you all that money, but you know it doesn't matter much to me, and you know I trust you to use it wisely."

"Nick, you're hopeless. If I'd had a son, I'd want him to be just like you."

"Tall, skinny, and hopeless?"

"Yeah, just like that."

Later, in Duck's living room, the two conversed on the couch.

"Reverend, I'm worried about you. You're not getting any younger. You're big, you're old, and your dad died of heart problems. I'd like to do something to help."

"Nick, you're not saying that because I should be helped. You said, 'I'd like to help.' If I was a random person in a hospital, would you try to help me?"

"I don't know. I'd like to."

"Of course you'd like to. You'd like to help everyone, but should you?"

"Well . . ."

"Nick, I'm old, and I've had a great life. Cora has already moved on and I'm ready any time the man upstairs calls."

"But, Reverend, I could easily prolong your life."

"Nick, the Foundation is in the hands of good people, my star pupil is marrying a great girl, and there's not any more I care to accomplish. Nick," he continued after a pause, "when you were a kid, we discussed the miracles Jesus did."

"Yeah."

"Do you think you've figured out how he did them? Is that what you do?"

"I've learned a lot of things, and my power to do good has increased exponentially, but there is a difference that I'll never fathom."

"What's that?"

"I'm a man. What I can do will always be finite. He is God. What he can do is infinite."

"Would that every man could learn that," whispered Reverend Duck.

The next day at ten in the morning, Nick and Press were married in a simple ceremony in Reverend Duck's large but unembellished chapel. Half of the town of Galena and many from Nick's alma mater in Joplin were in attendance.

It took a few hours for Nick to meet and greet all of them, and introduce them to his new bride. Press's parents stood behind them agog as Nick called each of the several hundred in the company by their first and last names, then explained their importance in his life. Nick tried not to rush, though he knew the schedule would be tight for the seven o'clock reception in Chestnut Hill.

By three thirty, they were all on the company plane headed to the Philadelphia International Airport. They were met in the noncommercial landing area by several stretch limos the Spurbecks had hired for the night. Nick felt as though he was in a funeral procession, but he and Press shared a limo by themselves, and she made sure his mind didn't wander too far.

The reception was at a club not far from the Spurbeck home. It was well attended by neighbors and associates from the University of Pennsylvania Medical Community.

Nick allowed himself to be referred to as Dr. Stringfellow so as not to diminish the family's standing in the community. As a matter of fact, there were several from the hospital that knew Nick and quite a few of his close friends from around the Eastern Seaboard.

It was midnight by the time Nick and Press got away to the airport where the company jet would take them via San Francisco and Honolulu to Narita International Airport in Japan.

Four weeks later, the happy couple came home to an open house hosted at Nick's place by Jemima Jones. Then it was back to work for the old married couple.

THE GRIND

Press was a few weeks away from completing her residency. It was shortened by her decision not to specialize. Consultations with Nick had convinced her that as a general practitioner she could do anything and more with his tutelage. She had come to accept his intellectual superiority but was comfortable with her equality in the relationship.

Press asked Nick to look at a patient who had delivered a child the previous day.

"Let's see the patient," he said.

"Our situation makes that a bit complicated," she replied.

"What do you mean?"

"She said up front she wanted a female doctor."

"But now she has complications; she would certainly understand."

"I'm sure she would, but you're a nurse. How would I explain being examined by a male nurse?"

"I guess that does complicate things. You'll just have to tell me the symptoms, and if I need more information, we'll have to run a relay."

"What does that mean?"

"I'll stand outside the door, and you can go back and forth examining and questioning the patient."

"That sounds like fun," she said sarcastically.

"You're the one into jogging."

"You never did teach me the pulmonary isometrics you talked about."

"There are a lot of exercise tips I could give you."

"Yeah, well, you'd better start tipping pronto."

"Not in the middle of a public institution. What are the woman's symptoms?"

"She's got a rash that looks like a sunburn covering her face and trunk, front and back. We considered the possibility of an allergic reaction to the anesthetic, but the birth was yesterday afternoon, and the rash wasn't apparent till this morning."

"Does it itch?"

"She says not really."

"How does it feel?"

"I hate having to ask a nurse for a diagnosis."

"I mean, what is the texture of the rash?"

"Very rough, not bumps but more like sandpaper."

"Fever?"

"Yes, 100.8."

"And a headache?"

"You certainly can be."

"Does she exhibit Pastia's lines?

"Yes, dark red lines in the groin and joint areas. Are you thinking of scarlet fever?"

"The worst since Rhett Butler fell in love," Nick said.

"Get serious." Press smiled.

"I'm terribly serious."

"I mean about the patient."

"Yes, I'd say it's a good possibility."

"But there's no sore throat or tenderness of the lymph nodes. And scarlet fever isn't normal in post-teen patients."

"In rare cases, the streptococcus pyogenes can enter by abrasions occurring in the birth process, causing a uterine infection."

"So that would account for the lack of symptoms in the throat."

"Yes, no sore throat, but in all other ways the same."

"It sounds plausible. A throat culture would probably not work then."

"No, I'd suggest a rapid antigen test. It's less reliable, but given the symptoms and the quicker results, I think it would be your best shot."

"And the treatment?"

"It's been okay, considering you think of me as a nurse," Nick said.

"I mean, how should I treat the patient?"

"I'm sure you'll be more than kind."

"I'm going to clobber you. What drugs would you prescribe?"

"I prefer clarithromycin."

"What about communication?"

"I think we're doing just fine."

"Of the infection, I mean."

"Oh . . . because of the uterine genesis, I think we'll not need to worry about her caregivers. She should be isolated now and for forty-eight hours after beginning medication. Of course she'll need to forgo breast-feeding."

"Do we need to worry about rheumatic fever or poststreptococcal glomerulonephritis?"

"We don't need to, but she might. With early detection, though, any such complications are highly unlikely."

"Sometimes you really try my patience."

"I thought I was trying your patients."

"Nick!" Press feigned exasperation.

"I love you," he said, planting a quick kiss on her forehead.

"Thanks, big fella. I'll check her out again, and if I feel like running a relay I'll get back to you."

STALKING

A couple of blocks east of Rainier Avenue and a couple of blocks south of I-90 sat the house of Jemima Jones. On Tuesdays and Thursdays, Tilly got a ride home from basketball practice around eight o'clock with a neighbor four houses down the block. This particular Thursday, a white van was parked a block away, and the driver noticed, as he had on Tuesday, that Tilly walked alone for the four-house distance. It wasn't much of a window, but with split second timing, he was confident he could make it work.

SHOWDOWN COMING

Doctors **Drosdick and Veshkov had** met several times in the lounge discussing details of Nick's downfall.

"Hello, Veshkov. I haven't seen Stringfellow around lately."

"No, he's been on his honeymoon. He got back a few days ago."

"How's it coming with the nurses' union?"

"That's what I've come to tell you. I've arranged for an audience with the local union board for Thursday at two."

"Fantastic. What's the plan?"

"You've said you could get another doctor or two who would be willing to testify."

"I've found one."

"Good, I've dug up a nurse who's complaining about the 'at large' designation that Stringfellow has. She's ticked at having to stay at one station while he gets to wander at will."

"That's great. One nurse will have a lot more sway with the union than a dozen doctors."

"I think with what we've got, we'll be able to demand his credentials from Human Resources. I already know from my sources that they're nonexistent. Furney will have to answer for that."

"The union will be furious over him inventing a classification that's not in the contract."

"I think Stringfellow's days are numbered, and they won't reach triple digits."

ANNOUNCEMENT

The group was together again for lunch.

"Press, what's it like being *married* to a human encyclopedia?" Cathy asked.

"He doesn't really know anything. He makes stuff up and bluffs everybody."

"Has he changed since you *married* him?"

"He's as strange as ever, but I'm getting used to it."

"Nick, has Press changed since you *married* her?" Cathy asked.

"Yes, everyone calls her Dr. Stringfellow. It's hard to get used to."

"I mean, is she a different person now she's *married*?"

"No, she's the same person, just a different name."

"Nick, you're hopeless. Press, can't you help this guy you *married*?" Cathy asked.

"He's helpless as well as hopeless."

"Cathy, why does every question you ask have the word 'married' in it?" Yukiko butted in.

"I thought you'd never ask," she said, pulling her left hand out from under the table. A beautiful ring was on one finger. "Isn't it gorgeous?" She showed a thin gold band with a tiny diamond.

"Cathy, that's so exciting!" Yukiko said.

"Yeah," said Nick. "Who's the lucky guy?"

That drew an elbow in the ribs from his wife.

"I neglected to say that since we've been married, Press has sharpened her elbows." That drew a harder elbow.

"Have you set a date?" Yukiko continued, casting a stern look Nick's way.

"No, but it will be sooner than later," Cathy answered, beaming.

DARPA

Nick was seated on the couch in his living room. Press had her head on his lap. They were both involved in some light reading, Nick on the history of Albania and Press with the *Journal of the American Medical Association*. There was an Albanian/English dictionary on the floor nearby.

"Do you always learn a language before reading a history?"

"Sure. If you don't, you always lose a lot in translation. Besides, it only took me thirty-seven minutes to finish the dictionary. Did you know that only 8 percent of the words in Albanian are native?"

"You mean, they've borrowed words for 92 percent of their language?"

"That's right."

"Did it say that in the introduction to the dictionary?"

"No, I could just tell as I was reading that the great majority had roots of Greek, Latin, Russian, and other languages I've studied. So I just added those up and divided by the total number of words, and it was 8 percent."

"That's pretty fancy statisticalization."

"Of course I only know about the words in the dictionary. I'm sure it wasn't comprehensive."

"You're too modest."

"How true."

Nick took an elbow to the thigh.

Presently, the doorbell rang. Press would have made Nick be a gentleman and get it, but she'd have to move first anyway. "I wonder who that can be."

She got up and opened the door as Nick peered around her to see for himself. There stood two men in dark suits. The nearest one was about six feet two and 220 pounds and looked to be about forty years old. The second was younger, in his late twenties, and thin.

"Mrs. Stringfellow, is your husband in?"

Press was still unused to being called Mrs. Stringfellow, and she paused to let it sink in. "He is. Who might I say is asking for him?"

"We're with the government. May we come in?"

"Uh, Nick," Press said, turning her head. "There are a couple of men here that say they're with the government. Shall I invite them in?"

"Sure, hon. I've been expecting them for months."

"Come in then."

The two men entered the living room. "Please have a seat," Nick offered as he rose to shake hands.

"Dr. Stringfellow, I'm Agent Kendall," said the older one, "and this is Agent Patterson. We're with the Defense Advanced Research Projects Agency—DARPA."

"I'm familiar with your agency. How can I help you?"

"Sir, we'll get right to the point. We're aware that you have achieved a massive technological advance in force field kinetics, and we'd like you to share it with your government."

"Force field kinetics? Gentlemen, I'm afraid you're mistaken. I have no new technology. I'm just a nurse at Harborview."

"We know that you're much more than that, *Dr.* Stringfellow," Agent Kendall said, emphasizing "doctor."

"Please, call me Nick."

"We know that you have PhDs in nuclear physics, electrical engineering, and mechanical engineering, as well as many other fields. We've read your work and consulted with a number of your professors, all of whom think you capable of nearly anything," Agent Patterson said.

"I admit I do have a reasonable education, but what is this force field matter you think you know about?"

"We have hard evidence that you have engaged a force field in defense of yourself and others," Agent Kendall said. "This type of breakthrough could be a tremendous advantage to our armed forces. We'd like you to share it with the department of defense."

"Obviously, any kind of force field would be an advantage. What kind of evidence do you think you have?" Nick asked.

"We'd like you to come downtown with us, where we'll show you the evidence and discuss the issue further."

"Am I under arrest?"

"Of course not, but it would be advisable to cooperate with us," Agent Patterson said.

"Well, I've always tried to be a good citizen, but I must let you know, I'm expecting some important personal business to require my time a little later. Let me get my coat."

Nick went to the hall closet and grabbed a windbreaker. "It looks like I'm going downtown, toots," he said as he leaned over to kiss Press good-bye. "Be in front of the Federal Building in an hour and twenty-three minutes," he whispered in her ear before walking to the door with the two agents. Nick had one of his feelings that he would need to be somewhere else before the night was over. He picked up his backpack, which was hung by the door, and walked out. The feds eyed the back-pack suspiciously.

FEDS

Nick was led to the seventh floor of the federal building and down to the end of the hallway. Agent Kendall swiped his ID card and opened a door to a spacious room filled with about three dozen desks, half of them occupied. Nick was then taken to what could only be called an interrogation room with a table, four chairs, and an obvious two-way mirror on one side. On the table were a PC and a projector. Agent Patterson motioned to a chair, and Nick sat down, laying his backpack next to him on the floor.

"Now, Dr. Stringfellow, we have a bit of film to show you." Agent Kendall booted up the PC and turned on the projector. Once the operating system was engaged, he turned out the lights and pressed a key. The projector shone on the stark white wall in front of Nick. The first few minutes showed Cathy walking along a dark street with Nick following. Filming from behind Nick, you could vaguely make out the two thugs as they accosted Cathy. Nick was there in a couple of strides, and after a few seconds of muffled conversation, it showed the men being flung against the wall. At that point, one of the DARPA men paused the film and turned to Nick.

"What was it that caused those men to fly against the wall like that?" the agent asked Nick.

"Maybe I startled them," Nick answered, feigning seriousness.

"Let's get real, Dr. Stringfellow. It would take a lot of energy to impel them backward like that." Agent Kendall was tilted back against the wall in his chair, when all of a sudden the legs slipped forward. He landed on his back.

"Sorry, Mom," Nick muttered under his breath.

Patterson tried unsuccessfully to stifle a laugh, but Kendall didn't see the humor. He struggled to find his dignity while righting his chair.

"Now, as I was saying, Dr. Stringfellow, it would take a lot of energy to impel them backward like that."

Not all that much, Nick thought. "Would you believe I'm an expert in martial arts?" he asked.

"I didn't see the slightest movement from you."

"Would you believe they jumped backward when they saw my ugly mug?"

"Don't mess with us, Dr. Stringfellow. We know you're very intelligent. We know you're highly educated. We know you were the cause of this event, and we know that you did nothing physically. What went on?"

"I'm stumped. You tell me."

"Okay, don't cooperate. It won't be good for your future. Patterson, show the next clip."

The next segment was in the same location, but the angle was different. Instead of filming from behind Nick, they were looking down from atop a building across the street. Nick, Cathy, and the two thugs were in a face-off about twenty feet apart. The flash of the guns was visible, and with the infrared film, the paths of the bullets could be seen as streaks in the darkness. Each could be seen to veer off suddenly as they approached Nick and Cathy. Once again, the film was paused, and the lights went on.

"How do you explain that, Mr. Stringfellow? Definitely not martial arts," Kendall said.

"Explain what? They shot at us and missed."

"Patterson, rerun that clip." He did so and paused it with the angled bullet streaks still visible on the wall screen.

"What made those bullets change direction, Mr. Stringfellow?"

"I couldn't say," Nick answered.

"Next clip, Patterson."

The two punks shot each other.

"Your explanation?"

"Obviously when they couldn't hit me, they turned on each other."

"Why can't you help us out?"

"I'm doing my best. I can't explain those things."

Finally they showed a clip of Brunk's van smashing into the hospital wall.

"Where were you and the girl, Dr. Stringfellow?"

"Obviously not there."

"But you were there moments before."

"I guess we moved."

The lights went on, and a third man joined them. He was of medium height, balding, with a tapered salt-and-pepper beard, and wearing a forest green turtleneck and a tan corduroy jacket. "Stringfellow, this is Dr. Sunesky, a physicist. Dr. Sunesky . . ."

"Yes, doctor, I've read some of your work. It's a pleasure."

"Thank you, and a pleasure to meet you, Dr. Stringfellow." He took a seat. "The agency has been tracking your movements since before you came to Seattle. You've been involved in several difficult to explain occurrences. We only have these last three on film, but witnesses have described quite a few others. Putting all the facts we know together, we can only conclude that you have devised some sort of force field generator."

"Force fields are only real in *Star Wars* or *Star Trek*, doctor. Certainly you don't believe science fiction," Nick answered.

"Dr. Stringfellow, you know that we know you have concocted a way of forcing objects through space without physically touching them. What is it? Electromagnetic pulse? Ultrasonic waves? Quantum chromo dynamics? Antigravity? A plasma window?"

"Doctor Sunesky, certainly you know that there have been no advances in any of those disciplines that would allow any kind of force field strong enough to move a physical object of greater than molecular size."

"There is surely no *known* advance, but among the top minds in each of those endeavors, you are respected as a technology leader."

"Stringfellow," Agent Kendall interrupted, "you have something that could be extremely valuable to your country. It's your patriotic duty to share it with us."

"Am I under arrest?" Nick asked again.

"Of course not," Kendall answered.

"Then I'd like to leave," Nick said. Something was telling him that he had urgent business to attend to.

"We're not going to allow that until you've explained these bizarre events."

"There's no explanation. Even if I had invented some kind of force field, how could I possibly transport the enormous apparatus necessary to use it?"

"That's what we're most curious about," answered Sunesky. "Experts in each discipline are still in the construction phase of such an enormous apparatus that they're hoping will be able to achieve success in minute force field effects. How could you make a monstrous breakthrough in kinetic technology and manage to miniaturize it so quickly?"

"I couldn't. Now may I go?" The urge to leave was getting stronger.

"Hold on, Stringfellow. You can't just walk out of here with the invention of the century unexplained. Did I tell you this is the United States government you're dealing with?"

"Yes, you did, Agent Kendall. And I love my country. Did I tell you I have nothing to tell you?" Nick's spiritual senses had him getting extremely agitated.

"Dr. Stringfellow, it's been noted that wherever you go, your backpack is always with you. May we look inside?" interrupted Dr. Sunesky.

"Do you have a search warrant?"

"Of course not. Couldn't you please just cooperate?"

"Sure. If you want to look in my backpack, go ahead," Nick said, handing it across the table. "There is certainly no scientific apparatus in there."

Sunesky unzipped the outer pocket, which was empty. Then he opened the main compartment. He pulled out four Twinkie ten-packs one by one and laid them on the table. "You're the original junk food junkie, Dr. Stringfellow," he said, fishing around and pulling out a sandwich bag full of carrot sticks, a collapsible umbrella, and a four-inch wad of one hundred dollar bills wrapped with a rubber band.

"You feel safe carrying around that kind of cash?" Kendall asked Nick incredulously.

"I've found that's the kind that works best."

"Well, that just adds evidence to the fact that you have some kind of protection."

"You can see I have nothing. Would you like to frisk me?"

"Yes, I would."

"Go ahead then." Nick stood and raised his arms like a giant condor.

Agent Patterson frisked Nick, and the only thing he came up with was a wallet. He emptied the contents onto the table: a driver's license, pictures of Uncle Stan, Aunt Lily, and Carrie Sue and Sally and their families, more one hundred dollar bills, and some cards giving the New York address and phone number of his lawyer.

"You can see I carry no scientific devices whatsoever. May I go now?" A stronger feeling was telling Nick to leave. It was hard for him to sit still. "May I?" He grabbing a package of Twinkies and began chomping on some Fantastic Focus Factors. "I'm starving. Would any of you like one?" Patterson immediately reached out his hand but retracted it upon the receipt of a very stern look from Kendall.

Nick had never attempted what he did next, but he'd never been in this situation before. He began a multidirectional concentration beam divided into four. Three for the men in the room and one for the technician he knew to be behind the two-way mirror. It was difficult to focus so minutely in four directions at once, but he had to make it work. Nick's thought waves entered the heads of the four DARPA men simultaneously. He began to massage the pineal glands at the center of their brains. He stimulated the activity of pinealocytes, which in turn ratcheted up production of melatonin, which plays a major role in human sleep cycles. One by one the men's eyelids drooped. They struggled to maintain consciousness, but their fluttering eyelids were shortly followed by nodding heads, and then they were out.

Nick grabbed his things, tossing them all into the backpack. While opening another Twinkie, he went to the door. It was locked. Concentrating on the imbedded tumblers, he flicked them one by one and tripped the latch.

NUMBER 4

Tilly was unconcerned as she passed the next-door neighbor's home. She'd just said good-bye to her friend, and her house was but a few steps away. She turned to take the walkway to her door when an arm encircled her waist and a hand covered her mouth. Her scream was totally muffled.

Kicking, she was carried around the front of a van and into the side door on the street. The man forced her to the floor, punching her in the gut. She gasped for air. With that gasp, he grabbed some pre-cut duct tape to cover her mouth.

Tilly punched and kicked as she writhed to escape his grasp. He had more pre-cut tape to wrap around her wrists. He slid them into a clasp-hook in the middle of the roof. She was still kicking, and when he grabbed one leg, she put the other knee into his face.

He swore at her and backhanded her head before wrapping her ankles. He put a burlap bag over her head and wound her neck with more tape. She was hung in a kneeling position. Try as she might, she couldn't free herself from the hook.

The man, whom she could only describe as dark, pulled the side door shut and slid into the driver's seat. He turned the ignition and pulled from the curb.

WALK OUT

Moving into the bullpen full of desks, Nick casually
walked to the door chewing on another Twinkie. He took the
elevator to the ground floor, forcing himself to walk nonchalantly. He
went out to the curb, where Press was waiting with the Impala idling.
He ran to the driver's side and scooted her over.

"How'd it go?" she asked.

Nick threw the car into drive and took off as fast as the law would
allow toward Rainier Avenue. "It was a waste of time. They think I have
some miraculous new invention. They have some video of me tossing
around a couple of thugs that tried to mug Cathy, and a shot of me
knocking some bullets off track so they wouldn't hit us."

"You never told me about this. You risked your life and saved the
fair maiden. Isn't that worth a mention to your wife?"

"I didn't see it as any big deal."

"Like you got shot at?"

"Well, it's happened a few times. Twice this year, as a matter of fact,
not counting the times with you in Japan."

Nick was taking corners at the speed limit, which left a screaming
tail of burnt rubber behind him. He wasn't sure exactly what he was
headed for, but he knew he needed to hurry.

"How do you corner like that without flipping us?" Press demanded.

"I read a book on high speed driving," Nick answered as if she
should have figured it out herself.

"Where are we going anyway?" Press asked.

"Generally southeast," Nick answered.

"I mean, why are we going this way, and what's the hurry?"

"Tilly's in trouble."

"How do you know that?"

"I just know. We don't have much time."

"Are we going to Jemima's house then?"

"To the neighborhood, at least. That's where the trouble is."

TRACTOR BEAM

Nick and Press arrived on Jemima's street just as a white van was turning a corner a couple of blocks ahead. "That's got to be him," Nick blurted, and he gunned the Impala in pursuit. "What a day for a daydream" was playing on the car's CD.

"Who?"

"The guy who is the trouble for Tilly."

"How do you know?" Press asked.

"I don't know how I know. It's just the way I always know. She's in there with him."

Nick was going near sixty when he rounded the corner, and the tires screamed their complaint. The noise alerted the van driver, who quickly turned at the next corner and floored it. "Nick, slow down! You'll kill us!" Press implored.

"Don't worry. The car has racing suspension, and I told you I read a book on high-speed driving."

The van was entering the on-ramp to I-90 when Nick careened around the corner. A group of teenagers was crossing the street in front of him. The tires yelled their complaints again as he smashed the brake pedal to the floor and fishtailed to a stop inches in front of a terrified group of kids. He leaped from the car. "Anyone hurt?" he asked, working his way to the middle of the pack.

"Anyone hurt?" a girl of thirteen returned. "Are you crazy? You could have killed the bunch of us."

"I'm really sorry," he gasped. "Could you please move aside? I'm in

271

a hurry," he said as he extended his lanky arms and herded them to the sidewalk. "I'm really sorry. Here, get yourself some teriyaki," he shouted, throwing them a one hundred dollar bill, pointing to the shop on the corner, and jumping back into the car. "It's an emergency."

About a mile and a half ahead, the driver of the van looked in his mirror and let out a long sigh of relief. He'd seen the group of kids and sped past just as they were about to step onto the street. He figured whoever was chasing him had made a mess of humanity.

When Nick pulled onto the freeway, the van was nowhere in sight. "He's already through the tunnel and gone," Nick said. "You have your seat belt on?"

"After the way you've been driving? I wish I had a crash helmet."

"Well, lean back against the headrest, pull that red knob, count for two seconds, and push it back in."

"What does it do?"

"It will make us go faster."

"How does it do that?"

"It's just a little booster fuel I concocted."

"Okay, here goes." She pulled back on it.

In the Chevy's specially modified carburetor, a small jet opened up and sprayed a homemade mixture of kerosene, paraffinic naphtha, and alcohol in with the gasoline.

In a flash, Press was depressed into the seat.

Nick fought to hold the steering wheel with both hands. He eased right to avoid a car and crept a foot up the side of the tunnel.

With the force of four g's smashing her backward, Press struggled to get her hand back on the knob. After straining for what seemed to her to be several minutes, she touched it.

Nick veered left to regain the road and had to rush right again as they overtook another vehicle.

It was all Press could do to push the button in. Instantly the car quit accelerating, topping out at over 240 miles per hour, though the speedometer pegged at 120.

"I told you to push it in after two seconds. You took 2.78," Nick said.

"Excuse me, I was distracted."

"Well, I hope you'll learn to concentrate better in the future."

"Sure, next time I'm going 300 miles per hour, I'll pay more attention."

The car slid to the left and grazed the sidewalk.

"We can't be doing a bit over 242."

"How do you know?"

"I calculated the top speed based on the fuel mixture, the gear ratio, the weight of the vehicle ,and the relative humidity."

"Just now?"

Nick cut back to the right. "Well, I'd figured out some of it before-hand, but had to adjust for your weight, and the humidity. I couldn't have known that until now."

Nick compensated, and the car zipped back to the left, nearly smashing into the rail on the other side.

"My weight? Are you implying that I'm heavy?"

"Of course not. That was only a minor adjustment in my calculations."

"Well, it's a good thing. It's these pants that make me look fat. I've only gained a couple of pounds since the wedding."

"I assure you I hadn't so much as noticed."

"You mean you don't pay attention to the way I look?" Press asked with an irked tone.

They flashed between a bus and a semi.

"That's not what I meant. You're as beautiful as the day we met and definitely callipygian."

"It seems to me I was angry that day. Are you insinuating that I'm angry now?"

"Of course not, I'm just saying you're always pulchritudinous."

"Thank you. That's what a wife needs to hear."

Nick recalled that he'd complimented her on her looks eleven times already that day but decided not to remind her.

Two cars that were side by side forced Nick to shuttle far to the left.

"How did you talk those G-men into letting you leave so quickly anyway?"

"We had a short discussion, and I suggested they sleep on it."

They shot through the tunnel and on to the floating bridge.

As they cleared the tunnel, the car seemed to float. Nick didn't dare hit the brakes but fought to steer past the few cars in his way while not shooting over the railing on the sides. He was dodging in and out as the lights of the other cars shot by like electric streamers with reverse rockets.

"I'm feeling woozy," Press said.

"It's the g-forces and swerving. I'm sure your equilibrium will adjust soon."

"Will we be doing this long?"

"A few more seconds, and we should find him."

"I think you should add some kind of gyroscopic stabilization to this rocket."

"I hadn't considered that."

"Now that you're married, passenger comfort should become a priority."

A car seemed to zoom toward them, and Nick had to make a quick adjustment.

"A gyroscope system would add a lot of bulk."

"Are you going to bring up the weight issue again?"

The Impala climbed the sidewalk on the north side, but as Nick compensated, they grazed the railing on the south. Press was in a daze induced by the terrific g-forces and the surreal nature of the high speed. Though the vehicle was still going upward of 200 miles per hour, she could see every detail of every object around them, even to the looks on the faces in the few cars they sped past.

"Two hundred and forty two is a lot faster in a car than in a plane."

"Actually they are identical speeds."

"I know that. I mean relative to other cars, it seems faster."

A car ahead, on seeing Nick's approach, tried to get to the side of the road. Again Nick had to make a speedy adjustment.

"I assure you that if we were flying a plane down the freeway it would seem just as fast."

"You're hopeless. What did those government guys think, anyway?"

"They thought I was using a force field."

"You never told me about this kind of telekinesis. Do you call it macro versus the micro you use when healing?"

"I hadn't thought of it, but that's a good description. If I'd told you all about me, there would have been no mystery, and you probably wouldn't have married me." He swerved again as a driver ahead hit the brakes.

"Probably not. What other dirty little secrets have you been hiding?"

"I'm not saying . . . there he is."

They quickly cleared Lake Washington and had slowed to about 120 as they approached the tunnel on Mercer Island. Nick was happy to get back to a manageable speed. Then he saw the white van taking the West Mercer Way exit. They shot past, but as they entered the tunnel, Nick began pressing the brake pedal. Slowly at first, and then as they decelerated past 60, he jammed it to the floor and cranked the wheel hard to the left. Press took the longest breath she'd taken since she pulled the knob. The Impala leaned left, its right wheels leaving the pavement. Nick released the brakes, then jammed them down again, spinning the vehicle 180 degrees.

"How'd you manage that?" Press gasped as the vehicle righted itself.

"I keep telling you, I read a book on high-speed driving."

"I've gotta read that book," Press remarked.

As they slammed back onto all four wheels, an RV was bearing down on them. Nick spun hard right, nearly grazing it as they passed. Then he turned hard left to miss the concrete tunnel wall. A couple of more cars had to be dodged as he made it to the off-ramp and once again did a squealing 180-degree turn. They climbed the ramp and saw the van disappear around a gentle turn about a half mile ahead. "We've got him now," he exulted with what approached an evil smile on his face.

Finally letting out another long-held breath, her face drained of blood and covered with sweat, Press asked, "What are you going to do when you catch him?"

"Hadn't thought about it," Nick answered. "I was a bit preoccupied. Get me some Twinkies."

Press leaned back over the seat. Nick accelerated to a speed of 89.47 miles per hour. Press unzipped the suitcase and grabbed a ten-pack. "More," Nick said.

They rounded the bend as the van disappeared around the next, about a quarter mile ahead. Press sat forward with half a dozen ten-packs in her arms. "Feed me!" Nick barked. Press ripped open the first ten-pack and fumbled with the individual wrapper of the first Twinkie. "Hurry," he urged.

"I've never stripped a Twinkie under pressure before," she whined, finally opening the first and stuffing it into his gaping mouth.

"I guess I should have married someone with better digital dexterity."

"I've performed countless surgeries. Isn't that dexterous enough for you?" She slowly got the hang of it, opening and then stuffing, continuously forcing them into his mouth as they closed in on the van.

"It's a different sort of operation, isn't it? I guess I'll have to put you through Twinkie training or get another apprentice."

Press crammed the next one into his mouth with increased force. "You're not all that great at eating them, are you? Haven't you ever seen that Japanese guy eat hot dogs? He'd put you to shame."

"He had a drink of water between bites. I'm swallowing them dry."

Nick slowed slightly to make the curve.

"This is Seattle. Stick your head out the window. You'll get all the moisture you need."

"I don't like your attitude. Gimme another Twinkie."

Press forced two more of the Stuffable Steaks of Strength into his mouth.

"Call Terry Kimura. Get him over here."

She opened the next one and ate it herself.

"Hey, I need those."

"Well, I'll need to concentrate in order to make a phone call and open Twinkies at the same time."

"You should buy your own."

"Washington is a community property state."

Nick approached the back of the van.

"Hey, you can't push him off the road! Tilly will get hurt."

"Doannnd warrrie," he mumbled through another mouthful. "I've gawwtt a plannn." Nick slowed the car to a safe 30 miles per hour, and miraculously the van slowed accordingly.

The driver of the van pressed down his accelerator, but it felt as if he were dragging a Caterpillar Tractor behind him. He shifted into second and revved the engine to the max, but the tires spun heedlessly, and he couldn't gain speed.

"Terry, get over to Mercer Island, West Mercer Way, quick! We're about to catch the kidnapper. He's got Tilly . . . What are you doing now? Not you, Terry. I was talking to Nick. Got to go." Press's eyes were fixed on the slowing van. It gradually began to pull away.

"More Twinkies!" Nick demanded, mouth now empty.

"I've been multitasking," Press complained and resumed her duties. Again the van and the Impala slowed, this time to about 10 miles per hour. They were traversing a tree-canopied stretch of road, with lights from the western shore of Lake Washington on their right. Nick pulled the car off to the shoulder, and the van, tight in the clamps of a Twinkie-powered tractor beam, pulled over in unison. Its tires were fiercely throwing up gravel until the driver obviously gave up and rammed it into park.

Nick threw open the door. "Be careful!" Press shouted hoarsely.

He cautiously closed the door and took a step forward.

Bam!

He heard the gun blast echo inside the van. He dashed forward and grabbed the door handle on the driver's side. It was locked. Focusing a thought wave, Nick smashed the window, pulled up the lock knob, and threw open the door.

BUSTED

The driver tipped out the door, gun in hand, barrel in mouth. Hitting the pavement, he flopped from his side to his back. Nick snapped upright as Cyril Veshkov stared lifelessly at him.

"Who is it?" Press shouted, jumping from the Impala.

"I think you'd better see for yourself," Nick answered.

He stepped around to the passenger side, slid open the door, and found Tilly, duct-taped, blind folded, and hanging from a spring-clasped hook on the ceiling of the van.

"Nick, it's Cyril!" Press shouted. "Is Tilly okay?"

"Right on both counts," Nick answered, slowly unwrapping her head. "Tilly, it's Nick," he said and gently guided her hands from the hook and unwrapped them. He took the tape from Tilly's mouth.

"Nick! I knew you'd come," she gasped, throwing her arms around his neck.

Press joined them for a group hug.

In about five minutes, the Mercer Island Police arrived, having been called by a neighbor who reported a gunshot.

Nick wanted anything but publicity, so when the cops arrived, he planned on making a quick statement and getting away. Unlike on most movies, he hadn't been stupid enough to pick up the gun and stare at the victim as the police arrived. The gun was still in Veshkov's hand, and he lay where he had fallen.

"What's happened here, sir?" the officer asked, having already called for backup.

"Our friend Tilly here got snatched by the driver of this van, and we followed him. I guess he gave up and shot himself."

Tilly was wrapped in Press's arms, "Is that what happened, miss?"

"Well, I didn't see Nick and Press behind me, but this guy grabbed me, taped me up, and took off. I was blindfolded, and after a while, we stopped, I heard a shot, and Nick unwrapped me."

"How did this guy have time to tape her up if you saw him kidnap her?"

"I didn't say we saw it happen. We were driving to her house when we saw this van take off in a hurry, so we followed."

"Why would you follow a van taking off from a neighborhood?"

"It was right in front of the house. We'd heard about previous abductions, so we were suspicious."

"Where did this take place?"

"Tilly lives in the Rainier District."

"And you followed him from there to here?"

"Yes."

"You wouldn't be connected to a reported rocket car on the I-90 Bridge would you?"

"We may have exceeded the speed limit a bit, but you can see this car's no rocket. It's just an old Chevy. Could we leave now? We'd really like to be getting Tilly home."

"I'm sorry, but all three of you have a long night of answering to do."

"Could you get a hold of detective Kimura of Seattle PD? He's leading this investigation, and he's a friend of ours. I'm sure he'll say we can talk later."

The officer leaned over and spoke into his shoulder mic, asking that Detective Kimura of Seattle PD be contacted immediately. Another cop car pulled up, and the officer directed them to sit in their car until he needed to talk to them further.

Nick's phone rang.

"Hello."

"Nick?"

"Jemima, hi."

"Nick, have you seen Tilly? She's not home, and the neighbors say they got back half an hour ago."

"Sure, she's here with Press and me. We've had a bit of excitement."

"Can I talk to her?"

"Sure . . . Tilly, your mom would like to talk to you."

"Mom, I was kidnapped and Nick saved me."

"You were kidnapped?"

"Yeah, a guy in a van grabbed me just as I reached our walk. He tied me up and was driving away when Nick got there and chased him."

"Where are you now, honey?"

"On Mercer Island."

"Mercer Island. Nick chased him that far?"

"Yeah, I didn't get to see it though. I was blindfolded."

"Who did it?"

"Nick says he's a doctor from the hospital."

"A doctor kidnapped you?"

"Yeah."

"You tell Nick to get you home right now."

"We have to talk to the police some more."

"Let me talk to Nick, honey. I love you. Thank heavens you're safe."

"I love you too, Mom."

"Nick, is everything all right?"

"Yes, Jemima. Tilly's fine. We're all fine."

"You bring her home right now."

"The police won't let us leave yet."

"How long till you can come home?"

"It won't be long. Terry Kimura's on his way here. He'll make sure we can get away."

"Good. If it's over half an hour, you call me so I won't fret."

"I will. Don't worry."

The second cop was followed quickly by the coroner's van. Within ten minutes, Terry Kimura was there, and after a few more questions, they let Nick, Press, and Tilly go home.

AFTERMATH

When they got back, Jemima gave Tilly a hug that lasted several minutes and nearly squeezed the life out of her. She was sobbing too hard to speak. Finally she let go of Tilly and grabbed Nick for another long squeeze. "Was this the same guy that kidnapped those other little girls?" she asked finally.

"I'm not sure, Jemima, but Terry Kimura should soon be able to figure it out."

"And you say he shot himself?"

"Yes, he's dead."

"If he wasn't I'd make him wish he was."

"Me too. I prefer to save lives, but some are better off gone."

"The Lord have mercy on his soul."

"He'll need it."

Word of Veshkov's crime and death circled the hospital at the speed of a NASCAR championship. The roar was nearly as loud. Some were shocked, others titillated, and some of those who knew him well were not unhappy. Sidney Drosdick was nothing but crestfallen. He'd lost his main ally in the hunt for Nick's head.

FAMILY TIES

Uncle Stan and Aunt Lily pulled their RV to the curb in front of Nick's place. The house next door was freshly painted sunshine yellow and had a manicured lawn and flowering lilacs. The roof had been retiled. Other homes on the block were in various stages of remodeling and rejuvenation. The yards would have made any park proud. The cobblestone street rivaled any in San Francisco, the sidewalk was level and crack free, and addresses had been neatly stenciled on the curb.

Stan was rather portly, with a thick head of curly dark hair. Lily still had a good figure and skin that belied her sixty years.

Press met them at the door and received a warm hug from each.

"Lily, how do you stay so young looking?"

She leaned into Press's ear and whispered, "Didn't Nicky tell you he invented Botox?"

"He never mentioned it."

"Just once I complained mildly about getting wrinkled, and a few weeks later there it was. It's like with Stan's Rogaine though. The version we use works way better than what's on the market. It's not FDA approved."

"Well, come in and take a rest. We didn't get to spend any time together at the wedding. I'm hoping you'll tell me all about 'little Nicky.'"

"Oh well there's not that much to tell. He's just a regular guy."

"Nick says the same about himself."

"He's always been modest and insisted that we be

"I'm his wife. Don't you suppose you could open u

"I guess that does make a difference. What would yo

"What was he like as a child?"

"Shorter."

"Funny. I mean personality wise."

"He's always been a bit of a prankster. He liked teasing his cousins."

"Aren't they both older?"

"Physically, yes, but mentally not since he was about two."

"He wasn't born mature was he?"

"Oh no, he was a teenager during the teenage years, all of those hormones and such. It wasn't possible to argue with him either, on account of his brain. But he never wanted to be anything but a model citizen."

"How about when he was younger?"

"I'll admit that the terrible twos were difficult, but he had them at about six months. When he was two, he was quite sobered by his mother's murder."

"I've wondered how he coped with that. He won't discuss it."

"He cried a lot. He's really not the crying kind (aside from that last scene in *The Dirty Dozen*). He sat on my lap, and I held him. We rocked in the rocking chair for days. After about a week, he stopped and said he needed to move on with his life. He hasn't talked to me about it since."

"How about his dad? Does he talk about him?"

"Occasionally he'd talk of trying to find him, but I haven't heard him say anything since he started college."

"He started college at eleven?"

"Yes, I'm sure he could have done the work at seven, but we couldn't let him go. Then we made him go locally at first, though all of the top schools recruited him. I'd drop him off and pick him up every day."

"Did he ever have girlfriends?"

"He had crushes on girls in his class, but they were always much older. Many of them really thought he was cute and tried to mother him. He didn't like that, being the smarter one. I wasn't even allowed to be a mother, just Aunt Lily. I think his memories of his mother are too dear. I don't know much about girls and him after he went back

.o graduate school. I know he dated, but he didn't say much about nyone."

"Lily, have you seen my iPod?" Stan yelled from upstairs.

"No, dear. Did you leave it in the RV?"

"Would you check for me? I'm in the tub."

BELLS AND TELLS

Cathy's wedding day arrived. It was a Saturday afternoon in the town of Issaquah. A house had been converted to a venue for such occasions. Nick had insisted on paying for the whole thing. Monty's mother didn't have much, and Cathy's dad had nothing but a small disability income and what Cathy provided. Press was in the master bedroom with Yukiko and Jemima helping Cathy get into her wedding gown. Nick was downstairs with Monty and the male members of the gang, wondering why it took four women four hours to get someone into a dress.

"Cathy, tell me about Monty and your dad," Press said. "I've heard your father is not real easy to get along with."

"He's not great in social situations, but Monty insisted a couple of months ago on coming in and meeting him. I usually try to avoid anyone coming in because Daddy can be cantankerous, but Monty was insistent."

"Did Monty actually ask permission to marry you?"

"Yes, he made me wait outside the night he proposed while he went in and talked with my dad."

"What did Monty say afterward?"

"He said my dad agreed."

"What did your father say to you once Monty had gone?"

"He gave me a hard time, as usual. He likes to keep me humble."

"Nick says he likes to berate and belittle you."

"Oh, it's not like that. He's in a lot of pain and he just gets mouthy sometimes. I can tell he's really concerned though about what will happen to him once we're back from our honeymoon. He's afraid I'll quit paying my share of the rent, and he'll be left out on the street."

"What *will* happen to him?" Jemima asked.

"I'm sure we'll be able to get by somehow. I'll keep paying his rent, and I can drop by each day to cook dinner and clean and make sure he's taken care of."

"That sounds difficult," Yukiko said. "You'll have a husband to watch over."

"And believe me, that's a lot of work," Press added. "That gets me to a point I've wanted to make. Nick and I have talked it over, and after you're back from your honeymoon, we intend to give you our house as a wedding present."

"What! You can't do that? Where will you live?"

"We can too do that, and where we'll live is of no concern. Nick has a bit of money put aside, and I'll have my doctor's salary. We'll be fine."

"To say Nick has a bit of money put aside is like saying it rains in Seattle," Jemima said. "I've never seen anybody chuck the bucks like Nick."

"He hardly spends a cent on himself," Yukiko said.

"Oh no, he spends it on all of the rest of us. Since Nick got here, my kids have been spoiled so bad they're rancid," Jemima said.

"Anyway, there's no use in arguing, Cathy. You and Monty are moving in after your honeymoon, and Nick and I are moving out."

"But Nick is already paying for the wedding and the honeymoon."

"You get what you deserve when you take on a friend like Nick."

"That means I'll be around to whip that father of yours into shape," Jemima added.

The crowd was about three hundred strong as the wedding got underway. There were friends of Monty's and of Cathy's from the hospital, Nick and all of his friends, and friends and family of Monty's that he'd grown up with.

Cathy's dad had sobered up and put on a tux. Dragging his bum left leg, half bent over from his bad back, he walked her down the aisle. Despite his condition, he had a look of pride in his eyes at the size of the crowd and the rich circumstances under which his daughter was getting married.

Nick stood next to Monty stage right, once again looking stately in a well-fitted tux. Nick hadn't seen Chuck Starr till then, but he somehow looked familiar. It was probably the resemblance to Cathy.

Having dropped his daughter off at the altar center stage, Chuck took his place on the left. He got a quizzical look on his face as he noticed Stan and Lily sitting in the front row, then seemed to shake it off as the ceremony began.

"I now pronounce you man and wife. You may kiss the bride."

Cathy threw her arms around Monty and practically knocked him over with a staggering kiss. The crowd cheered, and the hugging and kissing blossomed.

Cathy tossed her bouquet over her shoulder. It was caught by Yukiko. She glanced over at Terry Kimura, who quickly looked away.

Once the revelry quieted a bit, Cathy insisted they queue up in a formal receiving line: bridesmaids and her dad on her right and the groom, best man, and Monty's family next to Monty on her left.

As the line proceeded, Cathy introduced those she knew to her father and those she didn't know, mostly Monty's friends, introduced themselves to her and her dad. Not far into the group, a couple came up and Cathy said, "Daddy, this is Stan and Lily Bennett. They're Nick's aunt and uncle." Chuck turned mouse-skin gray. His hearing seemed to amplify as he heard Monty say to the guest ahead, "This is Nick Stringfellow, my best man."

"Daddy, are you okay?" Cathy asked as he staggered back from the line.

"I . . ." He put his hand to his head. "I think I need a drink."

"Daddy, you promised you wouldn't until after the wedding."

"I'm not feeling well. I've got to go."

The line moved on, and Monty and Nick turned their heads to appraise the situation. For the first time, Nick took a serious look at Chuck Starr. Stan and Lily were also staring at Chuck as if there was something hidden in the folds of his face. A profound pause permeated the room as the entire entourage seemed to sink into silence. Lily broke the spell.

"Chad Stringfellow . . . you're Chad Stringfellow!"

Chuck tried to bolt the scene as only a cripple can bolt. He tripped over a nearby chair and sprawled spasmodically on the carpet.

Stan stood over him, grabbed him by the scruff of his rented tux, and pulled him to his feet. "I've been waiting to get my hands on you for thirty years."

Cathy gasped, realizing the implications of this revelation. Her dad was Nick's dad. Her dad had murdered Nick's mom. Nick was her half-brother. Her dad would go to prison. Gravity overcame her. She fainted into Monty's astonished arms.

Nick stood speechless, an attitude previously reserved exclusively for speaking with beautiful women. He'd never expected to see his truant father again.

Nick had told no one but Cathy and Press the tragic story of his mother's murder, but the tale had been passed to all his circle of friends. Terry Kimura, as always, carried his gun and a pair of handcuffs with him.

"There's no statute of limitations for murder," he said as he approached the collared con. He stepped over to Chuck, still in the grasp of Stan Bennett, and began, "You have the right to remain silent . . ."

Press ran to Nick and threw her arms around his waist. "I can't believe you found your dad. That makes Cathy your half-sister!"

"Of course it does," he said somberly, "but I've never really had a father. She's just lost hers."

DROSDICK DEFEATED

Dr. Sidney Drosdick was again at Theodore Furney's desk. Veshkov's demise had been a blow to his crusade, but he was determined to put an end to Nick's career.

"I'm telling you, Furney, I'm going to get this Stringfellow fellow if it takes going over your head to the board of directors. I'll complain to the AMA. I'll take it to the newspapers!"

"Relax, Sidney. You won't have him bothering you anymore. Nurse Stringfellow has resigned, effective today."

Drosdick fell silent. "Well," he said with a self-satisfied look on his blubbery face, "that's different. I knew he'd fold to my pressure sooner or later. Guys like that have no intestinal fortitude. He meddles and messes with other people's lives, but he can't take it when confronted with his own foibles."

"Yes, Sidney, I'm sure your campaign to foil him is totally responsible for him leaving."

"Well, I'm sorry to have to do it to a friend of yours. He just shouldn't have gotten involved in issues way over his level of qualification."

"No doubt qualifications were a big part of your differences with him."

THE END

Nick **and Press had been** packing their things. (Nick now had several suitcases full as his wife insisted he dress with a bit more style. They were taking no furniture, but because of Press, the Impala would be pulling a U-haul.) They sat down on the couch to rest, and Press asked, "Where are we off to, Nick? Have you decided?"

"I'm not sure yet. I don't think it will be far, but it's somewhere east of the mountains. An old friend from Cle Elum called me a few days ago. I was thinking of stopping there and seeing what he was up to."

"That sounds nice. I've always liked that area . . . drier, but still in the mountains enough to be forested. I haven't gotten totally used to the idea of being a vagabond for the rest of my life. Being close so we can visit friends will be appreciated," Press said.

"I never said we wouldn't be close to friends. I have them all around the country. In fact, in most places in the world."

"I'm not nearly as notorious as you, Nick. I'd like to be able to see *my* family and *my* friends frequently."

"I guess I'm not fully accustomed to being tied to the old ball and chain." This earned him the customary elbow to the ribs. "Ouch, that hurt."

"It was meant to."

"We'll always have time to see our loved ones, and the corporate jet can pick us up on a few hours' notice," he said. "I've noticed you eating Twinkies and trying to push pencils around on the table."

"You think you have a monopoly on this thought wave stuff?"

"It takes lots of practice and a concentration level that's difficult even for me. You need to be cautious eating those Salubrious Segments of Sagacity."

"You are not the only one in the family with higher than average IQ. I can ingest as many of those Incomparable Ingots of Intelligence as I please."

"I'm not intimating you're incapable. It's just that you might need some tutoring to really get the hang of it."

"I assure you I can make a great deal of progress on my own, Mr. Stringfellow."

"Well, I'm just not sure you're ready for such power yet."

A pillow flashed across the room and hit Nick on the side of his head.

"Sorry, Mom," Press said with a triumphant grin.

THE BEGINNING

ABOUT THE AUTHOR

Lorin **Barber has an MBA** from the University of Washington and a bachelor's degree in Japanese language. He has had a successful career as a manufacturing executive. He has six children and, so far, eight grandchildren. He lives in a small town in the state of Washington with his wife of thirty-six years. In his spare time, you might find him panning for gold in the wilds of Washington. This is his first fictional work. Lorin would love to hear from his readers via Facebook or email: lorin@lorinbarber.com.